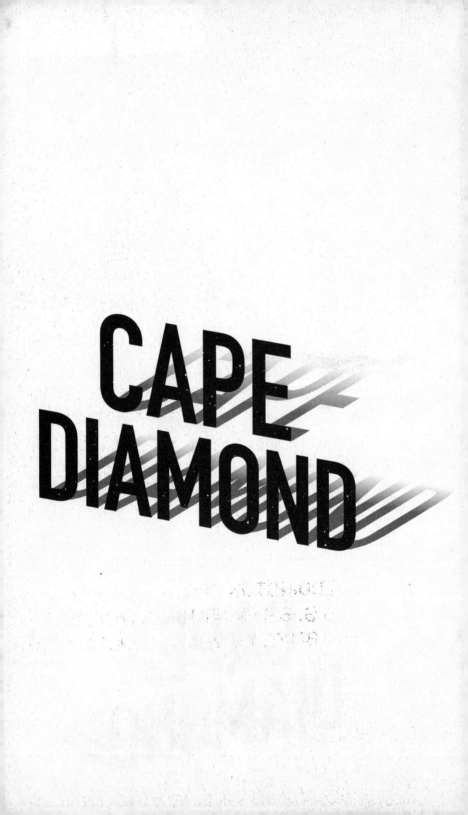

# CAPE
# DIAMOND

# RON CORBETT

## A FRANK YAKABUSKI MYSTERY

ECW

Copyright © Ron Corbett, 2018

Published by ECW Press
665 Gerrard Street East
Toronto, Ontario, Canada M4M 1Y2
416-694-3348 / info@ecwpress.com

Get the
eBook free!*
*proof of purchase
required

Cover design: Michel Vrana
Author photo: © Julie Oliver

Purchase the print edition
and receive the eBook free!
For details, go to ecwpress.com/eBook.

LIBRARY AND ARCHIVES CANADA
CATALOGUING IN PUBLICATION

Corbett, Ron, 1959-, author
    Cape diamond / Ron Corbett.

(A Frank Yakabuski mystery)
Issued in print and electronic formats.
ISBN 978-1-77041-395-5 (softcover).—
ISBN 978-1-77305-241-0 (HTML).—
ISBN 978-1-77305-242-7 (PDF)

    I. Title.

PS8605.O7155C36 2018    C813'.6
C2018-902541-7          C2018-902542-5

The publication of *Cape Diamond* has been generously supported by the Canada Council for
the Arts which last year invested $153 million to bring the arts to Canadians throughout the
country, and by the Government of Canada. *Nous remercions le Conseil des arts du Canada de son
soutien. L'an dernier, le Conseil a investi 153 millions de dollars pour mettre de l'art dans la vie des
Canadiennes et des Canadiens de tout le pays. Ce livre est financé en partie par le gouvernement du
Canada.* We also acknowledge the Ontario Arts Council (OAC), an agency of the Government
of Ontario, and the contribution of the Government of Ontario through the Ontario Book
Publishing Tax Credit and the Ontario Media Development Corporation.

PRINTED AND BOUND IN CANADA          PRINTING: NORECOB  5  4  3  2  1

MIX
Paper from
responsible sources
FSC® C103560
www.fsc.org

*For John Owens*
*True Gen writer and good friend*

## AUTHOR'S NOTE

This is a work of fiction. All places and characters are imagined. While the story takes place somewhere on the Northern Divide, there are no literal depictions of any city or town on the Divide.

*I will never reveal my dreadful secrets,*
*Or rather, yours.*

*Oedipus Tyrannus,*
Sophocles

# PROLOGUE

It happened during a lost season. The murders, the kidnapping of a little girl, the riots in Springfield. A season that was neither autumn nor winter but something in-between, with days of white sun and little wind, the hardwood trees carrying dry, sickly leaves and the rivers running low and black, a season where all the colour in the world seemed to have bled out.

Frank Yakabuski thought the lost season had something to do with what happened that week. When the proper reference points get lost, when the seasons up and walk away on you, he was of the opinion bad things would follow. Not everyone agreed. Those with a causation view of how the world worked thought it would have played out the same, nothing would have changed, because there was a plan and there was a goal and both had been set long before the lost season descended upon the Northern Divide and the first man was murdered.

But Frank Yakabuski also believed cause-and-effect people had little sense of place, that they lived in vacuums, connecting dots, forever disappointed in the sum of their actions. As a young cop, Yakabuski had worked peripherally on a case that seemed to involve obvious cause and effect. It brought him to High River in early spring, when the rivers were running wild, and you had to be careful where you trod in case you were swept away and never seen again, which could happen in High River. He had come to take custody of a mother charged with the murder of her only child, a four-year-old boy she had drowned in a bathtub.

The mother was young, only a teenager, and the evidence against her was damning. She was poor and had a crippling meth addiction. The boy had been taken out of her care by Child and Family Services twice before. On the day of his death, the mother had told several people she no longer wanted the child. The only mystery to the High River cops, and it did not seem like much of one as the mother was again high on meth that day, was why she had called 911 to report the child had drowned.

Yakabuski had taken her from her cell, and as they were walking to the squad car for the drive to Springfield, the girl stopped. She was a slight girl, with long black hair and a face that would have been pretty before she got high one night and took a razor to it. They stood in the parking lot behind the High River RCMP detachment for a long moment, Yakabuski not wanting to drag her the rest of the way. Eventually she said, "Do you hear it?"

"Hear what?"

"Listen."

Which he did, and after a few seconds he heard it clear enough. The sound of water coursing its way through the forests and over the streets of High River, down the creeks and tributaries leading to the Springfield River, water running in circles and turning on itself and wondering which divide to tumble over, which watershed to fill, so much coursing water in High River that spring there was a hum in the air that sounded like a faucet running.

"Why not the river?" the girl said, and after she said it, she started crying.

When they got back to Springfield, Yakabuski contacted the coroner and asked her to take one more look at the young boy's body. That's when they found the ruptured aneurysm in the child's brain. The mother was released a few days later.

Place matters. It is even possible the events of that lost season had more to do with place than they ever did with money, crime, vengeance, or any of the other explanations given at the time. For one week, the reference points vanished; the city of Springfield roiled around untethered, and a strange, deadly world came to visit.

# CHAPTER ONE

The first ones to cross Filion's Field that Monday morning were shift workers heading to the O'Hearn sawmill on Sleigh Bay. The field was on the west end of an escarpment that soared high above the Springfield River, and each worker would have left a high-rise apartment, lunch pail and coffee thermos in hand, then taken the shortcut across the sports field to be standing at the Sleigh Bay bus stop by 5:45 a.m.

The sun appeared that morning at 6:41, and so the men walked in the dark. Likely they walked with their heads down and eyes to the ground, in no hurry to greet the day, as they were shift workers heading to the O'Hearn sawmill on Sleigh Bay.

They could have missed it. When the workers were tracked down by police later that day — there were nine in total, all men — not one was interviewed for more than five minutes.

Next to cross the field were early-morning workers on their way to the city of Springfield: file clerks and security guards, dishwashers and parking lot attendants, construction labourers and split-shift bus drivers. By the time these workers crossed, the sun was in the sky, a winter sun that would have been more white than yellow, that would have shone through the birch and spruce at the edge of the escarpment and the canyon openings between the high-rise apartment buildings, casting shadows that would have lain directly in their path. Police were able to track down twenty-two of these workers. Each was interviewed at length. No one remembered seeing anything unusual about the east-side fence of Filion's Field that morning.

The last to cross were children, taking another shortcut, this one leading to a cut-opening in the fence and beyond that a trail through the woods that brought them to Northwood Elementary School. It was hard to get an accurate number for the children. Police estimated there could have been as many as thirty.

During first recess, a half-dozen boys returned to Filion's Field and that was when a police officer spotted them, throwing rocks at something tied to the fence, a target of some sort. The rocks arced in the air. The boys laughed. By then, the sun had risen high enough to be shining directly through the chain-link fence that surrounded the field, casting geometric shadows on the soccer pitch that replicated the metal mesh.

The cop's name was Donna Griffin, a young cop who had come to the North Shore projects to serve a family court warrant. She watched the boys, trying to figure out what game they were playing. Eventually, she started walking toward them. When she was spotted, the boys turned as one, like a herd of deer spotting a hunter. Then they took off as one, heading toward the hole in the fence and the path beyond.

The cop knew better than to give chase, as there was no way she was going to catch those boys. A couple of them had looked fast enough to make All City. She watched them disappear into the woods, and before the last child's back vanished, she realized no boy had turned to yell at her. Not one jeer or taunt when it was obvious she was not giving chase. A half-dozen boys. From the North Shore projects.

She kept walking. Was halfway across the pitch when the object tethered to the fence began to take shape, began to occupy time and space and become a thing defined. She stopped fifteen feet short of the object. The shadows fell across her, not in the pattern of chain-link, but as two large intersecting lines. She stared up at the fence and found herself wishing she had chased those boys.

# CHAPTER TWO

Frank Yakabuski sat in the kitchen of a bachelor apartment near the Springfield River. He was waiting for the teenage boy in front of him to speak. He had been waiting ten seconds and knew it was going to take more time.

He looked around the boy's kitchen. It was small and had a bad smell, but there was a window that would have overlooked a city park, except the boy had hung a Bob Marley towel there in place of the drapes he was never going to buy. Yakabuski felt pretty confident Bob Marley would have left the window open. Trees across the street. Good mid-morning sun. Yes, he would have done that.

What can you say about homage when it gets twisted around like that? Kid didn't know any better? Kid was given the towel? He sat and tried to figure it out. Eventually the boy said, "I fell, Mr. Yakabuski. Off the roof. How many times do I have to tell you that?"

Yakabuski turned away from the window.

"That's the story you're sticking with? After everything I've just shown you?"

"I was tripping on acid. I went to the roof of my apartment. I thought I could fly. That's what happened."

Five weeks ago, the boy had been found on the sidewalk outside his apartment building, beaten so badly he was still wearing a leg cast and an arm cast and, according to a doctor Yakabuski had spoken to earlier in the day, about to lose most of the vision in his left eye. The boy owed money to the Popeyes motorcycle gang. Many sources had confirmed it.

But his story, when he was interviewed in hospital, was that he had been high on acid and fallen off the roof of his apartment building. He had been released the day before and Yakabuski, the senior detective with the Springfield Regional Police Force, had come to the boy's apartment with his medical files to explain how the story was impossible.

When they had finished examining the x-rays he said, "So, maybe you can get these injuries from falling off the roof of this building, like you say. Problem is, you'd need to climb right back up and jump off three or four more times."

That's when Yakabuski had started waiting. The boy had dirty blond hair and doleful blue eyes, scabs on his forearms that bled from time to time, little trickles of blood that he wiped away, sometimes without looking. He was nineteen, and his name was Jimmy O'Driscoll.

"Unless you inherited some money when you were in the hospital, you're making a bad mistake," said Yakabuski. "You have the same problem that got you beat up in the first place."

"Don't know what you're talking about."

"How much do you owe them?"

"Not a clue what you're talking about."

"You have no criminal record, Jimmy. What you have is a serious meth addiction. Everyone can see that. Tell me what really happened, and we'll protect you. Get you some help."

"You can protect me? From the Popeyes?"

Yakabuski looked at the boy with sadness. Not frustration. Not disappointment. A familiar sort of sadness. He was watching how desperate people make stupid decisions. Jimmy O'Driscoll may as well have been a train wreck backed up ten seconds.

"There are no guarantees in this world. You're right about that, Jimmy. But don't you think some protection is better than nothing at all?" he said.

The boy didn't say anything. Yakabuski didn't say anything. They waited a little more.

But the cop saw soon enough how it was going to play out. Beads of sweat rolled down the boy's forehead, but then his body went rigid, the sweat disappeared, and a sneer worked its way onto his face. He was going to man-up. It would all be acting after this. Nothing genuine or worth noticing.

Maybe the boy had even convinced himself — in the short time it often takes desperate people to believe in impossible outcomes — that the Popeyes would reward him for his loyalty, for his refusal to turn on them, even after they had maimed him for life. At the very least, they would give him more time. Yakabuski began to gather the medical files.

"I'll need an explanation for the report," he said.

"An explanation?"

"An explanation for how you fell off a two-storey house and sustained the injuries you did. I need to write something down, Jimmy."

The kid thought about it. Scratched his arms. Thought some more. After a while he said, "It was really good acid."

Yakabuski wrote it down. He was about to push one more time when he received a text from the day-duty sergeant at the main Springfield police detachment, telling him he needed to get to Filion's Field.

# CHAPTER THREE

Springfield was built on the southern edge of the Great Boreal Forest, at the junction of three great rivers, and the north shore of the largest of those rivers, the Springfield, was always considered the outskirts of town. The North Shore was the place you could find what all cities pushed to the outskirts: cheap bars and cheaper housing, junkyards and one-bay auto shops, bad drunks and hucksters, thieves and junkies. It was French mill workers and Métis shantymen who first settled on the North Shore, coming in the early nineteenth century, in the heyday of square-timber logging in the Springfield Valley. After that it was Cree and Algonquin, more Métis, all displaced by the giant lumber companies that came in the late nineteenth century and needed the rivers to power their pulp mills, their sawmills, their matchstick factories.

By 1930, the shantytown on the North Shore was nearly

the size of the incorporated city of Springfield directly across the river. Every night people in Springfield would hear the sounds of fiddles and washboards drifting across the river, the barking of tinkers and shamans and rum-runners, the songs of drunken men stumbling in and out of the many taverns. Every morning, they would look across the river and see cookfires and smudge pots burning, and a slow-rising river mist that twirled around the cedar lean-tos, the bark-slab cabins, mist out of which would step voyageurs with their bright red sashes; crazed bushmen with long hair and leather britches; black-clad preachers as thin as lepers; boys with bowler caps and brightly coloured suspenders; temperance women from Springfield brought by boat, walking with hand-painted parasols and heavy gowns; everyone milling and jostling, disappearing and reappearing out of the mist and smoke that never seemed to leave the North Shore.

In 1936, the shantytown was razed by the city of Springfield in order to build a bridge. Because no one living on the north shore had deeded land, city workers simply showed up early one August morning with three barges of bulldozers and cement mixers, followed by another barge containing the sheriffs from Springfield, Perth, and Buckham counties. The sun was just barely above the treeline, the mist still heavy on the river, the cookfires not yet burning when the barges arrived.

The sheriff of Springfield County walked to the centre of the village and fired his rifle. In the quiet and hesitation of that morning, it made an empty boom, a sound without echo or reverberation that disappeared immediately. Yet it was enough to bring people from their beds, to awaken the men sleeping on the corduroy road outside Les Filles du Roi, and when enough people had gathered, the sheriff told the crowd they needed to be gone by noon.

When the men objected, the last barge arrived, filled with Irish thugs from Springfield, members of a street gang known as the Shiners. While the sheriffs kept their rifles trained on the crowd, the Shiners began to empty the homes, throwing belongings onto the mud road, taking whatever caught their fancy, setting fire to the homes when they were empty. Anyone who tried to stop the ransacking was beaten.

Some children were taken back to Springfield, where priests from St. Bridget's and some of the more devout members of the Temperance League were waiting to claim them. Everyone else gathered what was left of their belongings and marched away. Some marched right into the unincorporated townships and were never seen again. Most though, having some connection to the city of Springfield — whether by work, crime, or drinking habit — hiked up the escarpment that overlooked the North Shore, put down their belongings, and began to build another shantytown.

Thirty years later, the city came back to raze the second village. Not to build a bridge this time, but to build social housing for the lost souls atop the escarpment. It was mid-'6os idealism run amok, but before the city could be stopped, before anyone on the North Shore could be asked, eight high-rise apartment buildings had been built on the escarpment, seven thousand apartments altogether, with another two hundred row homes connecting the buildings like a charm bracelet. Though as far as Yakabuski could recall, there had never been anything all that charming about the North Shore.

· · ·

Once he was over the North Shore Bridge, Yakabuski turned right and followed a service road that ran beside the escarpment. When the road dead-ended at a municipal garage, he cut up LaPierre Street and made a right on Tache Boulevard. This was the main commercial street on the North Shore: thirteen blocks of taverns and corner groceries, nail parlours and dollar stores, all the businesses sitting in day-long shadows because of the high-rise apartment towers running parallel to the street.

The apartment buildings were lettered and identical in every way except for the graffiti. Yakabuski took an alley that ran between Buildings G and H and saw the patrol car. Then he saw a young police officer standing a hundred metres away from the vehicle. She had her cap in her hand and was staring at the east-side fence of Filion's Field.

Yakabuski slowed his Jeep to a crawl and leaned over the steering wheel to look at the upper-floor windows of Buildings G and H before popping the curb and driving across the soccer pitch, leaving the patrol car behind in the parking lot. When he reached the fence, he parked broadside to the apartment buildings, so the driver's door was facing away. He got out of the vehicle slowly, took one last look at the upper windows of the apartment buildings, and then motioned for the patrol officer to join him.

When she was standing beside the Jeep, he said, "How long have you been standing here?"

"Twelve minutes."

"Right here the whole time?"

"I have not left the crime scene, Detective Yakabuski."

She knew who he was. Yakabuski was no longer surprised by this. He had been with the Springfield Regional Police fourteen years, the first few years seconded to a joint task force with the Royal Canadian Mounted Police and the Sûreté du Québec, working undercover during the Biker Wars. He had befriended the head of the Popeyes motorcycle gang, Papa Paquette, and later testified against him in court, helping to send the biker to the Dorset Penitentiary for twenty years. He was well-known in Springfield after that.

But then two winters ago, he was sent to the remote town of Ragged Lake, high up on the Northern Divide, to investigate the murders of a squatter family. What he discovered when he got there was a secret meth lab owned by the Popeyes and the Shiners. The Battle of Ragged Lake was what the media came to call the events of the next three days. A journalist from Springfield had written a book with that title, and there was now talk of turning it into a movie. Yakabuski could not go anywhere in Springfield these days without being recognized. He leaned against his Jeep, looked at the fence, and said, "Where are you from, Constable?"

Donna Griffin looked confused. "Where am I from?" she stammered.

Yakabuski kept looking at the fence. He was staring directly into the sun, and he twisted his head to the right then far to the left. He shielded his eyes and stepped closer to the fence. Then he stepped back.

Tethered to the fence was the body of a man. A large man, dressed in an expensive three-piece suit. His legs were pinned together, his arms were outstretched, and his head hung down, touching his chest, so his face was obscured.

"What do you think happened to his head?" he asked.

"I'd say someone put the boots to him," answered Griffin.

"You've got a bad angle. I'll give you that."

"Detective Yakabuski, if I have done something wrong, please tell me what it is."

"You never told me where you were from."

The look of confusion came back to Griffin's face. She couldn't follow the narrative track of this hulking, Polish cop standing beside her. He was changing direction too often. Keeping her off-balance. Before she could answer, Yakabuski said, "I know you're not from around here for a few reasons. One, you're standing outside your patrol car in the North Shore projects with your back turned to those two apartment buildings. How long did you say? Twelve minutes? There are men living in those buildings, Constable, who would consider that a free shot."

"Detective Yakabuski, I'm aware of the dangers on the North Shore. It's the reason—"

"The second reason I know you're not from around here is because you've been doing all this while standing in front of Augustus Morrissey, who for some reason is tied to this here fence."

The young cop's face went white. She stared up at the dead man. "Are you sure?"

"Oh, I'm sure all right. Want to know the worst part?"

"All right, now I know you're having a go at me. How can there be anything worse than that?"

"It's worse because Augustus hasn't been given the boots. He's had his eyes cut out."

# CHAPTER FOUR

The border guard saw the vehicle shortly after 10 a.m. The sixth vehicle in lane four. A Falcon campervan with Texas plates, a raised roof, and travel stickers glued to the rear windows. All the windows tinted black, which you didn't normally see on a campervan.

The guard walked to lane four and tapped the window of the booth. When the other guard opened it, he said, "Thomas, you must do me a favour."

The guard in the booth was from Arizona, a young man with powerful arms and barbed-wire tattoos on both wrists. He didn't say anything right away.

"Switch lanes with me," the first guard continued. "There is a car in your lane I would like to put through."

The guard with the powerful arms broke into a smile. "The Miata?"

"Yes. I have put her through a couple times before."

In front of the Falcon campervan was a cobalt blue Mazda Miata, driven by a woman in her mid-twenties wearing a low-cut blouse and white denim shorts. She had a model's face and blond hair that blew in the wind the way blond hair like hers should blow in the wind.

"Let's hope you fuck up," said the guard in the booth, opening the door and stepping out. "A woman like that will leave you on a street corner begging your wife to take you back."

The two guards laughed. Neither one liked the other. The guard from Arizona thought it unfair so many guards of Mexican descent worked at the Brownsville, Texas, border crossing. The guard of Mexican descent thought the other guard was crude, stupid, and had a bad tattoo. But the woman was beautiful, and so the guard from Arizona played along. It would be entertaining, whatever happened.

• • •

When the Mazda arrived at the booth, the guard was thorough and officious, as he had been instructed in the email he received the day before, the one from an uncle in Mexico City he had never met but who so loved his nephew, he deposited money into his bank account every month. He ran the woman's driver's licence, passport, and vehicle registration through every imaginable computer check. The other guards were staring at lane four and smiling at how much time he was taking. When the guard waved her over for a full vehicle inspection, two guards actually laughed. They all turned and watched the Miata drive toward the security lanes and waited for the woman to step out of the car. They had yet to see the full view.

The campervan drove up and the guard took the passport offered to him through the window. He stared at his feet. Flipped to the tenth page and inked an entry mark, not bothering to touch his computer. He returned the passport, pushed the button that raised the draw-arm, and the campervan drove away, entering the four-lanes-merging-to-two melee of cars, motorcycles, cargo vans, trucks, and campers that had just entered the United States.

• • •

The driver of the Falcon set his cruise control at fifty-five and rolled down his window. Took a deep breath of this new country. Salt, shrimp, and gasoline, beef cooked on an open fire, the dung of a million gulls, pine needles — he picked out the scents one by one. Identified them. Categorized them. Nothing unfamiliar yet.

He drove north on the coastal highway, the Gulf of Mexico on his right, dotted with massive oil rigs and smaller pumpjacks, sailboats darting around them like white moths, attracted not to light but to the scent of fossilized dung and bones from millennia ago. The sun was high in the sky, and rays of heat simmered on the highway, layers of them, shimmering and moving across the asphalt like schools of silvery fish. Road signs appeared out of the rays as if they were flash cards seen in a hallucination.

He stopped for gas at a Texaco station, had coffee in the diner, and when enough time had passed, he went back to the Interstate. Twenty miles south of Corpus Christi, he started to look for the turnoff. He found it and turned away from the gulf, down a secondary road that soon turned to gravel, travelling past fields of sugar beets that stretched uninterrupted to the edge of the western horizon. The abandoned farmhouse he was looking for, used as a storage warehouse now, had beets growing to within two feet of its frame. The small road dead-ended at the rear of the building.

The Miata was already there, and he parked beside it. Checked to make sure there were no clouds of dust atop the fields of sugar beets. No vehicles moving. No one approaching. He sat in the campervan a long time, looking at nothing more than a field of sugar beets. Eventually, he left the camper, putting a screwdriver in his jacket pocket before opening the door. He stopped at the Miata to remove the licence plates, placing them atop the hood.

He entered the farmhouse and saw the woman had followed her instructions to the letter. A good worker. Hired in Heroica and sent to the most expensive salon in the city to turn her hair blond, the colour that most attracted American border guards. Now she was naked. Standing in the shadows and swirling dust of the abandoned farm, sunlight coming through the slats of the wood-frame building and touching her skin to form a geometric pattern. The driver stared at the woman for a moment, wondering if he had seen the pattern before. Whether it might be a portent for his journey.

But nothing came to him. The woman, thinking the man was enjoying the sight of her naked body, raised her arms above her head, a gesture that raised her breasts, pushed forward her pelvis. She was running both hands through her long hair when the man took the pistol from the waistband of his pants and shot her.

The bullet entered the forehead, just above the bridge of the nose. A perfect shot. But then the driver was a skilled marksman, and the woman could not have done much more to present herself as a shooting target.

He walked to where she had fallen, bent, and placed two fingers of his left hand against the right carotid artery in her neck. When several seconds had passed, he removed his fingers.

She had a beautiful body. It had been offered freely. She didn't expect men to turn away from such a gift. Which meant she was never suspicious. Meant she was killed with ease, the way beautiful people always seem to be killed. He stared at the body for another minute, then walked back to his van, picking up the licence plates along the way.

He drove until the sun started to set, then stopped at a rest area south of Houston. He went inside to a bank of payphones on the wall outside the men's washroom. He picked a phone with no one standing to either side. The number was memorized. The American change already in his pocket. The phone rang only once before being answered.

"You are on your way?"

"Yes."

"Six days?"

"Yes."

"I'll see you when you're here."

Nothing more was said. The driver hung up, got more change from his pocket, phoned another number, and had the same conversation with a different man. After that, he walked outside. The night air was cool, and there were no longer stars in the sky, just the low-hanging sheen of false light coming from the city of Houston. His disappearance was now complete. At that moment, not a soul on the planet knew where he was. Only two knew where he was going. And to one of those, he had just lied. He did not know which one. The answer would come to him during his journey.

# CHAPTER FIVE

Augustus Morrissey weighed more than three hundred pounds, and his body was strung to the top beam of the twelve-foot fence. Which meant he had to be lowered using the arm of an aerial fire truck, a process that took — from the time the call went out until the body was on the ground — more than two hours. By then, there were more than fifty police officers and medical personnel standing on the soccer pitch. Not all of whom needed to be there. Some of the cops weren't even on duty.

King of the Shiners. That's what Augustus Morrissey called himself, and no one ever argued with him. Out of fear. Out of knowing it was true. The Shiners were a criminal gang as old as Springfield. They'd come to the Northern Divide to work as labourers, building dams and reservoirs high up on the Divide and were marooned there when the company that hired them wouldn't pay their passage home. For years, the Irish lived on the Divide as little more than foraging animals, until a man named Peter Aylin organized them into a gang that terrorized the city for more than a decade. The Springfield Regional Police Force was formed in 1847 for the sole purpose of tracking Aylin down and bringing him to trial.

Augustus Morrissey had led the Shiners for forty years, a giant of a man who always dressed in three-piece suits and used a walking cane with a jewel-encrusted head, one he'd had specially made after reading about a similar cane being owned by J. R. Bath, a wealthy lumber baron who once lived in Springfield. It was rumoured men had been beaten to death with that cane, a story so well-known in Springfield most people were careful to keep their distance when first meeting Morrissey. To step back after shaking his hand.

Yakabuski had interviewed Morrissey once, when a man was beaten to death outside the Silver Dollar, the nightclub the Shiners owned in Cork's Town. Yakabuski stood six-foot-four and weighed 250 pounds, and it was one of the few times in his police career he was in an interview room with a bigger man staring at him from across the table. The suit Morrissey wore that day was houndstooth wool, and he looked like a Victorian couch that had decided to get up and walk. He smirked through most of the interview.

Yes, he was at the Silver Dollar that night. No, he never saw the unfortunate victim of the unfortunate homicide. Yes, he was acquainted with the victim. Not well. Billy Garret used to be a bartender at the Silver Dollar. And he did odd jobs. He once repaired the wharf in back of the

Silver Dollar, where Morrissey kept his boat. He had not seen Billy in several years. Was surprised to hear what happened.

"Surprised?" said Yakabuski, and Morrissey smiled serenely.

"A complete surprise."

"So you haven't seen Bill Garrett in years, but his body ends up in the yard behind your nightclub. Any explanation for that?"

Morrissey kept smiling, shrugged his shoulders, and, after thinking about it for a few seconds, said, "River was too low?"

Yakabuski watched as Morrissey's mutilated body got taken down from the fence, remembering the man's arrogance that day. All gone now. Long way gone for Augustus "King of the Shiners" Morrissey. Yakabuski had been in the army for fourteen years, a light infantry unit that deployed to Bosnia many times. He had marched into villages where bodies lay rotting in the street, half-eaten by the dogs that ran wild in the Balkans. As an undercover cop, he was present for the Lennoxville Purge, seven bikers murdered in a remote farmhouse, their bodies stacked like cords of firewood in a backroom until they could be weighted down and dumped in a lake. He thought if more people saw how some people ended their days, there would be less arrogance in this world. Generally better behaviour all round.

The inspector in charge of the Ident department, an old-school cop by the name of Fraser Newton, had arrived at the crime scene and was examining Morrissey's body when Yakabuski walked over to get a closer look.

"You were first on the scene, Yak?" Newton asked, not bothering to turn away from his work.

"Patrol officer called it in. I was first after that."

"No one around, I take it?"

"Only the patrol officer."

"You notice the crowd we're holding back at the perimeter?"

Yakabuski looked over at the yellow crime tape that now encircled the soccer pitch. No one was standing there except cops and paramedics.

"When was the last time you were at a murder scene, victim outside, and there wasn't a single gawker?"

"Not sure if it's ever happened."

"Hope you're not counting on getting much from the canvass of those apartment buildings."

"Never was. It's all up to you, Newt. What do you have?"

"He's had his eyes cut out. I didn't think they still did shit like that around here. How do you figure they got his body up there?"

While waiting for Morrissey's body to come down, Yakabuski had walked the soccer pitch, looking for blood stains, tire tracks, any clue as to what had happened the previous night in Filion's Field. He had walked the perimeter of the fence, and he now pointed to a clump of trees by a service road on the other side.

"I found fresh vehicle tracks on the other side of the fence. Standard issue winch for any Jeep would have done it, so long as you had enough cable. Throw it over the fence and winch him up."

"And to get him tied like that?"

"It's a chain-link fence, Newt. You climb it."

"Well, we have multiple stab wounds here, Yak. Some blunt-force trauma. I suspect one of the stab wounds will be the cause of death. He wouldn't have been killed here. Not enough blood on the ground."

There was an Ident cop on a ladder, taking photos of the fence where Morrissey had been hanging. Yakabuski could see that blood coming from his head had trickled down the edges of his coat and left a silhouette mark on the metal links. He had seen photos that looked somewhat like it. Shadow outlines of people living in Hiroshima on a hot August morning in 1945. The ground itself, though, as the Ident inspector had said, was relatively blood-free.

"Your best guess on time of death?"

"Around midnight, I would suspect," said the inspector. "Full rigor hasn't set in. He was probably put up on the fence around three or four in the morning. Who's going to tell Sean?"

"I am."

"You think that's a good idea? At the sight of you, he'll probably lose it."

"My case. My notification."

"You can delegate a thing like that."

"Don't want to." Yakabuski looked one more time at Augustus Morrissey lying on the gurney. His heft was so great, the gurney had been ratcheted down to its lowest setting, but even then it was stretching the fabric and seemed at risk of collapsing.

"You want to see how he's going to react, don't you?"

"Might be worth seeing."

"Well, I wouldn't want to be in the middle of that little experiment." Newton stood up and motioned for one of his Ident cops to come over and start the official examination of the body. "Is it true no one called it in?"

"It's true."

"A man hanging from a fence in a kid's sports field and no one calls it in. These projects are fucked." He spat on the ground and walked away.

# CHAPTER SIX

It was the second week of December, but the city of Springfield was still waiting for winter to arrive. Most years, it would have blown into town weeks ago, come by way of a single storm. The snow would stay and that was that. For days afterwards, city plows would be turning over chunks of snow with bright red sumac frozen inside. But every so often there was a year when the snows were late to come, when the wind laid on the other side of some ridge it couldn't climb out of, and you had this false season.

Like everyone else in the city, Yakabuski had begun to look for signs of the seasons about to change. On his way to Cork's Town, he slowed at the apex of the North Shore Bridge to look upriver and down. No cloud on either horizon. The sky the same faded-denim blue it had been for weeks. Another sunny, windless day, temperature twenty degrees above the seasonal average. The *Springfield Sun* seemed to be running out of ways to remind people how odd it all was. They had already run front-page photos of children swimming at a beach and people windsurfing on Buckham's Bay. One of the television stations had run a video that was shot at an O'Hearn sawmill, showing workers swatting away a mid-morning invasion of gnats. But it had been several days since the last weather story, and Yakabuski suspected the reporters were running out of things to say. Like everyone else in Springfield, they were now in a holding pattern, waiting for the anomaly to go away, for the natural world to come back.

. . .

The Shiners had owned a tavern at the corner of Belfast Street and Cork's Town Road since 1837. It was burned down by the newly formed Springfield Regional Police in 1847. Burned again during the Conscription Riots of 1917. When it first opened, it was called Mother McGuire's, the Shamrock Hotel after that, and since 1944 the Silver Dollar, a nightclub that to many in Springfield was as much of an institution as the Grainger Opera House or the Georgian-designed city hall.

The Springfield River was directly behind the Silver Dollar and to the right of it was an empty lot a developer in Toronto bought many years ago, thinking he would build riverside condominiums, until Augustus Morrissey visited one day and explained if such a building were ever erected, the developer would be dropped from the top floor on the day it opened.

To the right of the nightclub was the Blue Bird, a diner frequented mostly by residents of a nursing home run by the diocese of St. Bridget's. The diner closed every day at 4 p.m., and Augustus had made a deal with the owner years ago to not have his dancers begin their sets before that time, to avoid overlap between customers. The owner of the Blue Bird was appreciative and never complained about anything he saw or heard at the Silver Dollar. Morrissey didn't mind helping the diocese, and figured girls willing to dance in the daytime weren't worth the money anyway.

It was a fifteen-minute drive from the North Shore projects to Cork's Town, and Belfast Street was crowded when Yakabuski arrived — people entering and exiting the taverns, standing on street corners talking and waving their arms, cutting across the street as though it were closed to traffic. Saturday-evening foot traffic on a Monday afternoon. The news was already out. Augustus Morrissey had been found murdered on the North Shore. Yakabuski turned down the alley that ran between the Silver Dollar and the Blue Bird, parked his Jeep, and headed to the front door.

. . .

The doorman in front of the Silver Dollar stood six-foot-three and weighed close to three hundred pounds. His name was Eddie O'Malley, and he was wearing a checkered suit that pinched his shoulders and rode three inches too high on the sleeves. His tie was green, with a knot so tight it looked like a cat's-eye marble. On his feet were polished black shoes that looked like wake boards and on his head a fedora hat perched so high it resembled a boy's beanie, or a smoke stack on the roof of a Cork's Town triplex. O'Malley had been tending door at the Silver Dollar for more than a decade.

"Evening, Eddie," said Yakabuski when he reached the front of the nightclub.

"Evening, Mr. Yakabuski."

"Is Sean in?"

"He expecting you?"

"I reckon he is."

"All right. I'll take you back."

The inside of the Silver Dollar had the smells of any nightclub in Cork's Town: beer, melted cheese, tobacco, Aqua Velva, hairspray, and Charlie perfume. It had the same noises too: clinking pool balls and chiming video-lottery terminals, the clicking of change-belts, the laughter of men who rarely laughed, the laughter of women who laughed too much. What made the Silver Dollar different were its provenance and its size, easily the largest tavern in Cork's Town. Yakabuski followed the bouncer's massive back as it weaved between the tavern tables. Although the entertainment wouldn't start until later that afternoon, the room was already full, and most of the patrons took a moment to watch them pass. Some leaned over their tables to whisper something. A few in the farthest corners of the room stood up to point.

O'Malley looked over his shoulder and said: "How did Augustus end up on the North Shore, Mr. Yakabuski? That doesn't make any sense to me."

"Me either, Eddie. You seen anyone from the North Shore in here recently?"

The bouncer gave a chuckling snort but didn't bother answering. It was the sort of question you could do that with. They walked to the end of the bar and then took a left, down a hallway that had another doorman standing in front of a velvet rope. Eddie waved at the man, and he stood aside. They went down the hallway, which had a half-dozen office doors, and stopped at the last door on the right. Just before knocking, a quizzical look came over O'Malley's face. He put down his raised fist and said, "When was the last time you saw Sean, Mr. Yakabuski?"

"It's been a while."

"Since what happened to Tommy?"

"Why? What happened to Tommy?"

The bouncer looked confused. "You killed him, Mr. Yakabuski. You don't remember that?"

The look on O'Malley's face was sad to see: a pained contortion, all the man's mental prowess turned to the problem of figuring out how Frank Yakabuski could forget he was the one to kill Sean Morrissey's cousin and best friend, Tommy Bangles, up at Ragged Lake.

Yakabuski regretted the joke immediately. He felt small and cruel, as though he had just bullied a child or made a lewd joke about a woman who had briefly left the table.

"Of course I remember what happened to Tommy, Eddie. I was just trying to . . . forget it. I'm sorry. I haven't seen Sean since then, no."

"Shit. I should have thought about that. I should really tell him you're here before we walk in."

"He was annoyed?"

"Annoyed? Mr. Yakabuski, I never seen him anything like it. He trashed his office. It had to be completely redone."

"Well, we're standing in front of his door right now, Eddie. Why don't we just knock and walk in. See what happens."

"Oh man, I should have thought about that. Why don't I think about these things?"

The doorman was hitting himself on the head. How could he forget something like that? *Thump. Thump.* When are you going to remember the important stuff? *Thump. Thump.* The fedora was hanging on O'Malley's head by some invisible thread. In between blows, Yakabuski pushed open the door.

# CHAPTER SEVEN

Sean Morrissey was sitting behind a large metal and chrome desk, his head turned to some papers, and when the door opened, he raised his head slowly, no surprise registering on his face when he saw Yakabuski standing there. After a few seconds he said: "I was wondering if it would be you."

"Senior detective. It's my case."

Morrissey was dressed in a charcoal grey suit with a gleam to it that let you know it was expensive, even if you knew nothing at all about suits. A white shirt but no tie. Cufflinks with a blue gemstone that looked like a summer sky after a good, hard rain. His hair curled around his collar, and there was just a tinge of grey around his temples. He kept staring at Yakabuski but didn't speak.

O'Malley had stopped hitting himself in the head and was standing with the fedora in his hands. "I'm sorry, Mr. Morrissey. He said you were expecting him. I figured with what happened to your dad and everything, I figured that it was . . . you know . . . true?"

Morrissey held up his hand and the doorman stopped talking. Then he curled his fingers over and flicked them upwards. Did that twice, and the bouncer left the room, closing the door behind him. After flicking his hands, Morrissey went back to doing nothing at all. Yakabuski knew Sean Morrissey well, had questioned him in the holding cells at the police station during at least half-a-dozen criminal investigations, and after he thought enough time had passed, he said, "You dishonour your cousin, Sean."

Morrissey's body twitched, and his eyes flashed with an anger so malevolent there seemed to be millennia worth of antipathy staring across the desk at Yakabuski.

He continued, "You dishonour Tommy by pretending his death was something it was not. Tommy Bangles died on his feet, in battle, the way he would have wanted and the way you always imagined he would go. He died a soldier's death. It was not unfair. It was not an insult to his memory. It is your desire for revenge that does that."

Yakabuski strode into the room until he was standing directly in front of Morrissey's desk and said, "We need to talk about your father."

Morrissey continued staring a few more seconds before saying, "This soldier's death you talk about, we must take your word for it, right, Yak? Everyone else in Ragged Lake is dead. You were last man standing? Do I have the story right?"

"If you wanted people still standing, maybe you shouldn't have sent Tommy."

For the first time there was motion on Morrissey's face that wasn't a flash of anger. A thin smile. After that, a bending of the head. The gestures of a man enjoying a good memory. Before long, he stretched out his right hand and said, "Take a seat, Yak. Tell me what you know about my father's murder."

He was taking control. Yakabuski didn't mind. The questions were going to be the same.

"I don't have cause of death," he said, sitting down in a chair in front of the desk. "He was stabbed and beaten. Sometime last night. Can you think of any reason your father would be over on the North Shore?"

"No. I can't remember my father ever going up there. Why would he?"

"Are the Shiners doing any business up there?"

"You expect me to answer that?"

"It would be nice if you did."

"The North Shore is a cesspool. You know that. Why the fuck would I have business up there? I'd have to burn my suit every time I came home."

"When was the last time you saw your father?"

"Day before yesterday. We played euchre at St. Bridget's."

"Can you think of anyone who would want your father dead?"

"No sane person."

"That's a no?"

"That's a search Google. You can come up with your own list."

"Any trouble recently?"

"No. My dad was retired."

"That's right, you've been running the Shiners for, how many years is it now, Sean? Four?"

"Never heard of anything called the Shiners. I've been in

charge of my family's business holdings for about four years. You're right on the date."

Yakabuski wrote something in his steno pad. Flipped back a few pages. "I have a couple different birth dates for your father."

"I'm not surprised. He came over from Belfast. Probably made his documents in the hull of the ship."

"I have his age as either seventy-six or eighty-one. Do you have a preference?"

"He'd probably like to be younger."

Yakabuski wrote it down. After that he rubbed his neck, trying to work out a kink. He looked around Morrissey's office. There were no photos anywhere. No wood, a lot of chrome and white paint and two Japanese prints of plants that looked like they would die if you ever tried to grow them on the Northern Divide.

"So, you have no idea what your father was doing on the North Shore," he said. "No idea why anyone would want him dead. No theories, speculations, or possible explanations for the murder. How am I doing so far?"

"Pretty good. You should be a detective." Morrissey leaned back in his chair and cradled his hands behind his head. A full smile was now on his face.

"Well, let me ask you a question that you will be able to answer, Sean. What are you going to do about this?"

"I'm going to have a funeral for my father."

"After that?"

"Bury him, I suppose."

Yakabuski closed his steno pad. "You don't want to answer, Sean, that's fine. But I would caution you against taking matters into your own hands."

"You're cautioning me?"

"That's right. The smart move here would be to stay away and let us catch whoever it was that killed your father. I'll keep you updated on the investigation."

"Let you avenge the death of my father?"

"You should consider it."

"Let the man who killed my cousin avenge the death of my father? I'm considering whether you're drunk."

"I don't blame you for being angry, Sean. But if you start any trouble in those projects, if you send any sort of crew up there, you will be making life difficult for a whole lot of people, and you will be shut down."

"Did you come here just to give me that warning, Yak?"

Yakabuski rose from his seat, gave his back a stretch, and said, "Why would I ever give a man a warning? I thought you were from around here."

Both men smiled. Yakabuski turned to leave but before he reached the door Morrissey said, "A question from me, Yak. That seems fair, doesn't it?"

Yakabuski turned to look at him. "What would you like to know?"

"Is it true, what I've heard about my father's eyes?"

"It's probably true."

"You know what that means, don't you?"

"I know what it could mean. Or what it used to mean. It might not mean much of anything anymore."

"A coincidence? That's what you're telling me?"

Yakabuski saw the anger returning to his face. He gripped the pen in his hand with so much force the knuckles were pinch-white.

"Maybe I will give you that warning, Sean. Stay away from

the North Shore. You and any crew you might be thinking about sending up there. Get in the middle of this investigation, and I promise you'll regret it."

O'Malley was still standing on the other side of the door when Yakabuski opened it. The doorman walked him back through the tavern, two women unfurling a white rug on the stage and a DJ in the booth beside the bar testing a hand-held microphone.

# CHAPTER EIGHT

Dusk came quickly in Springfield. Came each day when the sun slipped behind the western haunch of the escarpment on the North Shore, a process that took — from when the sun first pressed down on the roofs of the apartment buildings to when the world went dark — about forty-five minutes. Give or take. Depending on the time of year.

It could be witnessed just about anywhere in Springfield, and it was a sort of unofficial clock for the city. When the sun hung above the escarpment and started sliding down the backside of the projects, people knew they had less than an hour before twilight. Mothers would call their children in from backyards. Girls needing to walk through the back streets of Cork's Town or one of the city parks would start heading home. Night-shift cabbies would finish their suppers and walk out to their driveways, their backs already hurting.

A dozen times a day, most people in Springfield would look up at the cliffs on the North Shore and calculate the distance of the sun to the top of the apartment buildings, judging what was left of the day. From the corner of Belfast and Derry there was an unobstructed view of the North Shore, the apartment buildings across the river looking like the turrets of some castle tucked high on the Scottish coastline. The sun had just started its descent when Yakabuski reached the intersection, and he stopped his Jeep to watch.

Sean Morrissey was Augustus's only child but looked nothing like his father. Although he had bulked up, as a young man you would have called him slight. He had fine features and curly black hair he wore long. More than one person had said he looked like Jim Morrison, an effect Morrissey encouraged by wearing leather pants, white shirts, and alligator boots for most of his twenties, until he switched to expensive suits, at the demand of his father some said, although Morrissey seemed as comfortable in the new suits as he had in the jeans and the leather.

Though there was no physical resemblance to his father, Sean Morrissey was a Shiner in every other way. The first entry in his police record was 1985, when he would have been eleven years old. He had broken into the back of Quinn's Tavern and stolen eight crates of liquor. All whisky. They had joked about that at the police station, and the boy had asked the cops what he was supposed to steal, "Beer?"

He said it with such a sneer the desk sergeant got stomach cramps from laughing. Morrissey was released into Augustus's care and never stopped stealing, in any meaningful way, for the next twenty years. In the '90s he ran a heist crew with his cousin Tommy Bangles, robbing jewellery stores and banks

43

up and down the Divide and as far away as Montreal and New York State.

A lot of the stores were robbed at night, with Bangles finding the way into the building and Morrissey emptying the safe. The Anthony's vault in Montreal was one of their jobs, the head of security for Anthony's fired three days later, still insisting it was impossible. Other jobs were straightforward smash-and-grabs, with Morrissey holding a sawed-off shotgun on sales girls who should have been more frightened than they were. The cousins took only the best gems in the store, both Morrissey and Bangles having good eyes for that sort of thing, and then they were gone in whatever time they had given themselves, working off a stopwatch, never caught in any roadblock or on any surveillance tape outside a shopping mall, mysteries no cop could ever figure out.

Although it was no secret around Springfield who was doing the robberies. The Popeyes motorcycle gang tried to muscle in on what the cousins were doing, seeing Sean as a possible weak link in the Shiners organization. The privileged and reckless son of Augustus, a boy who would crumple at the first swing of a bat. "Put the fear of God into those boys," Papa Paquette had said when he dispatched a crew to track them down and explain how things worked if you were a thief in Springfield. The Popeyes needed to have their tithe. It was a scheme that looked good on paper. It should have worked. But as with many schemes that look good on paper and should have worked, there was a variable missing. In this case the variable went by the name of Tommy Bangles.

The two Popeyes in the crew cornered the young robbers on Mission Road one evening, forcing Morrissey's Cadillac to the curb. The Popeyes were big men, with the thunderbolt tattoos of men who worked security for the gang. They exited their truck with sawed-off shotguns shouldered and lecherous smiles on their faces, strode toward the car they had just run off the road.

Tommy Bangles exited the passenger-side door and strode to greet them. When the bikers were fifteen feet away, Bangles drew his handgun and shot them. Then he walked up to the men, as they lay writhing on the ground, and shot each two more times in the head. Morrissey already had the sedan turned around when Bangles got back into the passenger seat. He switched out the clip in the handgun, stuck it back in his waistband, and said to his cousin, "You didn't need to hear what they were going to say, right?"

"No."

"That's what I thought."

The next crew Papa sent for the boys was more cautious, more methodical, looked for a way to ambush Morrissey and Bangles, pistols pushed to their heads before they knew what was happening. Another scheme that looked good on paper. Problem this time was the crew couldn't find the cousins. They did stakeouts at the Silver Dollar, at the high-rise apartment building where Morrissey lived, at the walk-up apartment on Belfast Street where Bangles lived. Nothing. They ran computer checks on their credit cards. Nothing. Straight-armed several of Morrissey's girlfriends. Nothing. After six days of searching, they finally found his Cadillac sedan in a long-term lot next to the airport. Papa sneered when he heard that news. "So they have run."

"Looks that way."

"Augustus will be proud. His son starts a fight and then runs away like a punk."

"They're both fuckin' punks. Turn-tail-and-run fuckin' punks."

That was the last conversation Papa had with his crew. The next morning, the men were found on the front stoop of the Popeyes' clubhouse, their bodies riddled with bullets. In the mouth of one man was shoved a parking stub for the long-term lot. When the stub was brought to Papa, he laughed.

So it had been *his* crew that was ambushed. Lured to an isolated parking lot by a car Morrissey knew the Popeyes would eventually find. All they had to do was hunker down and wait. They had been hiding in the woods nearly a week.

Papa stopped the hustle after that. Sent word to Morrissey through an intermediary that the game was finished, no debts outstanding, well-played, and maybe they could do business one day. To those closest to him, he said Sean Morrissey and Tommy Bangles were Shiners you needed to respect, the Tough Men from lore, and it didn't look like that gang of Irish misfits was disappearing anytime soon if that was the next generation. The Popeyes needed to be smarter if they were ever going to get rid of those bastards.

And Sean Morrissey *was* smart. Smart enough to already be wondering about his father's eyes. Both of them scooped out as neatly as dollops of ice cream dispensed by some pimple-faced teenager standing behind a dairy counter. Yakabuski watched until the sun slipped behind the escarpment and night had come again to the city of Springfield. He started his Jeep. He knew the person he needed to see, and he called on the way to let him know he was coming.

. . .

George Yakabuski had been a cop in High River for thirty-three years, until the day he went to a Stedman's department store to purchase mosquito netting for his hunt cabin and was followed two minutes later by a stick-up crew from Montreal. Yakabuski's father watched two of the crew take up positions by the front door while another two started walking toward the back office.

He caught up with the two heading to the office and yelled, "Cops, put your hands where I can see them," thinking that was all that needed to be said, all that needed to be done, being old school like that, even though he wasn't carrying his service pistol.

When the two robbers heard him yell, they turned and stared at him. Craned their necks to see if they might be missing something. Then they took out the sawed-off shotguns hidden beneath their coats, pointed them at Yakabuski's father, and fired. They left him for dead in the toy aisle, Teenage Mutant Ninja Turtles and My Little Pony toys scattered around his prone body.

But George Yakabuski didn't die. He was a big man, like his only son, and he took the shotgun blasts not in his chest but his hips and lower spine, the metal shards missing every internal organ but ensuring he would never walk again.

He had left High River three years ago, to be closer to his doctors in Springfield, and he now lived on Albert Street, where there were many subsidized apartment buildings and police responded to calls just about every night. A cop's pension — especially when most of it went to medical expenses — did not allow for much better than Albert Street. He lived in one of the better buildings for that street, and Yakabuski tried not to let his father's home address worry him more than it should. Although he hadn't decided yet where that line might be. He spoke to his dad just about every day. Never went a week without seeing him.

Yakabuski had a key to the apartment and let himself in. He found his father sitting in front of his kitchen window, a teapot on the table and an empty cup in front of the seat where Yakabuski was expected to sit. Although Yakabuski's father had once been one of the largest men in High River, there was hardly any indication of that today, little more than the rolls of skin beneath his chin and the length of his useless legs, which ran past the foot rests of his wheelchair and which he usually had covered with a blanket.

"Long day?" he asked, when Yakabuski was sitting at the table.

"Didn't start out that way. Took a bit of a turn."

"The North Shore projects. That's about the last place in the world I would have imagined Augustus Morrissey ending his days."

"You interviewed him a few times, didn't you?"

"Several times. You'd get dead Shiners up in High River from time to time. They'd turn up in some farmer's field or in the trunk of some burned-out car ditched down a back road. So someone had to come down to Springfield and talk to Augustus. Listen to him talk his sweet bullshit and smile at you, a lawyer sitting beside him who probably got paid more for a day's work than most cops make in a month."

His dad motioned to the teapot, and Yakabuski poured himself a cup. It was herbal tea of some sort. He didn't care much for herbal tea. His dad didn't care for herbal tea either. A doctor said he should drink it.

"I've heard some things that weren't on the radio," continued his dad. "The fact you're here makes me think they must be true."

"The body was in pretty bad shape."

"The eyes?"

"Both gone. Nice and smooth. Probably about as clean as you can do a thing like that, I figure."

His dad stirred his tea but didn't speak.

"Didn't look like a first-time thing to me," Yakabuski continued. "It looked ritualistic."

"Is there a reason you're not coming right out and asking me, Frank?"

"I'm not sure. Maybe asking the question will make it real, and I don't want it to be real."

"Well, I can't blame you for that."

His dad took a sip of the tea. His lips winced and his eyes closed for a second. He put down the teacup and pushed it away from him. "I'll say it then. Cutting out a man's eyes was a form of desecration once practised around here by people who came to the Divide a long time ago. It's done to make sure your enemies spend all eternity blind and lost in purgatory. There's still some people in Springfield who would believe in that sort of stuff, and you'd most likely find them on the North Shore."

"Have you seen it before?"

"Never. I've just heard about it. The same way you've just heard about it, Frank. These are old stories. About as old as they get around here. I suspect someone is just being a copycat."

"What if that's not the case?"

"What if this is real, you mean? What if the North Shore Travellers have just killed Augustus Morrissey and hung him from a fence in Filion's Field?"

"Yes."

His dad laughed and adjusted the blanket around his legs. "Then you've got a shitload of problems, Frank."

# CHAPTER NINE

The driver of the campervan was known by many names, but most people in Heroica, the Village of Heroes, his hometown fifty miles south of Brownsville, knew him as Cambino. He spent the twilight hours of his first day on the road thinking of the woman he had killed. Not with regret. Not with remorse. Idle thoughts about where she had gone wrong. Why fate had decided her time on the planet should end in a sugar-beet shack on the outskirts of Corpus Christi.

Cambino figured she had brought it upon herself. Life had been too easy for her. Her experiences had been too limited, likely little more than accepting the gifts and sexual demands of rich men. Without adversity, you are weak. Unprepared for what is coming.

It was nearly 8 p.m., and the sun was setting to the west of the coastal highway, throwing shadows across the road that grew and twisted until they were lost at sea. Traffic was heavy with trade vans making their way between the rigs and ports that dotted this stretch of the gulf, and long-haul truckers who knew enough to avoid the midday sun in Southeast Texas were just awakening and bringing their rigs back out on the highway.

He knew his disappearance had now been confirmed. His brother would have made the necessary checks throughout the day. The beachfront home in Cancun. The penthouse in Mexico City. All his vehicles and planes would have been searched. All his women as well.

Once Raphael had confirmed the disappearance, his brother would have taken control of the family business. Started the protocols that needed to be followed. His brother could no longer sleep in his bed at his villa in the gated community outside Heroica. Could not sleep anyplace for three consecutive nights, a rule their father had taught them both and which they had adhered to all their adult lives. His brother would not search for him. Nor would Cambino's enemies, who once saw his disappearances as a weakness, a way to take advantage of the family. They no longer believed that, and they no longer tried to find him. He could disappear at will.

To disappear is to have power. Another thing his father taught him. The philosophy. The technique. His father had learned from his own father, a trench fighter from the first Great War, a small man with large hands covered with yellow veins, expressive hands that flapped like the wings of a bird, full of life and creativity. His grandfather once told Cambino he never purchased cigarettes in the Great War, even though he was a man who had always smoked. When Cambino asked how that was possible, his grandfather explained that when you lit a match in the trenches, a sniper from the enemy side would see the light, aim his rifle as the flame was brought to the mouth of the second smoker, fire when the third man bent toward the light.

"You never needed to buy cigarettes," he laughed. "You could pluck them, unlit, from the mouths of every third smoker. All you needed were matches."

So his father had learned from the trench fighter, and one day it was Cambino's turn to learn the trick of disappearance. How to become a ghost and strike from the shadows. How to disappear before the eyes of your enemies. If you can do this, his father said, you will have a powerful tool that is beyond all imagining, for men who can disappear are considered demons by other men and have dominion over other men merely by having their names whispered into a frightened ear.

His father thought the skill of disappearing was the most graceful of all the various forms of power. When Cambino was a young man, his father disappeared for two years, after a gang from a neighbouring village went to war against his family. Hjs father could not be found, although he struck back almost every night. By the end of the war, the other gang surrendered without conditions. The three brothers that led the war knelt like madmen in the piazza of their village, feverish, and delusional from sleepless nights, from two years of waiting for death from an enemy they never saw, and everyone in their village accepted their executions as a necessary thing. Cambino's father moved behind the men with his handgun, and no one who watched — and the entire village was rounded up to watch — was sure if the brothers were even aware they were leaving one world for another.

"The trick is to make it real."

"What do you mean?" asked Cambino.

"You must be prepared to never come back. It is the only way the trick works."

Disappearance was the first of many things his father taught him. When he was ready, his father also taught him the philosophies and techniques of death. How death is another powerful tool, not so serene, not so graceful, but still a beautiful and powerful tool and one that, like disappearance, rarely needed to be used. It was sufficient in most cases simply to let your enemies know you had brought it with you.

A useful tool: that was how Cambino had been taught to see death. Not as something to fear or deny but as something to embrace and turn to utility. It was why he travelled in this campervan, with its stainless-steel fillet tables and its reciprocal saws, its ligatures and carving knives, its buckets of bleach and its commercial-size freezer. It was not ostentation. It was not depravity. It was simply the acceptance of death as a tool, by a man who needed a quiet place to work.

# CHAPTER TEN

The North Shore Travellers were one of the great mysteries of the Divide. Most people were unsure if they were even real. Those who believed said they were descended from Central European gypsies, from a fierce sub-sect of the Yenish or the Roma, no one was quite sure, but they were gypsies that did not travel in caravans with red and white flags, inviting people to come and have their fortunes told, their ironware repaired, their pockets fleeced.

They were criminals who plundered and killed to get what they needed, gypsies who scared other gypsies, who travelled in caravans that flew black flags and that decamped every night on high land, wagons and horses not circled but positioned like an artillery line, ready not to defend but to charge. In time, people began to call the black-flagged gypsies "Travellers."

In the seventeenth century, Travellers were in the port

cities of southern France — in La Rochelle and Brouage — and it was then that they boarded ships going to the New World. They were there during the voyages of Samuel de Champlain and de La Salle, and some believe Champlain's great scout, Étienne Brûlé, was a Traveller. It was a story with the whiff of truth to it, as Brûlé was an urchin from a tent city on the outskirts of Paris, and he disappeared into the woods as soon as he reached the New World. Something a Traveller would do.

The Travellers had an affinity for the New World no other settler could match, had skills and passions that were transposable and served them well. For nearly two centuries, the fur trading companies of the New World used them as guides and explorers, as deep-bush trappers, and, when it was necessary, as private militia, to protect their furs as they were brought to market. Many of the Travellers wore red sashes around their waists, and before New France fell, they were often called by the French translation of their historic name — voyageurs.

That was the story. If you believed it. And there was not much on the public record to make you believe it, until one night, fifteen years ago, George Yakabuski raided a brothel in High River. In the backroom of the brothel was a meeting room of some sort, what newspapers later described as a church, and Yakabuski's father thought that was a fair enough description of the room.

There was what looked like a pulpit set up in front of twenty wooden chairs, fanned out like the pews of a church. There was a gold cross behind the pulpit and several smaller crosses scattered around the room. Old photos were on the walls, showing gypsy caravans in the foothills of some distant mountain range — Poland perhaps — and by the shores of an ocean that might have been the Atlantic, on either coast. A couple of the photos looked like they could have been taken in bush camps somewhere in the Springfield Valley. On the wall behind the pulpit was a black flag with a red rose and a five-turret castle. The oddest thing about the room, though, were the blood stains.

The High River cops found them everywhere. On the cedar-planked walls. The pulpit. Several of the gold crosses. It was not until the next week, though, when the preliminary forensics report came back, that the true horror of the room became known. According to the report, the bloodstains came from seventeen different people. Given the spray patterns, it was certain all seventeen had been killed or suffered a catastrophic injury in that room.

Some of the stains were more than a century old.

"Everyone had a shit fit when the forensics came back," said George Yakabuski, forcing himself to take another sip of tea. "I worked that case and pretty much nothing but that case for the rest of the year. Land registry records had the brothel being owned by a numbered company here in Springfield. Most of the investigation ended up over on the North Shore."

"What did you learn?"

"I learned that they're real, Frank, that's what I learned. The North Shore Travellers. The Ghost Gypsies. The Rose and Castle Gang. Whatever you want to call them. They came over here centuries ago, and they're still here. Most of the gang is spread out along the old fur trading routes. There's a weird religious part to all of it too. The Travellers consider themselves guardians of the nomadic life, but they're criminals all the same. They make their money smuggling, running a few brothels way up north, and collecting money from families that have been giving them money for centuries."

"Who's their leader?"

"Man by the name of Gabriel. He owned that brothel in High River. The numbered company traced right back to him."

"Gabriel? Like the angel?"

"You'd think that, but no. His name is Gabriel Dumont. That's the same name as Louis Riel's military commander during the North-West Rebellion, the buffalo hunter who took down ten cops at the Battle of Fish Creek. People who have seen him say he looks like the first Dumont. I have to take their word for it. I never saw him."

"You didn't interview him?"

"Interview him? Fuck, I couldn't even find him. He had a lawyer from Montreal who answered all our questions about the building. Without any known victims, we sort of had our hands tied."

"What beef do you think the Travellers could have had with Augustus?"

"Could be anything, Frank. The Shiners and the Travellers have been here forever. Lots of shared history. Remember it was the Shiners who evicted everyone on the North Shore. That's where most of the Travellers would have been living."

He took another sip of his tea, looked at the teapot as though he wanted to pitch it through the kitchen window, then he looked at his son and said, "This is a strange case you have, Frank. Augustus Morrissey being dead is a good thing. Anyone would tell you that. And the Travellers, they don't cause a lot of visible trouble. Why don't you hold your cards for a day or two and see how this one plays out."

"You don't think it will escalate?"

"It might not."

"A one-time settling of accounts between the Travellers and Augustus because of some old beef no one can remember? He's not a working Shiner, which makes a big difference to those guys, so maybe Sean doesn't have to start a war. Is that how you see it?"

"It's real easy to see it that way, Frank. How was Sean when you saw him?"

"I couldn't get a read on him."

"That sounds about right. You'll know Sean Morrissey is pissed when something blows up."

"He asked about the eyes, though. He's thinking the same thing we are."

"So let him think. You look tired, Frank. Why don't you call it a day?"

"I need a name, Dad. Who should I talk to on the North Shore?"

"What are you going to do with a name at this time of the night? Go home and get some sleep, Frank."

# CHAPTER ELEVEN

Yakabuski couldn't sleep.

He sat on his living room couch and stared out at the Springfield River. His apartment was in the Queen Elizabeth Tower, one of the oldest high-rises in Springfield. Most of the tenants in the Queen Elizabeth were seniors, the lobby often filled with women using walkers and men wearing pyjamas. Most people found it an odd place for Yakabuski to live, but he loved the view from his living room.

He knew much would be made the next day about Augustus hanging on that fence until mid-morning and no one on the North Shore calling it in. He had listened to a call-in show on the way home, and people were already talking about it: What was wrong with people over there? Can you imagine? I don't know why we spent taxpayers' dollars building those apartment buildings. Have you seen it over there?

Funny thing about the North Shore was it didn't get as much police activity as you might suspect, nothing like Albert Street, or Cork's Town, or some parts of the French Quarter, which had a lot of abandoned buildings these days and so had a lot of crack houses and pop-up meth labs and squatters so scary you felt sorry for the cockroaches. Maybe it had something to do with the Travellers being there. More likely it had more to do with the North Shore being home mostly to people with lousy jobs and no luck to speak of.

It didn't surprise Yakabuski that no one had called 911. If you weren't from here, you could misunderstand what it could do to you, living someplace so indifferent to your welfare it could kill you any day of the year. Not because of anything out of the ordinary either. Just because it was February. Or just because a windstorm came up suddenly when you were fishing in the middle of a lake. Or just because a spring flood came in and you were caught standing in the wrong spot.

For most people, living on the Northern Divide meant you kept your head down and didn't go looking for trouble, knowing there was enough coming down the road you didn't need to bring in the extra work. You kept your own counsel. Made your own decisions. There was a lot to be said for an attitude like that. Until an entire community could walk by a dead man hanging from the fence in a children's sports field and do nothing about it.

Yakabuski knew that wasn't being cowardly. That wasn't being mean-spirited. That was just being beat up for so long you'd lost sight of the right reference points.

He kept staring at the river, thinking of the murder of Augustus Morrissey, surprised to see the green-and-red navigation lights of a pleasure craft far out in the main channel. The middle of December and there was a boat on the river. He watched the lights go under the North Shore Bridge and disappear. He kept sitting on his couch, scanning the river for more lights, but no other boat appeared. "So there's only one lunatic in the city tonight," he muttered. That didn't seem at all right to him, but eventually he got tired of waiting and went to bed.

. . .

The sun appeared at 6:45 a.m. the next day, and by then Yakabuski was already in his kitchen, feeling more alert than he had the right to feel after only four hours of sleep. He had showered and shaved and was staring at liquid bubbling in the glass bead of a percolator. He waited until the liquid was a dark peat colour and turned off the gas. Took one of the two cups stored in the cupboard beside the stove and poured himself a coffee. Added milk and sugar. Took a sip. Closed his eyes, and, as he did many days, wondered if this might be the highlight.

Any visitor to Yakabuski's apartment could have easily guessed he was ex-military. Excluding the furnishings, everything in his apartment looked like it could fit into a kit bag. It was little more than books and toiletries, two drawers of T-shirts and underwear, a closet with one suit, half-a-dozen shirts, and some winter gear. The furnishings consisted of a double bed with one nightstand holding one metal alarm clock and one lamp, a kitchen table and two chairs, his living room couch and a coffee table. His television was a Sony Trinitron with an antenna and converter box that brought in three channels. He had Wi-Fi and a laptop, but only used them for work. The camp percolator he used to make coffee every morning he had owned since he was a teenager.

He finished his coffee and checked his email before leaving the apartment. He opened two that had come in overnight. One was from his sister, asking him to call her. Another was from Newton, the Ident inspector, asking Yakabuski to see him as soon as he got to work.

. . .

He phoned his sister from his Jeep. It was early in the day and he wasn't expecting her to answer, but she picked up on the first ring.

"Frankie. There you are. I've been trying to reach you. Didn't you see I called you a bunch of times yesterday?"

"Sorry, Trish, it was a busy day. But I'm phoning you as I'm driving into work. That should count for something."

"It does. So tell me everything you know about what happened on the North Shore yesterday."

"Trish, you know I can't do that."

"Are you kidding me? Augustus Morrissey is murdered and you can't tell your kid sister anything? You know Tyler was up most of the night taking phone calls. He won't tell me anything either."

.Trish was Yakabuski's only sibling. Their mother had died when Trish was a baby, and they were about as close as siblings could be, although right then Yakabuski was wishing he had followed his first instinct to keep ducking her calls. He had known what she was phoning about, and if he hadn't been curious to know what her husband had been doing yesterday, he probably would have kept ducking. In one of those quirks of fate God comes up with sometimes to keep families interesting, Yakabuski's sister had married Tyler Lawson, one of Springfield's top criminal defence lawyers. His biggest client was Sean Morrissey.

Like the adults they wanted to be, Yakabuski and Lawson had agreed to live with this strange set of facts, if not as friends, at least as respected adversaries, the way Crown attorneys and defence lawyers in Springfield had agreed to get bombed every Friday afternoon at Kelsey's Roadhouse.

"I think Tyler would be a better source for you, Trish. Who was he taking phone calls from, by the way?"

"Frankie! You know my husband can't talk. Attorney–client privilege and all that boring stuff. But you're free to talk! So is it true? Did the old bastard have his eyes cut out?"

"Trish, come on . . ."

"Just say yes. It was practically in the newspaper. They just didn't come right out and say it. So you wouldn't be telling me all that much, and you know you're going to tell me something eventually — you *know* you will — so if you're in such a big hurry, you should just tell me now."

And then she broke into laughter. The over-the-top sales pitch had become too much even for Patricia Lawson, a former real estate agent so successful she had brokered out the business years ago. Now she collected commission from people she didn't even know, as she drunkenly, and happily, told her brother during Christmas dinner last year. And she was right, as she usually was. She would get something from Yakabuski if he didn't end the conversation soon. He had never met a person quite as relentless as his sister.

"I still think your husband is the best one to help you, Trish."

"Christ, Frankie, why don't you think about your kid sister for once? What is even the *point* in being Frank Yakabuski's kid sister if I can't get better information than the freakin' newspaper? You're *embarrassing* me. Do you know how many times I'm going to be asked about this today?"

"Then try acting coy, Trish."

"What do you mean?"

"I mean smile and act as if you know something but don't actually speak."

"Are you serious? That's what you're giving me? Freakin' coy?"

"I'm at the detachment, Trish. Got to let you go."

. . .

Yakabuski used his access card to open the parking lot gates. He was not even out of his Jeep when a man started walking toward him. He was standing behind the vehicle when Yakabuski closed the driver's door.

"Detective Yakabuski?"

"Yes."

"It's a real honour to meet you, sir."

The man extended his hand. Yakabuski gave the hand a quick shake, and the man started walking with him.

"My name is Mike Gardner. I work in Ident, with Inspector Newton. He sent me down to get you when you arrived."

"He already sent me an email."

"I know. The inspector wanted to make sure you came and saw him as soon as you arrived."

"How long have you been waiting?"

"Little over an hour."

Which meant it would have been dark when Gardner started waiting. Yakabuski flashed the young cop a quizzical look. What in the world had Newton found?

# CHAPTER TWELVE

The Forensic Identification Department was in the basement of the main detachment in Centretown. It looked like an Apple store, if Apple ever built a store in a windowless basement. A large white room with white desks and white chairs, steel accents coming from the microscopes and the lasers and the display terminals. Yakabuski was surprised to see the chief of the Springfield Regional Police Force sitting in a chair, drinking coffee from a travel mug and looking impatient.

"This must be important," said Yakabuski.

"Not sure yet what it is," said Bernard O'Toole. "I was cc'd on the email. You should reply to those, you know, Yak."

"He asked me to come. Here I am."

Yakabuski took off his coat and placed it on a desk next to O'Toole's winter parka, which looked brand new. The chief was nearly the same size as his senior detective, and the parka took up the entire surface of the desk.

O'Toole saw him looking at the parka and said, "I keep checking the calendar and it keeps telling me it's winter. So I keep bringing the coat. Fuck, I bought it more'n a month ago."

"Can't be too prepared, I suppose."

"Yeah, well, winter is going to come in an afternoon, and you're going to look like an idiot in that leather coat of yours."

The two men raised their travel mugs and took a sip of coffee. It seemed almost a toast.

Just then, Inspector Fraser Newton came into the room. Unlike the senior detective and the chief of the force, Newton was a small man, with thick glasses and hair that had been receding since birth. He was dressed in a white lab coat and carrying an armful of files.

"Ahh, you're both here, good." He put the files on a table, waved at them to join him. "Anyone care for a cup of coffee?"

O'Toole and Yakabuski held up their travel mugs.

"Very good, then, we'll get right to it. It's been a late night down here. Let's start with cause of death for Mr. Morrissey — internal bleeding due to a laceration of the heart. It would have been a bit of a race to claim that title. Every internal organ was perforated. We have at least five potentially fatal stab wounds. Swelling on his brain would have killed him within a day or two. Depends how long the Morrissey family would have wanted to leave Augustus hooked up to life support. He took a vicious beating."

Newton opened one of the file folders and spread out some 8 x 10 photos of the body. With a flawlessly sharpened 2B pencil, he pointed out some of the wounds. There were two head-on mug shots with the recesses of Morrissey's eye sockets circled. There were question marks next to the circles.

"Time of death was late Sunday night, probably around 11 p.m.," he continued. "He wasn't killed at Filion's Field, as I told Detective Yakabuski yesterday. Body would have been transported there between 3 a.m. and 4 a.m. Monday morning, I would estimate. You're not going to move a body that size in any vehicle smaller than a good-sized sedan. I would suspect a truck or an SUV. There was a bit of pooling beneath the body, so it probably wasn't transported that far. It's quite possible the vehicle came from one of the high-rises."

"So we'll start looking for trucks or shitty old SUVs registered on the North Shore," said O'Toole. "My money is on a pickup."

"We can do better than that," said Newton. "There were tire impressions on the other side of the fence from where Augustus was hung. Detective Yakabuski is probably correct that a vehicle with a winch was used to get him up on that fence. Preliminary analysis of the treads would indicate it's a Bridgestone Dueler H/L 400 tire. That's a common tire for light SUVs and some pickups. Dakotas use that tire as stock."

"That's good work, Newt. Thanks for working so late."

"You're welcome. Out of curiosity, do you think everyone on the North Shore registers their vehicles?"

O'Toole laughed. His travel mug was nearly empty, and he was coming to life.

"Fuck, you're funny, Newt. You give people good news, then you try to take it right back from them."

"Exactly. How do you think I've survived down here for thirty-five years? 'The answer to your question is maybe yes, maybe no. You'll need to check back with me later.'"

They all laughed, and O'Toole reached for his parka. He stood up and started walking toward the door, stopped after a few steps, and looked back, wondering why Yakabuski wasn't following. His senior detective was still staring at the photo of Augustus with the circles around what should have been his eyes. Yakabuski looked up and said, "What else did you find, Newt?"

The Ident inspector looked at him in surprise. "Cause of death. Time of death. Model, make, and name for the tire the killer probably had on his truck. You want more than that?"

"I don't *want* more, Newt. I know *there is* more."

"Why do you say that?"

"Because you've got a big fat file there you haven't opened yet. And as interesting as all this is, it doesn't explain why you had someone stand in a parking lot for more than an hour just to make sure I came and saw you right away."

Newton looked annoyed. Then he started to laugh. "I had this big climax all worked out. I was going to wait until you were both at the door and then I was going to say, 'Oh, there's one last thing.' Like Colombo used to do. Remember that show?"

"Newt, it's an early start to what's going to be a long day. What else did you find?" said O'Toole.

Smiling, the inspector opened his last file and shuffled through some photos until he found the one he was looking for. He placed it on the table and slid it across for Yakabuski to see. "We found this in Augustus's mouth," he said. "Would have been put there post-mortem."

Yakabuski and O'Toole looked at the photograph. Eventually Yakabuski said, "Is that a diamond?"

"It is indeed. Uncut, unpolished, right out of the ground I'm told, but it is indeed a diamond. Do you see this line running right down the centre of it?"

Yakabuski and O'Toole looked to where the flawlessly sharpened 2B pencil was pointing. There was what looked like a suture mark down the middle of the rock.

"That's another lucky break for you gentleman. With almost all diamonds, you can't tell where they're from. The internal heat and pressure needed to form a diamond wipes away all traces of any other mineral. That's why blood diamonds are such a problem. There's no way of telling if they came from some slave mine in Sierra Leone, or some legitimate mine in South Africa.

"This diamond is different, though," the inspector continued. "That line you're looking at is actually a vein of red quartz. It's beyond rare, I'm told, to see this in a diamond, but it happens from time to time, and only with red quartz because it's one tough little mineral. Know where the world's largest deposits of red quartz might be, Yak?"

"Canadian Shield."

"That's right. This diamond is from the De Kirk mine at Cape Diamond. It's all in this report." Newton took a sheaf of papers from the file and slid it across the table.

"The gemologist is Joshua Edelson, from the Anthony's store in Centretown. He was down here most of the night. We probably owe him a dinner or something. He has physically inspected the diamond and sent photographs to the head gemologist at Anthony's in Montreal. Both men agree the diamond is from the De Kirk mine at Cape Diamond."

O'Toole was starting to flip through the pages of the report. Yakabuski had yet to bother, was still looking at the photograph of a grey stone with a ragged red line running down the middle of it. It wasn't attractive. Didn't look like it held the light of the inner earth. It was just big and odd.

"What else did you find?" he asked.

Newton didn't bother feigning surprise this time. He sighed and said, "Last page. Bottom line."

O'Toole flipped to the page. The caption at the bottom read *Estimated Auction Value*. He looked up from the paper and said, "One-point-two million dollars?"

"The conservative estimate. Could be more. Depends how good the person is that's doing the cutting. Not sure if that one is such a lucky break for you gentlemen."

# CHAPTER
## THIRTEEN

The Arkansas state trooper was in his mid-forties, had mirrored sunglasses, a slight paunch over his belt, hair cut so short it resembled the hard fuzz you find sometimes on kiwis or deep-rooted turnips. He was what central casting would have sent if you requested an Arkansas state trooper. Still had the rank of patrol officer, first class, after twenty years working I-55.

He saw the campervan twenty miles south of Memphis. He watched from a vantage point atop a small mound of earth next to a service ramp to the Interstate. The spot gave the trooper a long view of northbound traffic. He ate the tuna sandwich he had brought for lunch and watched the camper as it approached. The sun refracting hard and white from a raised metallic box that had been added to the roof. Driving a perfect speed limit.

When the camper passed, he saw the Texas plates. The

tinted windows. He watched it travel down the highway. Start to shake and waver in the heat waves, the sun refracting off the roof, a shimmering white light that seemed to have landed there.

He put the car in gear and drove off the mound of earth. He stayed in the right-hand lane, moving in and out of traffic, vehicles slowing to the speed limit, and was behind the camper within a minute. He ran the licence plates and quickly got a report back that told him the vehicle was properly registered and licenced to a numbered company out of Brownsville, Texas. No tickets. No moving vehicle violations.

A perfectly clean vehicle. Driving a perfect speed limit. The state trooper kept following, curious now to see what the driver might do, because everyone did something eventually. Some motorists slowed to below the speed limit. Or watched out their rear-view mirrors until they started to drive erratically, crossing lanes and kicking up gravel. Some were so unnerved they pulled over and stopped. But the driver of this campervan did nothing. Cruised along as though the cop car was not sitting ten feet off his rear bumper. The state trooper pushed a button on his console and his sirens sounded.

It was a hot day. The trooper could hear crickets and tree frogs when he opened the door of his patrol car, so many it sounded like a choir. The heat hung on the horizon like sauna clouds. He walked up to the camper on the driver's side. Stopped when he was even with the rear bumper, and standing five feet out, shouted, "Open your window please. Then keep your hands on your steering wheel, where I can see them."

The tinted window swooshed down, and the trooper saw the side profile of a man, ball cap on his head, hands gripping the steering wheel at ten and two. He didn't look that big. The trooper started walking, making a wide circle so he approached the driver from the front of the camper.

"I'm going to need to see your licence and registration. Do you have any firearms in the vehicle?"

"What am I being pulled over for, Officer?"

"Keep your hands on the steering wheel. I repeat — do you have any firearms in the vehicle?"

"No."

"None in the glove compartment? None in the cab?"

"No."

"All right. Licence and registration, please."

The driver pulled a wallet from his back pocket. Handed over a Texas driver's licence and a registration card. The trooper looked at them and said, "Where are you coming from?"

"Brownsville," said the driver. Despite the heat of the day he was wearing a white, long-sleeved shirt, buttoned to his Adam's apple. *He looks Mexican*, thought the trooper.

"Where are you off to?"

"Chicago."

"That's a long trip. Your reason for going to Chicago?"

"Work."

"What do you do, Mr. Michaels?" the trooper said, looking again at the driver's licence in his hand.

"I'm a facilitator."

"What does that mean?"

"I solve conflicts. Labour disputes. Corporate reorganizations. Those sorts of things. I was going with the flow of the traffic, Officer. Is there a reason I was pulled over, but no one else?"

"A campervan matching this description was picked up on our traffic plane going eighty-five. Just ten miles back," the trooper lied. "I'll need to see inside the camper. Can you step out of the vehicle, please?"

The man sat still for a minute, as though considering it. The cop unhooked the lapse on his holster. The driver opened his door and stepped out.

"I doubt very much if that was my camper your traffic plane saw. They would have photos, yes?"

"Yes, they would. I still need to see inside the camper."

"Of course. You are just doing your job." The driver walked to the sliding side door of the camper. He unlocked it with a fob on his key chain, pulled back the door, and stepped aside so the trooper could look in.

It was dark. The tinted side windows let in little light, and the camper was cut off from the cab by a partition of some sort, something the trooper did not think came standard on a Falcon campervan.

"You can inspect the camper if you like," said the driver, his voice soft and pitched low, oddly pleasing. "It's all right with me."

"Don't think I need your permission, Mr. Michaels," said the trooper, and he peered more closely inside the camper. His eyes had adjusted somewhat to the darkness, and he saw a sink and chrome items of some sort hanging from the wall. Cooking utensils?

"You didn't do any hunting in Ouachita, did you, sir?"

"No."

"Because that's a national park, and you'd be in a heap of trouble if you did that. Even if you're Mexican, you'd still be in a heap of trouble. Can't say you didn't know about the hunting laws."

"I know that."

"Step back a little further, please."

The driver did as he was told. Then watched the state trooper step carefully onto the drop-down step that led into the camper, watched him rise and enter, turn on his flashlight, and then gasp. It was the gasp that was his undoing. The time it took to inhale breath and collect his thoughts, as he looked at the array of rifles and steel knives, reciprocal saws and metal restraints — no more than four seconds — but that was too much time. The side door was already sliding shut as he turned.

For another four seconds, the state trooper stood there, not comprehending what had just happened. Then he rushed the door and shook the handle. Banged furiously on the window.

"What the fuck are you doing out there? If you don't open this door right fuckin' now, you fuckin' wetback, I swear to God I am going to stomp your fuckin' . . ."

And then he stopped yelling. Saw the driver come into view. The back of him, as he walked casually toward the patrol car, lifting the ball cap off his head and running his fingers through his short black hair. When the man reached the car, he leaned his upper body through the open window and ripped out the dashboard camera. Took the keys from the ignition. After that, he leaned further through the window and took the half-eaten tuna sandwich sitting on the passenger seat.

The trooper stood back from the camper window, shielded

his eyes in the crook of his arm, and fired his service revolver: Three times, point-blank, at the tinted window.

When he opened his eyes, his body gave a jolt. It was a reflexive thing, something that happened without thought or awareness, as he stared at the window and saw the three slugs imbedded in the glass, not so much as a crack in the pane. After that, his body started shaking. Although the trooper did not know it at the time, his life of planned movement and rational thought, purpose and determination, had ended. It would all be reflexive after this.

Cambino stood on the other side of the unbroken window, eating the tuna sandwich. When he finished, he licked his fingers, one by one, and then he went back to his seat and continued driving. It remained a beautiful day, with high cirrus clouds and crickets singing from the scrubland. The banging on the metal plate that separated the camper from the cab stopped after a few minutes, and Cambino turned on the radio. He looked at the fuel gauge and calculated how much time he had. Then he began looking for a good secondary road where he could turn off and begin his work.

# CHAPTER FOURTEEN

Yakabuski and O'Toole stood in the basement hallway out-side the Ident Department. O'Toole carried the gemology report rolled up like a tube. He hit his knees with it while talking. A hard swat every once in a while.

"Well, if we didn't already know this was going to be a rat fuck, I'd say that rather confirmed it," he said. "What are we looking at here, Yak? Some sort of robbery gone bad?"

"Strangest robbery I've ever seen. Someone kills Augustus and *leaves behind* a million-dollar diamond?"

"Million-point-two," corrected O'Toole. "Conservative fuckin' estimate."

He kept swatting his knee with the gemology report, looking at the paper with disgust. People were starting to arrive for their 8 a.m. shifts and trying not to stare at the chief of the force and his senior detective whispering in a hallway. O'Toole held his unused parka under his other arm and looked at the coat with the same disgust he looked at the gemology report. He tried to take a sip from his travel mug, then shook the mug and smacked his dry lips. He looked at the mug with disgust too. There was nothing O'Toole was carrying or thinking right then that pleased him.

"I had a dream last night about Augustus getting his eyes cut out," he said. "He was a sorry excuse for a man, but I would not wish that dream on my worst enemy. I couldn't sleep afterward, so I turned on the computer and started going through Intel reports on the North Shore Travellers."

"Find anything interesting?"

"It was all interesting. You know there's never been a conviction of a Traveller in court? Some of them have been convicted, and done time, but never as a member of a gang called the Travellers. A lot of prosecutors won't even use the word, in case a jury thinks they believe in Big Foot and boogeymen as well. It's just like the Mafia was fifty years ago."

"Was there anything in there on Gabriel Dumont?"

"He was all over the place. The most visible member of the gang. He was raised on the North Shore and he's never done time. There's a youth record with two convictions for assault, and two charges as an adult, both for assault as well. One was a bar fight in Sault Ste. Marie that was ruled self-defence, and the other was an odd one from the States. Dumont was arrested at a protest in Fargo, North Dakota, a demonstration outside a National Park Service office. He hit a police officer. The Americans deported him instead of going through the bother of a trial."

"He's an activist?"

"Don't really know what the fuck he is. Here's the mug shot from Fargo." O'Toole reached into the inside pocket of his parka, took out a sheet of computer paper, and handed it to Yakabuski. "It's fifteen years old, but it's the most recent photo we have of the guy."

The man in the photo, with booking numbers beneath his chin, had a full black beard and long black hair to match, hair so long it fanned out over his shoulders, which ran from edge to edge of the photo. The skin that was showing consisted of little more than red scars on both cheeks, protruding from the top of the beard. He seemed to have a smirk on his face, but there was so much hair it was difficult to be sure.

"Quite the photo. How was that cop in Fargo?"

"He was all right," said O'Toole. "Although I gather the Americans were quite glad to dump Mr. Dumont the other side of the border."

"Do we have intel on where he's living now?"

"Nothing solid. He hasn't been on the North Shore for years. He was picked up on some wiretaps in Edmonton two years ago. Some bikers out there were looking for a pilot. Travellers are some of the best smugglers in the world. Did you know that? They've been doing it for thousands of years, and they hire out."

O'Toole stared at his travel mug and gave it a vicious shaking, as though there might be enough coffee stuck to the sides to free up one last sip. After a few seconds of shaking he tipped it upside down and tried. After trying, he looked at the mug as though he wanted to punch it.

"We need to find him," said Yakabuski. "I'd like to bring in someone from another department to help with research."

"Is there no one in Major Crimes you can use?"

"We're swamped right now. And this would be straight computer research."

"Who did you have in mind?"

"The patrol officer who found Augustus's body. Donna Griffin."

O'Toole looked surprised. He looked at Yakabuski, turning his gaze away from the useless parka and the useless travel mug and said, "Why her?"

"Couple of reasons. Did you know she graduated top of her class at George Brown? She got damn near one hundred percent in every computer course she took."

"You've read her file?"

"You know what she found yesterday. A lot of cops never see anything like that in a thirty-year career. I wanted to make sure we weren't looking at any potential problems."

"You were looking to see if she could handle it. Whether she might go off the deep end."

"Danger to herself or others is the phrase."

"But you didn't find any red flags?"

"None. Although parts of her file were odd. Her family is rich, did you know that? Her grandfather was some sort of shipping tycoon. I can't imagine anyone in her family thinking she's making smart life decisions right now, working as a cop delivering family court warrants in the North Shore Projects."

O'Toole laughed and shifted the parka to his other arm. "If I had a family like that, I'd listen to them. I'll clear her from the sked down in patrol. When do you need her?"

"Now."

• • •

Donna Griffin was already in the detachment, getting ready to start a twelve-hour patrol shift, when the day-duty sergeant found her and told her she was off the schedule. Senior Detective Frank Yakabuski wanted to see her, and he hoped Griffin hadn't done anything to piss that guy off. When Griffin arrived at Yakabuski's office door, he waved her in.

"I've asked for your help in the Augustus Morrissey murder investigation. Are you okay with that?" he said.

"Working a homicide case? I'm more than okay with that. That's why you needed to see me?"

"Yes."

Griffin looked momentarily confused. She had blond hair and a full, round face, what was probably called cherub when she was a child, maybe something less kind when she was a teenager. She wore little makeup and had rose-tinged cheeks, not from blush but from being outdoors. Yakabuski imagined her slopping around in Welly boots as a teenager, in some overpriced riding academy outside Toronto. The look of confusion on her face gradually drifted away and was replaced with one of concern.

"I'm beginning to think you don't trust me, Detective Yakabuski," she said. "Are you doing this just to keep an eye on me? Just how badly did I screw up yesterday?"

"You're here, Constable Griffin, because I think I can use you. If I thought differently, you wouldn't be here. If I thought you were a complete disaster, you wouldn't be here. So ask yourself: does the answer to your question matter that much?"

Griffin was silent a few seconds, then she stood more erect and said, "What can I help you with?"

"Have you heard about the diamond?"

"What diamond?"

And so Yakabuski told her about the diamond found in Augustus Morrissey's mouth. Despite her best attempt to act professional in front of the man who ran the Major Crimes section of the police force that employed her, she couldn't help but mutter "holy shit" when Yakabuski told her the diamond's value. Then he told her about the Shiners and the Travellers, some basic biographic material on Sean Morrissey and Gabriel Dumont, and the theories he and O'Toole had discussed in the hallway.

"We figure a diamond of that value, shoved in the throat of a man that has just been killed, has a limited number of possible explanations," he said.

"Fuck you," said Griffin.

"That would be one. Show everyone Augustus wasn't killed for money, that it was something personal. What else could it mean?"

Griffin was now sitting in the wooden Henderson chair in front of Yakabuski's desk. She gave it some thought. Eventually, she said, "I apologize for my language, but — fuck off."

"That would be number two. In that scenario, shoving that diamond down Augustus's throat isn't like pissing on his body. It's a warning of some sort, to the Shiners. You better back off."

"Why a diamond?"

"That's where you come in, Constable Griffin. I read in your file that you're good with computers. I need you to find some sort of connection between the De Kirk mining operation in Cape Diamond, the North Shore Travellers, and the Shiners. Go through land registry documents, business licences, court records, whatever you can think of that might show a connection."

"Is there a workstation I can use?"

"The chief has cleared you a desk in general pool in Major Crimes. You know where that is?"

"I do."

"Phone me right away if you find anything."

· · ·

The phone on Yakabuski's desk rang thirty-five minutes later. He saw the extension number, and when he picked up he said, "You can't be that fast."

"Well, they're not exactly trying to hide it."

Griffin's voice was breathless and hurried and Yakabuski imagined her leaning into the phone to speak. He was not at all surprised when she started to whisper.

"I ran Gabriel Dumont's name through land registry records for the townships around Cape Diamond, like you suggested," she said. "I got a hit right away. He owns a house ten miles from Cape Diamond."

Yakabuski leaned back in his chair. He hadn't expected it to be this easy. "How long has he been living up there?"

"According to the land registry, he's owned the house since 2004. But there's more. Once I had an address, I ran Dumont's name and home address through some government data banks. His home address is the same address as a Métis group up there: The Upper Divide Métis Assembly. They're not recognized by the federal government, the Cree, or any other Métis group, but their incorporation papers list three hundred members and Gabriel Dumont as president."

"You got all this in thirty-five minutes?"

"I stopped to buy a coffee in the cafeteria on my way here," said Griffin, and her voice sounded smug. "The group filed a land claim last year. It's for most of the Francis River and *all* of Cape Diamond."

. . .

Yakabuski's father was still in bed when his phone rang at 10:30 a.m. Yakabuski didn't bother with any pleasantries or any patient attempt to prod him into alertness.

"Ident found a diamond in Augustus's mouth," he said. "It was put there after he was killed. It comes from the De Kirk mine at Cape Diamond."

"A diamond? Why the fuck would . . ."

"It's worth more than a million dollars."

George Yakabuski stopped talking. He pushed a button on a remote lying on his side table and the top half of his bed began to rise. When he was in a sitting position, he said, "Shit, Frank, whatever is happening on the North Shore, it's about money. The Shiners just got some sort of warning. This is going to escalate."

"That's the way we read it too, Dad. So I need a name from you."

"Frank, those guys scared the shit out of me when I was investigating them fifteen years ago. I don't mind telling you that. Travellers almost *are* boogeymen. Do you remember the old song?"

"Of course I do: 'Beware the Traveller in the woods; Hidden 'neath a blackened hood; Evil comes a Traveller's way; Never light, never good . . .'"

"Well, it's not just a kids' song, Frank. Travellers are weird. They're not bikers. They're not Shiners. They're into this black magic shit. I wasn't sleeping much by the end of that investigation."

"Dad, I'm the senior detective on this police force. What would you be doing right now?"

George Yakabuski hesitated before answering. Then, in a voice that had lost its urgency, replaced by the cadence of weary acceptance, the sort of sound parents have been making since the start of time, he said, "You need to see Tete Fontaine. He runs the brasserie on Tache, in front of Building C."

"He's a Traveller."

"Yes. He's also a cousin to Gabriel Dumont. Be careful around that son of a bitch, Frank. When I say don't turn your back on him, it's not just an expression."

# CHAPTER FIFTEEN

Fontaine's Brasserie was built in 1937, the year after the Springfield police arrived on the North Shore and evicted everyone. It was one of the few buildings allowed to stand when the city came back thirty years later and did it again. It survived because the construction workers building the high-rise apartments needed a place to drink, and because the four exterior walls of the brasserie had been built with squared timber salvaged from the bottom of the Springfield River. Fontaine's Brasserie could have withstood a cannon blast.

It was another warm afternoon, and Yakabuski drove his Jeep with the windows down, thinking it was not right to turn on a vehicle's air conditioning in mid-December. Not that the air conditioning or heating worked all that well on his vehicle, which was one of the six original prototypes for the Jeep Rubicon, sent for testing to the Springfield Police's search and rescue department, and bought by Yakabuski at a police auction eleven years ago. He didn't care that the Rubicon was interior-climate impaired. He loved that it could climb a tree.

He slowed again at the apex of the North Shore Bridge to look at the sky. It was the same faded-denim hue of the day before. Glancing down the south shore of the river, he had a good view of the city of Springfield: The spires of St. Bridget's, always surrounded by smoke because of the many chimney spouts in Cork's Town. The sawmills and factories in the bays and inlets stretching to the west. The business parks and trucking terminals to the east.

The North Shore looked barren by comparison. From any sort of distance, even the apex of the bridge, you saw nothing but the apartment towers. Once he was over the bridge, Yakabuski turned down Tache Boulevard, drove past small stores with chipped brick façades and hand-painted signs. The signs were always changing. Many businesses on the North Shore had trouble paying their rent within the first month, and so they were gone by the second.

But there was some permanence to the street. There was Côté's Dépanneur. Lévesque's Hardware. The St. Jean Baptiste Society meeting hall. At the end of the street, the Church of the Redeemer, a poorly funded parish church the diocese of St. Bridget tended to forget was even there. And right in the middle of the street was Fontaine's Brasserie, the largest building on Tache, made of so much notched and squared pine, it resembled a small fort.

Yakabuski had no trouble finding parking on the street, and when he walked inside the restaurant he found only two old men sitting at a table near the back and a man standing behind the service counter bar to the left. The two old men were dressed in dark green factory clothes, and when they saw Yakabuski they began to take fast sips of their espresso. The man behind the service counter stared at him but didn't make any sort of movement.

When the two men finished their coffee, they went to the service bar and Yakabuski waited by the front door until they were finished paying. The brasserie smelled of coffee and bread and grilled meat. The floor was wide-plank pine, painted dark brown, although the paint was mostly gone now. The windows in the restaurant were all along the front, offering a view of a former nail parlour across the street, a *For Lease* sign hanging in the window.

As the old men waited for their change, Yakabuski took a closer look at the man behind the counter. He was tall and lanky, with black hair he greased back, wearing a flower-patterned shirt and blue dress pants. The shirt looked to be silk, and he had it unbuttoned halfway down his rib cage, revealing a concave chest and more black hair. The chest hair was curly and knotted in tufts, not greased like his head. After the two men left, Yakabuski strode to the service bar. He saw now that the flowers on the bartender's shirt were red roses connected by green vines that snaked and twirled and occasionally erupted into white buds. The man's chest hair looked like mulch between the flowers.

"Mr. Fontaine?"

"*Bien oui*, my friend," he answered, speaking in the thick French patois so common on the North Shore.

"I'm Detective Frank Yakabuski with the Springfield Regional Police. I'd like to ask you some questions about the body we found in Filion's Field yesterday."

Fontaine was smoking and he took a long, slow draw from

his cigarette, eyeing Yakabuski through the curling smoke. Then he placed the cigarette carefully in a metal ashtray on the lunch counter. "Body? You mean t'at Shiner, Augustus Morrissey. You cryin' tears 'bout t'at one, Detective?"

"Don't know if that matters much. My job is to investigate homicides."

Fontaine pressed his lips together and gave Yakabuski another long look. When he spoke he said, "You're bigger t'an I t'augt you'd be. People told me you wuz big, but I figure it wuz bullshit. Never seen a bohunk big as you."

"And I've never seen anyone on the North Shore wearing a silk shirt. So it's a day of wonders. Did you know Augustus Morrissey?"

"Everybody know Augustus fuckin' Morrissey."

"Did you have any business dealings with Augustus Morrissey?"

"A Shiner?"

"Is that a no?"

"T'at's a I'd go down on my mot'er 'fore I shook t'e hand of a fuckin' Shiner." Fontaine scratched his chest and smiled at Yakabuski.

"So that's a no. I appreciate your candour, Mr. Fontaine. Let me return the favour. I don't think there's much that comes onto the North Shore from the outside world. This place is as cloistered as a monastery. I figure a man like you would know something about what happened the other night at Filion's Field."

"A man like moi? Did you jus' insult me, Detective?"

"Augustus had both his eyes cut out. Ever hear of something like that?"

"Everyone know t'at old story."

"You're right. Early settlers on the Divide were sometimes killed in their cabins, their eyes cut out and taken as a keepsake, by a travelling gang of cutthroats called the Travellers that didn't want to see the land settled."

"Maybe t'ey had a good idea. Look what happen t'us when you guys wanted a fuckin' bridge."

"That's how I figured you'd feel. So why did Augustus have to die?"

"I don't know 'bout no dead Shiner. Ot'er t'an a dead Shiner be always a good t'ing." Fontaine kept scratching his chest. From time to time he would grab a clump of black hair and pull on it.

"Do you know where I can find Gabriel Dumont? I'd like to ask him these questions."

"People tol' me you wuz big. No one tol' me you wuz funny."

"You have no way of reaching Gabriel Dumont? He's your cousin, right, Mr. Fontaine? We can continue this conversation down in the cells, if that is your preference."

"Your cells don't scare me. I can do your cells standin' on ma fuckin' head."

"You probably can, Mr. Fontaine. So why don't we avoid the drama? You tell me what you know about the North Shore Travellers and a land claim your cousin has filed up in Cape Diamond, and I go home. You stay here. We all have a good day. That work for you?"

"You t'ink t'e Travellers kill Augustus Morrissey?" Fontaine stopped scratching. Wiped the side of his hand over his mouth. "T'ey just boogeymen."

"I believe in the Travellers enough today to bring you

down to the cells for questioning, Mr. Fontaine. You got any plans for the next three days?"

"You got no cause."

"I've got Augustus Morrissey hanging from a fence on the North Shore. I've got all the cause I'm ever going to need in this city. So what are we doing here?"

Fontaine lit another cigarette. Blew smoke rings toward the square-timber ceiling, the wood dark and nicotine stained, oozing juice, like the hull of a once-great sailing ship lying in the darkness of an ocean bed. There was the stillness of deep sea in the room. The same sort of beyond-mute quiet. Same sort of languor. Fontaine moved his cigarette twice to the ashtray and back to his lips, his movements slow and deliberate, the smoke circles drifting around his head, his eyes shutting and closing, the hand without the cigarette scratching his chest, his groin, his lips, wiping spittle across a lecherous smile and finally he said, "I get in touch wit' Gabriel. You gotta card?"

# CHAPTER SIXTEEN

Yakabuski called Griffin on the way back from the North Shore and was surprised to learn she had no more information than she'd had that morning. She sounded just as surprised.

"Gabriel Dumont's name doesn't pop up anywhere else that I can find. Not around Cape Diamond, anyway. There's just the deed to the house and the land claim. Some of the names from the Métis association seem bogus, by the way. I'll know for sure in a couple hours."

"What about the Shiners? Any record of them being up there?"

"Nothing so far."

"You're including timber and mineral rights?"

"I am."

"And known Shiner associates?"

"If you mean the Popeyes, yes. I've been watching out for that."

"What about De Kirk?"

"Squeaky clean. Company's name hasn't appeared on any civil court filings, no labour code violations, no insurance claims that I can find, which should mean no diamonds have gone missing. Can't find any record of a De Kirk employee being arrested since they started mining up there. No incident reports with the Reserve Police at Kesagami or the RCMP detachment at Fort Francis."

"So they haven't been acting like a company that's getting robbed or getting scammed."

"No sign of it," agreed Griffin.

Yakabuski hung up and continued driving. It seemed to him the investigation into Augustus Morrissey's murder was now primarily a geometry problem, a search for the angle or missing line that would connect the Shiners to the Travellers to De Kirk. Many homicide investigations were similar, and the mathematical conceit appealed to Yakabuski, who thought if you focused on the missing connection hard enough, the geometric line might actually appear, like a vision in a dream. He believed it had already happened to him. The missing link would come as cognitive thought, but it was so palpable, so wondrous and obvious, it may as well have been a physical thing, hitting him on the head and asking what took so long.

He put his mind to the problem, rolling through the known facts and likely outcomes in the homicide investigation of Augustus Morrissey, a.k.a. "The Squire," a.k.a. "King of the Shiners." He was killed and his body put on display on the North Shore, after his eyes were first cut out and a million-dollar diamond was shoved down his throat. Who cuts out eyes? A Traveller. Who has access to a million-dollar diamond? Someone who owns a diamond mine. The person

Yakabuski had at the top of his list of suspects was a Traveller who owned a home ten miles from a diamond mine. That didn't give Dumont access to the diamonds, but it was hard to believe it was a coincidence.

Those facts connected nicely, but where did the Shiners come in? They must have heard of the scam being run at Cape Diamond — whatever it was — and tried to run some sort of hustle on the Travellers. That would fit the known facts. That was a nice geometric shape. Only things missing were the actual crime that was being committed, the people who were doing it, and how they were getting away with it.

Yep, just missing that. The shape blew away.

Yakabuski had started the problem one more time when his cellphone rang. He looked at the number and didn't recognize it right away. Then it came to him. Jimmy O'Driscoll. The beating victim he had interviewed yesterday morning before going to Filion's Field.

"Jimmy," he said, "I wasn't expecting to hear from you so soon."

"You'll be glad you did, I'm betting, Mr. Yakabuski. You're one of the detectives investigating the murder of Augustus, right?"

"That's right. Know something about it?"

"I know who can give you the name of the killer. Is that something?"

The second figure he had been working on collapsed in a jumble of lines and busted angles, like the crash of a kid's pick-up sticks game after someone went one move too far. *Maybe this wasn't a geometry case*, thought Yakabuski.

• • •

O'Driscoll said they couldn't meet at his apartment, and after they went through a list of possible meeting places (some too public, some too far) they settled on the alley behind Belfast Street, by the back door of O'Keefe's, in two hours. It was dark by the time Yakabuski arrived, and he parked his Jeep near the river and walked up to the alley. It was framed by the backs of buildings on Belfast Street and a row of abandoned warehouses and forward-steerage buildings on the riverside. The only security cameras were on Belfast. The alley was gravel, but Yakabuski made barely a sound as he rounded one of the abandoned buildings and made his way to the back door of O'Keefe's. When he got there, he scanned the roofline of the buildings on Belfast, then the roofline of the abandoned buildings by the river. He could see blue light coming from the rear of the Silver Dollar, a block away, and heard voices in the distance, probably by the shore of the river, young voices, drifting in and out of audio range on the gusts of warm wind that blew down the alley.

"You can come out, Jimmy," he said softly.

A few seconds later, there was the rustling of cardboard, then the sound of unsteady footsteps, and Jimmy O'Driscoll peered his head around a dumpster.

"Which way did you come in?" he asked.

"From the river. I didn't come down Belfast."

"Good. There were people here just a few minutes ago. Junkies I think."

"There's nobody here now, Jimmy."

O'Driscoll peered up and down the alley one more time, then stood up and let a cut-open shipping box slide off his back. He was wearing the same T-shirt Yakabuski had seen him in yesterday. Same pants, the left leg of the jeans cut open to make room for the walking cast. Same blood-trickled pattern of red lines on his forearms. Had a dirty pad of gauze hockey-taped to his left eye. That was new.

"How long have you been here, Jimmy?"

"'Bout an hour."

"That's a long time to be hiding under a box. Someone came and saw you last night, didn't they?"

O'Driscoll started picking one of the scabs on his forearm. Tilted his head, as though he was trying to recall something. When he spoke he didn't answer Yakabuski's question. He said instead, "So what can you do for me, if I help you find Augustus's killer?"

"That's a pretty big if, Jimmy. Why don't you tell me what you know, and I'll see what it's worth."

"Information like this is worth something. Trust me. You should be able to do better'n wait-and-see."

"If you're looking for money, Jimmy, some sort of confidential-informant payout, I'll see what I can do. But there's a part of me that thinks that would be a big mistake, giving you money. I'll find you dead in this alley in two days with a needle in your arm."

"I don't want your money. I need you to keep me away from the Popeyes. Until I can clear up a few things."

Yakabuski looked at the boy in front of him. For maybe the first time, he took him seriously — that maybe this wasn't a paid-informant scam being run by a strung-out, frightened junkie whose time on the planet was probably being measured in days now, if he knew the Popeyes. What Jimmy O'Driscoll was proposing made sense. If he had something Yakabuski needed, he would barter it for protection. The boy would never take help if it were freely offered, because he was from Cork's Town and stuff like that never happened. Something like that was unnatural and not to be trusted. But quid for a quid, scratch for a scratch, eye for an eye — that was time honoured.

"Will you testify against them?" asked Yakabuski. "Is that on the table?"

"I don't know, man. I don't fuckin' know. All I know is I gotta go deep underground for a little while. Can you help me or not, Mr. Yakabuski?"

"I can probably help you, Jimmy. So who is this guy you know?"

"We have a deal? You can hide me somewhere? That's what you're saying?"

"That's what I'm saying. So, who's the guy?"

"My granddad. Terry Maguire."

Yakabuski tried not to look surprised, although O'Driscoll was looking right into his face when he said the name, and right after that he smiled, so Yakabuski must have let something show. Terry Maguire. A name from the past, the former security chief for the Shiners, a cold-blooded executioner and one of Augustus Morrissey's closest friends, until Terry Maguire vanished from Springfield more than twenty-five years ago. Most cops on the force, including Yakabuski, had only heard stories of the man. Everyone assumed he was dead, probably killed by Morrissey for some sort of transgression.

Terry Maguire. This was starting to become a case with so many notes, colourings, and nuances from the past Yakabuski found himself thinking if a Hank Williams song started playing right then he wouldn't be surprised. Might not even bother looking around to see where the sound was coming from. Terry Maguire, the crazy, homicidal "Tough Man" of

Cork's Town from two generations ago, a Shiner people used to cross the street to avoid, the Tommy Bangles of his era, supposed to be dead and lying at the bottom of the Springfield River with a Shiner necktie around his neck, a look of either surprise or pain in his eyes, although the eyes would be long gone and no expression would be registering today.

"Your granddad was Terry Maguire? The Shiner?"

"He *is* my granddad. He's still alive, Mr. Yakabuski. I spoke to him just this morning."

"Christ, Jimmy, the courts ruled your granddad was dead years ago. No one has seen him in decades."

"He ain't dead, Mr. Yakabuski. I talk to him every month. I've seen him a bunch of times too. Saw him just last Christmas. He ain't that far away anymore. And he told me he knows who killed Augustus."

"Because he's the one?"

"No, he ain't the one. But he knows who done it. You interested?"

"This is what you're trading?"

"Yes. If you think that's a fair trade." O'Driscoll looked at the cut-up box he was standing on, then down the alley, and up at the night sky, where there was a waxing moon one day shy of being full, a soft, yellow light out on the water. O'Driscoll looked out at the water as well, before scanning the rear of the buildings on Belfast Street. He was avoiding eye contact. Scratching his arms and wiping away blood. He looked about as beat-up as a man could look, wondering if he still owned something in this world that someone else might want.

# CHAPTER SEVENTEEN

Far up on the Northern Divide, close to the Arctic seas, three men entered a house not far from Cape Diamond. It was a large house, the exterior walls built of notched pine, the roof of cedar shake, large bay windows in front that looked out on the Francis River and the lower reaches of the Chute de Savard rapids. Class-five rapids, so there was often a howl in the air when you approached this house. The men entered and made their way toward a back room. Two of the men wore light grey uniforms with white piping on the legs and the crest of a company from the Northern Divide on the shirt pockets. One of the uniformed men was tall and sullen. The other fat and jovial. The third man was Gabriel Dumont.

The back room was large, running the full width of the house and occupying about a third of the floor space. Dumont fished in his coat pocket for the key that unlocked the only door. He was dressed in the hides and skins of animals: a caribou-hide trench coat; black leather pants and knee-high, deerskin breeches, beaded and strung with some sort of sinew; beaver-pelt gloves and hat, the hat seeming almost unnecessary because of all the hair — matted and wild black hair that spread over his shoulders and hung down his back. When he had the key, he unlocked the door and turned on an inside ceiling light.

The bulb was low wattage and cast a mustard-yellow light that seemed almost token in the cavernous room, just enough light to reveal shadowy objects and possible walking paths. There were wooden crates stacked against the left wall, so many crates they were in rows, and workbenches of some sort beyond that, the kind auto mechanics might have. The right half of the room was less cluttered, with tables by the open door of a kitchen, the sort of kitchen you might find atop a hockey arena, and in front of the tables were twenty chairs, fanning out like church pews, and in front of the chairs, a lectern. Behind the lectern was a gold-coloured cross the size of a man, and a black furled flag, both driven into a base of dark knotted wood. On the walls were many black-and-white photographs. Candles sat on side tables set up at the end of each row of chairs.

"Just the three of us tonight," said Dumont, and the men took off their winter coats and hung them from a coat tree next to the door. The men in uniform took their seats before the lectern and a girl appeared. She carried a round tray with three rock glasses, a bottle of Scotch, and a small ice bucket upon it. She stood next to the door, not entering the room any further. The fat man turned and waved at her. She did not wave back. She was a pretty girl. Looked to be no more than sixteen or seventeen.

Dumont strode to the lectern and spoke for about ten minutes. He started in French but then switched to another language, one with slashing consonants and guttural sounding vowels that were sometimes stretched so far they sounded like a moan. It was an old language of pain and attack and the men in the chairs felt sad when they heard it, as they always did. There was no ceremony this night. No lighting of candles. No singing of old songs. After he was finished talking, Dumont strode to one of the tables and the two men got up and followed him. When they were seated, the girl came and poured drinks.

"Nathalie," said the fat man. "Do you understand what Gabriel has just told us?"

"Of course I understand, Pierre," she said, smiling and offering him the silver tongs, the fat man taking the gesture as an act of fondness, when really the young girl did not want to do more work for this man than necessary. He could get his own ice. "I was taught the old ways the same as you were taught. My mother was one of your instructors. Do you not remember?"

"Of course I do. You used to tag along. You're not so young anymore, are you Nathalie?"

She smiled and took back the tongs. She left the bottle on the table and went back to standing next to the door. The fat man watched her walk away.

"A toast then! To our success!" yelled Dumont and the three men raised their glasses, gave them a clink, and began to drink. The tall man took only a small sip of Scotch and placed his glass gently upon the table. Dumont and the fat man drained their rock glasses and slammed them down.

"This has been a long time coming," said the fat man.

"This will avenge all the wrongs we ever suffered. Can you believe it? *We* are the avengers. The ones that were chosen. People will be writing songs about us forever."

He laughed and ran the back of his hand across his mouth. Licked the Scotch he had managed to wipe up and laughed again. He was still laughing when it occurred to him he was the only one.

"You want the songs, don't you?" said Dumont.

The fat man sat a little straighter in his chair. "Of course I do. We are about to become folk heroes. Who *wouldn't* want that?" He looked over at the girl by the door. Gave her a wink. Turned to Dumont and gave him a similar wink. "There are advantages to being a folk hero, Gabriel. Life becomes easier for you. You would know this."

He poured himself another drink. Motioned for the girl to come over with the ice. When she didn't move right away, he raised the rock glass to his mouth, was halfway there, still staring at the girl, when he heard Gabriel say, "You act as if the songs are already written. Yet you have done nothing."

His hand stopped moving, the rock glass suspended halfway between the table and his mouth. "What do you mean?"

"People tell me you have become boastful. That you are spending money you do not have and running up debt that does not worry you. People are beginning to wonder why that would be."

The fat man finally took a sip of his Scotch, then he put down the rock glass, ran his left hand through his hair and said, "Thank God that's all this is. You had me worried there. I have not said anything about what we are doing, Gabriel. Not a word. I promise you there is nothing to worry about."

Dumont threw back his head and laughed. A loud sound that boomed and echoed in the cavernous room many times before fading away. Then he slapped his knee and said in a voice filled with humour and goodwill, "Pierre, my dear old friend, do you believe the only way people can find out something about you is when you *tell* them?"

Dumont took a sip of his Scotch, slapped his knee a few more times, kept laughing. The fat man tried to laugh along with him, but stopped trying when Gabriel leaned forward in his chair, placed his right hand behind the man's head, and with his hands tightly gripping the man's hair, said, "I need you to think for a minute. I need you to take your time answering the question I am about to ask you, because it is a very important question. Maybe the most important question you have ever been asked, so take as much time as you need. Time does not matter. You must be sure of your answer. Pierre, in your drunken boasts, in the folk songs you have heard in your dreams — have you once mentioned Springfield?"

Dumont released his grip and beads of sweat formed on the fat man's forehead. His hands started to tremble, and he reached for his drink, then thought better of it and pulled his hand back. Rested it on his lap. After he had done all that, he said, "I have not."

"You are sure?"

"I am. Not once have I mentioned Springfield."

"So that part, at least, you have managed to keep a secret."

"I have kept it all a secret, Gabriel. I promise you . . ."

But Dumont raised his hand and the man stopped speaking. The third man at the table, who had yet to speak, finally reached for his rock glass, took a long sip of his Scotch, looked at the fat man, and said, "What of his family?"

"They are Travellers and have done nothing wrong. Family is why we are doing this. We will all share the bounty of the land."

"We do not have much time. How can he be replaced?"

"I will make the arrangements."

"What of our partners? Should they be notified?"

"I don't see why."

The tall man nodded, finished his drink, and said, "Very well." Then he put on his winter parka, the peaked cap that went with his uniform, and left the room. The girl followed him. When they had gone, Dumont rose from his seat, a nine-inch Buckmaster hunting knife already pulled from the sheath he always had tied to his leg. He flipped the knife from hand to hand.

"Try not to be too sad about the songs. When I sing them, many years from now, I will think of you. Maybe not the fame you had expected, but still something, yes?"

The man sitting at the table did not speak, did not move, even as a large black stain spread across the groin area of his uniform.

# CHAPTER EIGHTEEN

That night Yakabuski had a new dream, which was rare for him, something that must come with age, he figured. Most of his dreams now were of the recurring kind, or so poorly remembered when he awoke that they were little more than vaguely recalled emotions. But that night he dreamed of Augustus Morrissey having his eyes cut out and timber rafts burning on the Springfield River, men in bowler hats diving into the river to try to escape the flames. Barges pulled up to the North Shore and people marched by gunpoint into the mist, the men carrying the rifles wearing oilskin trench coats and badges pinned to their collars with the same insignia he had on his badge. He saw Bernard O'Toole, looking as sad and mammoth as Atlas, blocking the sun and pointing with his rifle toward the mist.

He saw eight apartment buildings appear on a bluff, rising as quickly as spring hay. Heard an Algonquin chant, so far away in his dream he could only make out the rhythm, none of the words. After that he saw a gypsy caravan moving down the Northern Divide, a black flag flying from the lead wagon and all the light of the known world disappearing as the caravan passed. He saw a rocky peninsula jutting far into a great river, sparkling like a swath of starry sky that had fallen to earth; after that he was floating, not sure where the lines of the physical world could be found, where the planes, divides, watersheds, and dimensions had gone, drifting somewhere between all of it.

At five in the morning he awoke, and the dream stayed with him several minutes, something else that had become rare in recent years. He knew there would be no more sleep that night. He went and made a coffee and watched the sun appear over the Springfield River, a thin red line to the east that lengthened and started to shimmer, and then broke over the treeline as a bright red ball that would soon turn white and then hang low in a cloudless sky for the rest of the day.

. . .

A phone ringing high on the Northern Divide has a different sound than a phone ringing in Springfield or somewhere down south. When you're phoning up north the ring has a weak and distant sound to it, a sound muddied by audio static, by crazy changes in pitch and resonance, a sound that seems lonely and weak and always at risk of slipping away.

The frail chime rang out from the four speakers suspended from the ceiling corners of the conference room of the main detachment of the Springfield Police. There were eight people in the room. Besides Yakabuski, O'Toole, and Fraser Newton from Ident; there was Jack Laurier, the inspector for Criminal Investigations and Yakabuski's direct boss; Max Ferguson, who was Newton's direct boss; Samantha Dillon from the coroner's office; and two RCMP officers from Toronto who had shown up late yesterday, after the Mounties had received a forensics-lab request for DNA testing on blood taken off a $1.2-million diamond.

No one had requested they show up. But the diamond had caught the Mounties' attention. They were sitting in on the conference call as observers. The phone chimed and chimed and the various people in the room leaned into the phone console in the middle of the oak table, as though this might help make the connection. O'Toole drummed the table with his fingers. Yakabuski again read through the opening paragraphs of the Upper Divide Métis Assembly's land claim for Cape Diamond, which Griffin had printed off and left on his desk.

Then the chiming stopped, there was a metal click, and a woman's voice said, "Good afternoon, De Kirk Mines. How may I direct your call?"

O'Toole straightened in his chair. Yakabuski put down his papers and stared at the console. It was O'Toole who spoke.

"Ma'am, this is Chief Bernard O'Toole, with the Springfield Regional Police. I have a conference call scheduled with your general manager."

"Oh yes, Mr. Merkel is expecting your call. I'll put you right through, sir."

Some more metal clicks, and then a man's voice said, "John Merkel."

"Mr. Merkel, this is Chief O'Toole, with the Springfield Regional Police. I have some people in the room with me. I won't bother going around the table. I know you're pressed for time."

"It *is* rather a busy day, Chief, thank you for mentioning that," said Merkel. "I gave a rather lengthy statement to one of your detectives, yesterday. Are you aware of that?"

"I am, sir. And I'm glad the detective has brought you up to speed on what is happening down here. We're investigating a rather gruesome homicide, so again, I appreciate you taking the time to talk to us."

"Well, yes, of course. Anything I can do to help. I am just not sure what more I can add to what I have already said."

"I can help you with that one, Mr. Merkel. That's one of the reasons I'm phoning. We are now in a position to confirm the diamond found on the body of our victim came from the Cape Diamond area, almost certainly from your mine."

"Who is the gemologist who has told you this?"

"Mr. Joshua Edelson, here in Springfield. He is a licenced cutter and appraiser."

"I would like to see his report."

"I can send it to you. Not a problem. I'll send you his estimate as well."

"That should be part of the report."

"Well, yes, I guess it is. You're right about that."

O'Toole looked at Yakabuski and rolled his eyes. It was rare to see O'Toole taking part in an investigative conference call. Rarer still to see him have this much patience.

"What is his estimate?" demanded Merkel.

"One-point-two to one-point-six million dollars."

"He can't be serious."

"He certainly seems to be. This is all new to me, but that was one mother-sized diamond we found in the throat of our victim."

"Well, I would have to see the report. Although, again, I still don't see what this has to do with us."

O'Toole didn't reply. He looked at his senior detective and gave a small nod.

"You don't see that?" said Yakabuski.

Merkel paused a beat before answering. "That's right, I don't. Your victim was not an employee of De Kirk. The crime happened in Springfield, not at Cape Diamond. The diamond was not stolen from us."

"What makes you so sure about that?"

"With whom am I speaking, please?"

"Detective Frank Yakabuski, Mr. Merkel. I'm the lead investigator."

"It would be nice if you identified yourself."

"It would be nice if you answered the question."

Although they had a bad connection, there was no way of missing Merkel's gasp. The two Mounties looked at Yakabuski and smiled. Rattle the man's cage. Always a good interview technique.

"Detective, I don't appreciate your tone. Is this how you normally speak to people?"

"When I'm on a conference call it can be. I don't care for them much. So what makes you so sure you haven't been robbed, Mr. Merkel?"

"All right. If you insist, Detective, I'll go through it with you. Just once, so please listen carefully. Is this call being recorded?"

"It is."

"Good. Then your notes won't be a problem. Detective, every one of our miners is searched when they come off shift. We're not shy about it, I can assure you. It's a complete strip search, with x-ray scans. Every diamond we mine is numbered and registered, and we check our stock against our mining manifest every morning. It is a visual inspection. Not a computer check.

"The only transportation link in and out of the mine is by air, and we're the only ones who fly here. Before leaving, the miners have another four-stage search at the airport. They are not allowed carry-on luggage. One checked bag, and those are thoroughly inspected. As for the mined diamonds, we warehouse them and fly them out every quarter, again, using one of our planes. We contract out none of our security or transportation. Our plane goes straight to New York City, where a customs inspection is done on the tarmac. When the diamonds have been cleared, we load them into an armoured car and take them directly to the vaults at our New York office.

"In eighty-seven years, De Kirk has never been robbed while transporting or mining a diamond. Nor has a diamond ever failed to match up perfectly with a shipping manifest. This is what makes me so sure we have not been robbed, Detective Yak-a-bus-ki." Merkel dragged out the last name.

There was silence in the room. The RCMP officers shuffled their feet and looked embarrassed, as though they had just wasted someone's time. O'Toole started chuckling and had almost started to laugh when Yakabuski said, "Mr. Merkel, I get that you're in love with your security protocols. They sound beautiful. But that doesn't change the fact someone is robbing you. Now, I need to get up there and see that mine. We've hired a plane and a pilot for the day. How does four o'clock this afternoon work for you?"

# CHAPTER
## NINETEEN

The address Jimmy O'Driscoll had given Yakabuski was for an apartment in the back of a brownstone in Fergus Glen, thirty miles downriver from Springfield. The street was one block from the river, and you could hear the Lemieux Rapids in the distance, see terns diving for fish in a shoal. Yakabuski walked up the rear outer stairs until he stood before the apartment door. There were cardboard cases of O'Keefe stacked on the landing, the rusted wheel of a clothesline that probably hadn't worked in years. In the backyard, there was a picnic table and a green plastic sandbox in the shape of a turtle.

The man who answered the door looked to be in his eighties. He was wearing a white undershirt that hung loose on his belly. Through the armpit holes and over the neckline Yakabuski could see thick tufts of white hair. The man was only an inch shorter than he was and he held the door open a long time before saying, "You're bigger than you look in photos. I thought I'd be bigger."

"You probably were at one time."

"That's not saying much. Are you here to arrest me?"

"I'm not aware of any warrants for your arrest, Mr. Maguire. Would you like to confess to a crime?"

The old man gave Yakabuski a hard look, but it wavered in a few seconds and he started to laugh. "Anything I'd like to confess. That's good."

"You never know. I'm here because of your grandson, Jimmy. He suggested we talk."

"You've seen Jimmy?"

"Last night. He's in bad shape. He's actually at my ice fishing hut right now, getting some sleep."

"He can't go back to his apartment?"

"I wouldn't think so."

"Yeah, we talked about that. He wasn't sure what he was going to do. Can you help him?"

"Perhaps. Am I coming inside?"

Maguire stared at him a moment, then he pushed the screen door, a quick shove, not holding it open for Yakabuski, who had to catch the edge of the door before it slammed into him.

"You're coming inside," he said.

· · ·

The windows in the apartment had the blinds drawn and the only light came from side-table lamps in the living room. Just enough light to show off a corduroy couch, a brown leather

La-Z-Boy, some fold-away television trays, one of which was set up permanently in a corner, covered in a linen cloth, and on top of that a dozen different prescription medicine bottles. Maguire sat in the La-Z-Boy. Motioned for Yakabuski to sit on the couch.

"I'm still surprised I outlived Augustus," he said when Yakabuski was seated. The old man's breath was laboured, and he spoke in clipped sentences. "He may still have a contract on me. I don't know how Sean feels about things like that. Whether executions should be passed down from father to son."

"Most people think you're already dead, Mr. Maguire. You were declared legally dead fourteen years ago. I looked it up."

"I did a good job of disappearing, didn't I? I always kept that in my back pocket. My get-out-of-Dodge plan."

"Where have you been?"

Maguire thought about it a minute, then shrugged his shoulders as if to say "why not," or "what the fuck," and said he'd lived out west for nearly twenty years, spent most of that time working at a sawmill in Sooke, on Vancouver Island. He had a good union connection, and his name never appeared on the books. Then he got homesick and started migrating back, careful not to get too close, staying two days' drive from Springfield for many years. His sons and grandchildren started to come for visits. He moved to Fergus Glen a year ago.

"I wasn't as worried about Augustus by then," he said. "I had other worries to take his place. I'm betting you know what they are."

"Are you undergoing treatment?"

"Not anymore. Stage four. I take pills for the pain. That's all I can do. Like I said, it's a real surprise, outliving Augustus."

"So what was the falling out about?"

"Stupid stuff. That's always the way though, isn't it? The thing that fucks you up is never the thing that should fuck you up. You always get blindsided."

He laughed. Went to pat his belly. A quick look of surprise flashed across his face as his hand kept pushing down on the old T-shirt, looking for skin but not finding it.

"Are you telling me you can't recall why you had to get out of Springfield?"

"Fuck, of course I can recall. I told Augustus he had a situation he needed to take care of. I showed him the damn videotape. I was chief of security. It was my job to know shit like that. Turned out showing him that tape was pretty stupid."

"Are you going to tell me what you're talking about?"

"No. I'm not part of this deal. This is about Jimmy. And you solving the murder of that fat fuckin' cow."

"All right. Jimmy says you know who killed Augustus. Is that true?"

"That's true."

"You flat-out know. Not rumours. Not best guesses."

"Are you a serious guy, Detective Yakabuski? Jimmy says you're a serious guy. I hear from people who should know these things that you're a serious guy. So why are you insulting me? I just told you I know. So what can you do for Jimmy?"

"I can get him into Ridgewood. The hundred-day program. If he wants to get clean, he can do it there. To be honest, Mr. Maguire, I would probably try to do that anyway. I'm going to need my ice fishing hut."

The old man laughed. "The season's going to start as soon as God remembers it's winter."

"I'm hoping."

The old man looked pleased. He was cut from the same cloth as his grandson, same cloth as a lot of people on the Divide, who held to a world view that said you don't offer favours and you shouldn't go around looking for them either. Yakabuski would want his ice fishing hut back. That made sense to Maguire. The two men were now bartering.

"I can't guarantee the Popeyes after the hundred days," continued Yakabuski. "But bikers tend to have short attention spans. If Jimmy cleans up and leaves town for a while when he gets out, I'd say he has a decent shot of getting clear of this."

"Leave those bastard bikers to me."

"You can't do anything rash, Mr. Maguire. That can't be part of our deal."

"Relax. I'm going to pay Jimmy's debt. I have money coming. I've already made the arrangements."

"That's rather decent of you."

"Think so? How much money do you think I need right now?" The old man gave Yakabuski a sour look. He went to pat his stomach again, but stopped as his hand approached the T-shirt. "Here's what I'm willing to do. I'm not going to tell you who killed Augustus, because if I did that you'd just walk out of here and make an arrest. Which means I would need to testify in court, on account of you not doing any of the work. Your evidence is me."

"We can take an affidavit, Mr. Maguire. You won't have to testify in court."

"The other thing I'm not going to do is let everyone know

117

I just turned rat-fink informant for the Springfield Regional Fuckin' Police."

The two men stared at each other. There was a resolve in the old man's eyes that Yakabuski knew would be as firm and unmoving as the north shore escarpment, as tough and unflinching as any set stone. Maguire had been staring down cancer for years, Yakabuski figured, and the chances of him changing his mind probably ranged from nil to none.

"I think we have a problem," he said quietly.

"I don't think so. This is the deal I'm willing to make, Mr. Yakabuski. You help out Jimmy, and I'll give you the only clue you're going to need to solve this murder."

"You've been watching too much television, Mr. Maguire. You're going to give me some sort of riddle? Is that what you're thinking of doing?"

"Not a riddle. I'm going to give you a name. Find that person, and you'll find your killer."

"You realize I'll probably help Jimmy whatever we decide here. I've already told you that."

"I know. But I think you will take better care of my grandson if we make this deal."

There it was again. That Northern Divide world view. Maguire needed to barter for his grandson's protection otherwise it wouldn't be real, wouldn't be the sort of thing you could hang your hat on, as people around Springfield still said. Extracting something from Yakabuski was the only way Maguire could feel good about what he was doing, the only way he could convince himself he might just have protected his grandson from the beasts and monsters that lived around here.

"We have a deal, Mr. Maguire. Who do I need to find?"

The old man smiled.

"Katherine Morrissey."

"And who is she?"

"Sean Morrissey's mother."

# CHAPTER
## TWENTY

The mountains were not tall enough to have exposed rock on the summits. From base to peak, it was a dense forest, mixed woods of jack pine and scrub spruce, oak and hickory. At this time of year, many of the leaves had fallen, but the mountains were still green. Mist rose from the valleys and the gullies to hang like smoke rings around the girth of the hills.

Cambino drove through Arkansas, and although the land was sparsely populated, the highway was immaculate. A perfect, dark-black asphalt highway winding its way through the green mountains. This was an immense land, green, lush, and wet. The Mississippi River could be seen from time to time far to the east, and Cambino could not imagine there ever being a drought here, or famine in any real way. Wildlife was abundant. The rivers were plentiful and clean, not at all like the slow-moving, oil-slicked rivers of his youth. A man with a good rifle and a strong back could survive with ease in land such as this.

Yet the people were poor. Cambino glimpsed their houses occasionally through the trees that bordered the Interstate, rough-timber and Typar-wrapped houses, with cars on cinder blocks and thin hounds that barked at shadows and other things they would never catch. When he left the Interstate, which he did from time to time, as he was making good time and could not arrive earlier than expected, Cambino drove through small town after small town where men sat on milk crates at four-corner gas stations, and every second store was shuttered. At truck stops near the Interstate, children sold lemonade and cookies beside the ramps, close enough to the passing vehicles to be coughing out diesel exhaust most of the day.

Cambino wondered how such a thing was possible, to be born in a land like this yet live in poverty. He drove and considered the problem, searching for the disconnect, where the formula deviated from the logical conclusion: a free man in paradise will be rewarded. But the answer never came. The people remained a mystery to him, exiles in their own kingdom, reaping none of the bounty of the land, no more physical claim or linkage to the land than the shadows that came sliding off the mountains every day at dusk, to go skittering down this perfect black highway.

• • •

Both of the men from the North wanted the same thing, and as Cambino drove from Arkansas into Missouri, he thought

121

again of what a coincidence that was, although as a man who did not believe much in coincidence, it must have been something else. Fate? A joke from God? He could not decide. But the men had approached him separately, independent of one another, with an identical plan. Betray and kill the other man. Because both men had been business partners of Cambino for many years, he had listened, and because it was a good plan, one that made sense to him, he had agreed.

Yes, I will kill him for you.

The men had given similar motives for the killing and this amused Cambino. The man they wanted dead did not deserve the spoils of the crime they were plotting. It would be like tossing pearls before swine. It was the argument of many a thief with a back-end scheme, and the betrayal did not offend Cambino. He believed if you were not strong enough to protect what you had stolen, you should not have become a thief.

He would need to decide soon. To which man had he lied? He needed a test, some way of knowing which man was unworthy, which man the planet no longer needed. A test for courage, or devotion, or beauty would be futile with these men. They did not possess such things. Cambino needed to see them for what they were. And devise his test accordingly.

$$\cdot \; \cdot \; \cdot$$

Later that morning, Cambino pulled into a Chevron station near Charleston, Missouri, and filled the dual tanks of the Falcon. The sun sat at a sixty-degree angle on the eastern horizon, and the awning over the pumps offered no shade. He went inside and paid in American cash. A Texas A&M ball cap pulled low on his face. He never spoke to the clerk at the register, only shook his head no when the teenager asked if he wanted a receipt.

As he was walking back to the camper, another teenage boy, pumping gas into an old Camaro, yelled at him, "Hey, is that a Falcon camper?"

Cambino nodded and kept walking.

"Shit, it looks brand new. I thought they stopped making those back in the '90s."

He stopped. To say nothing would seem suspicious.

"Nineteen ninety-six," he yelled at the boy. "Mine is from the last production run."

"Cool-looking van. It looks brand new. I've never seen one with tinted windows. How much did that cost you?"

"Not much. I have astigmatism. Bright light hurts my eyes."

"Shit, that explains it. I didn't think it was even legal to tint them that dark. I tried to have my car done, but the DMV wouldn't allow it. Fuckin' jerks."

Cambino wasn't sure if he was supposed to reply. People spoke so freely in this country. Making comments at a gas pump that would get them thrown in jail in Heroica. He nodded and resumed walking, deciding nothing needed to be said. But as he unlocked the van with an electronic fob the boy yelled, "Whoa, keyless entry? That's not stock. What all have you had done to that thing?"

"Just the keyless entry," Cambino said, working to keep the frustration out of his voice. "You can get it done at Walmart."

"Sweet. You know, my dad used to own one of those campers. Would you mind if I had a quick look inside?"

Cambino hesitated before opening his door. Briefly considered it. But could not come up with a workable plan that also had the Camaro disappearing from the gas station and so he said, "I'm in a bit of a hurry, son. Maybe another time."

# CHAPTER
## TWENTY-ONE

As he drove back from Fergus Glen, Yakabuski took a closer look at the Springfield River than he had that morning, when he was rushing to meet Terry Maguire. The water sat unmoving. No current. No wind. Low and black at a time of year when it should have been frozen, should have been a ribbon of white with ice fishing huts out on the middle channel. The willows that leaned over the water had mouldy yellow strands that looked diseased in some way. There were no bright colours anywhere that Yakabuski looked.

As he drove, Yakabuski thought of what Terry Maguire had told him, after saying Sean Morrissey's mother was the key to learning the identity of Augustus's murderer. When Yakabuski had asked her age, the old man did the math in his head and said sixty-four. Maybe sixty-five. Somewhere around there. When he asked what part of Springfield he should start looking in, Maguire had said only that she was "nearby." To every other question, he shook his head and said that was all Yakabuski was going to get. They didn't bother shaking hands when he left.

When he reached the detachment, Yakbuski went looking for Donna Griffin. He found her at a general pool desk in Major Crimes, staring intently at an Excel spreadsheet she had on her computer screen. She was still wearing her patrol uniform. The only one in uniform in the general pool area.

"Any more luck?" asked Yakabuski, pulling a chair from a nearby desk and sitting beside her.

"Nothing, I'm afraid. This is a list of timber rights that have been granted around Cape Diamond. Nearly every company is numbered. I'm working my way through the list."

"Take a break from that. I need you to track someone down. Her name is Katherine Morrissey, mid-sixties, she lives in Springfield, or somewhere nearby."

"Who is she?"

"Sean Morrissey's mother."

"Really? I've been reading up on Augustus, but I haven't read anything about a wife."

"I never knew he had one," said Yakabuski. "It must go back a few years. I don't know if anyone should be surprised by that, given everything else we're looking at in this case."

"There *are* a lot of things about this case that are old, aren't there," said Griffin, turning away from the computer screen and looking at Yakabuski. "The North Shore Travellers, Terry Maguire. Even the name Gabriel Dumont, it's right out of the history books. Do you think it means anything?"

"Of course it does. Means there's nothing young around here anymore," said Yakabuski, and when Griffin looked as if she was about to seriously ponder his answer, he laughed and stood up. "Katherine Morrissey. Call me if you find anything."

• • •

Earlier that day, Yakabuski had called up Tete Fontaine's police record. The first entry in it was when Fontaine was twelve years old, arrested for beating up two other boys in Filion's Field. At twenty-two he was sentenced to five years in Kingston Pen for manslaughter after beating to death a man who had stolen food from the brasserie. The most interesting item, though, was a non-arrest from five years ago. Fontaine had badly injured two Popeyes when the bikers showed up one night at the brasserie, looking for off-sales, and Fontaine refused to sell them any beer. Refused to sell them any because — and here the police report had four eyewitnesses quoted — the bikers stank. And they had ruined perfectly good leather jackets by cutting out the arms "like fuckin' Cocos." When the bikers objected to the lack of service by putting their fists through Fontaine's wooden walk-in beer cooler, he cut them from belly to sternum with a twelve-inch Bowie knife he kept behind the service bar. He left them bleeding and moaning on the floor of the brasserie, then hectored the paramedics when they arrived for taking so long "takin' out ta fuckin' garbage." A man protecting his property. No charges laid.

Yakabuski figured Fontaine dressed in silk shirts because he wanted people to know he could do a thing like that. Dress in flower-patterned silk shirts on the North Shore and no one would bother him. It was like pissing your way down the street. But he was no dandy, and it would be an unlucky man who mistook him for one. As those two Popeyes found out.

When Yakabuski entered the brasserie, Fontaine was again standing behind the service bar. He was wearing pressed jeans this day, and a black shirt with a western motif on the shoulders, antlers and knotted rope. Cigarette smoke hung heavy around his head, and he did not move in any noticeable way as Yakabuski approached.

"I'm heading up to Cape Diamond today. I hear your cousin lives around there," said Yakabuski, when he was standing in front of the bar.

"Gabriel live many places. I doin' all I can to find 'im, *mon ami*."

"Oh, I doubt that."

Yakabuski sat on one of the stools at the lunch bar, a heavy chrome swivel chair with a roun,d padded seat the colour of cherry. It had metallic flakes in it. A hard poly-plastic veneer that had cracked and formed topo maps during the half-century the chair had been in use at the back of Fontaine's brasserie, but it had never torn. Never broken. A half-century of worn-down comfort in that chair.

His father used to take him to brasseries like this in High River, where the beer was stored in walk-in coolers, kept cold by squares of ice and dark-wood framing; where there was sawdust spread on the pine floors by the cash and the front door to absorb the melting ice. Any time his father took him, there was the aroma of vegetable soup and malt vinegar and wood burning in an airtight stove in a corner somewhere. If they visited on a Saturday afternoon, there would be men sitting around the airtight, playing cards and talking. Later in the afternoon they would start to play music. Fiddles.

Spoons. Washboards. Yakabuski shifted his weight on the stool. There was not a position that seemed uncomfortable to him.

"Are your sur long sandwiches any good?"

Fontaine spread his arms wide. "*Mon ami*, you insult me agin'. Ma sur long sandwich keep honest men workin' all day."

"And dishonest men?"

"In your wife bed all night."

"I'll take one to go."

"I t'ink you need two."

Fontaine turned to start working the griddle. He poured some oil from a bottle on the counter, then dipped his spatula into a bowl of congealed bacon fat and started working the spatula across the griddle, working the fat in with the oil, letting it melt together as he stroked the griddle, moving square by square, as methodical as a field retriever, as precise in his hand movements as a string-instrument musician. The muscles in his back could be seen rippling beneath his shirt as he worked. As tight and sinewy as the ropes on his shoulder piping. Yakabuski knew muscles like that didn't just happen. Muscles like that almost never happened.

"The wake for Augustus is this afternoon," said Yakabuski. "Funeral is tomorrow. There are a lot of people coming into town for it. Might be a smart idea to keep a low profile the next couple of days."

"You t'ink I scared of a fuckin' Shiner?"

"No. Still might be a smart idea."

Fontaine laughed and threw strips of pork on the grill, some onions and tomatoes. Flipped the pork a few times and then slid his spatula under the grilled meat and vegetables, slid everything into a cut-open baguette, sliced the whole thing in half, and carefully wrapped the two sandwiches in sheets of waxed paper. He put them in a brown paper bag and put the bag in front of Yakabuski. He wiped his hands and lit a cigarette.

"How much?"

"On t'e house."

Yakabuski took a twenty from his wallet and put it on the counter. "Your cousin has a land claim for all of Cape Diamond. You ever been up there?"

"Many time. Good fishin' in t'at stretch of river."

"Just go for the fishing?"

"What else t'ey got up t'ere?"

"Quite a few diamonds. Like the one we found shoved down Augustus Morrissey's throat."

"I hear 'bout t'at. Maybe some kind boy do it to make sure his stinkin' body get pick'd up."

Yakabuski stared at Fontaine through the curling smoke. He seemed a happy man. As he walked away, Fontaine picked up the bill Yakabuski had left on the bar and shoved it into the pocket of his jeans.

# CHAPTER
## TWENTY-TWO

The plane circled Cape Diamond before landing. A full, 360-degree bank that let Yakabuski see the entire mining operation. There were corrugated metal hangars and heavy trucks travelling over the tundra, what looked like a large silo, likely the entrance to the mine. He counted fourteen bunkhouses and two cookhouses, judging by the steam rising from them. A row of ten metal trailers he thought would be offices. What might have been a hockey arena. What might have been a church.

Diamonds were found twenty years ago on this peninsula, thirty miles north of the Kesagami Reserve. A geologist working for De Kirk made the find. He was taking soil samples on the Upper Divide when he heard stories on the reserve about a peninsula that jutted far out on the Francis River, one you could see some nights because of gemstones twinkling in the dark. The first diamond to be taken out by

De Kirk was mined with the geologist's camp spade. Forty-four carats. When it reached New York, the clarity was rated "flawless."

De Kirk sent a full advance team to the Northern Divide within days, to secure mining rights for the area. The company had its headquarters in Johannesburg and had been mining diamonds a long time. It knew a strike the size of the one on the Francis River meant more money than the company could discreetly move around and keep secret from the various state revenue agencies with which it dealt. More money than any member of the corporate board could spend in one lifetime.

Dynastic wealth. That's what had been discovered on Cape Diamond, and so De Kirk spent money freely when it arrived on the Divide, knowing they would lose more money each day they were not allowed to mine than they could ever spend in bribes.

The provincial government was shown projected tax revenue that exceeded the taxation base of every forestry company on the Divide. De Kirk offered to pay the tax in quarterly instalments, first instalment to be paid the day the mine opened. There was no need for actual cash flow, the company's financial people explained to the surprised government bureaucrats who had come to Johannesburg to negotiate terms. They were confident of their numbers.

As for the Cree and Métis in the area, they were offered most of the jobs in the new mine. The Kesagami Band Council was also given five percent of the net revenue, paid out quarterly, with an annual guarantee of forty million dollars. The Cree did not have clear title to the peninsula, but they had a land claim, and De Kirk entered the annual payment as an advance against future revenue. In truth, the company did not care if the land claim was ever settled. Five percent of net was a workable expense. Whether it be called an advance against future revenue or a payoff.

Nine months after that first diamond had been dug up, De Kirk was pouring the foundation walls for the mine shaft. The provincial premier, the minister of northern affairs, and the entire Kesagami Band Council turned out for the ribbon-cutting ceremony.

. . .

The plane landed and taxied to a metal hangar, where a thin, middle-aged man dressed in white coveralls and a hard hat was standing there waiting for them with a clipboard in his hands. A ramp was wheeled to the plane and the door opened. When Yakabuski was on the tarmac the man with the clipboard walked over to him.

Once there, the man tipped his hard hat to the back of his head and said, "John Merkel. You've just the one bag?"

"Just the one."

"No one else on board?"

"Just the pilot."

"Very well. Let's go. Did you bring the report?"

Yakabuski slid his packsack off his back, opened the top pouch, and took out a manila envelope. He gave it to Merkel. The man ripped it open and took out an 8 x 10 black-and-white photo of the diamond. He examined it carefully. Took a pocket magnifying glass from the breast pocket of his overalls and examined it again. He was walking at a brisk pace. When they were in front of the metal silo he stopped walking and slid the photo back into the envelope.

"It looks like one of ours," he said.

"Glad we won't be wasting a lot of time arguing about that."

"Still doesn't mean we've been robbed."

"It's an uncut diamond."

"Everything we ship is uncut. Perhaps it was stolen after we shipped it."

"And it turns up in Springfield? Someone steals it in New York and ships it back to Springfield? Does that make sense to you?"

"It's strange, I'll grant you that, Detective Yakabuski. But it still doesn't mean we've been robbed. Here, I'll show you how impossible your theory is. Your timing is good, by the way. There's a shift coming up top in ten minutes."

Merkel swiped an access card and opened a large metal door. Inside they walked down a hallway with a metal floor that reminded Yakabuski of navy ships. Administrative offices, it looked like, ran down both sides of the hallway. They rounded two corners and came to another metal door that needed Merkel's access card to enter. Inside there was the roar of heavy machinery, and men wearing white overalls just like Merkel's were moving quickly up and down catwalks that either disappeared into the earth or rose high into the frame of the silo.

Merkel leaned his head toward Yakabuski and shouted, "This is the main power station for the mine."

Then he turned away and kept walking. Yakabuski considered himself a fast walker, but it was only his larger stride that was letting him keep up with Merkel. At the end of the power room, there was another large metal door. This door required not only Merkel's access card but also a retina scan.

Inside this room there was no roar of heavy machinery. No engineers in white overalls. The layout of the room was so familiar it startled Yakabuski. A long, rectangular room with what looked like a glass window running down one of the longer sides. Only it wasn't a glass window. It was a two-way mirror. It looked like a room where you brought people to look at a police lineup. In the room were six beefy looking men in security uniforms, each sitting at a desk positioned in front of the mirror. There were laptops on every desk.

"Detective Yakabuski, I'd like you to meet Johanne Kurtz, our head of security." The beefiest of the six beefy men stood up and shook Yakabuski's hand.

With no discernable sign of joy he said, "Pleasure to meet you." Then he sat back down.

"Forgive him, we're just about to start," said Merkel, and just then a door opened in the room on the other side of the mirror. A man dressed in the same sort of overalls as Merkel, only dark orange with no insignia on the chest pocket, walked into the room. He was followed by nine other men wearing the same orange overalls, all with soot stains on their faces and hard hats under their arms. Each man was Cree or Métis, it looked to Yakabuski.

Kurtz leaned into a microphone sitting on his desk and said, "You can start."

There was apathy in the faces of the miners as they stripped. They took off their workboots first and placed them in a plastic tub. Each man had a tub. Then they unzipped their overalls, let them slide off their backs, kicked them free, and put these also in the tub.

"We keep close track of each worker's clothes. All their possessions, actually. There is no overlap. Nothing is missed."

When the workers were naked, Kurtz leaned back into the microphone and said, "The screen please."

The men lined up in front of a full-body scanning machine, the kind of x-ray machine they have in airports. The men waited, and one by one they went behind the screen. Security guards tapped keys on their computers, looked up as the men turned, bent over, sometimes asking them to bend again, sometimes asking them to step out from the screen and then back, peering closely into their computer monitors after each command.

"If one of our workers gets a kidney stone," Merkel said with a smile, "we will be the first ones to know."

Yakabuski looked at the workers and tried to ignore the bile rising in his stomach. Looked at them as they stripped and bent and got computer examined by people in crisp white clothing who never had to bend, never had to be examined, who flew in and out of Cape Diamond on two-week shifts and who would be gone from this place as soon as the diamonds were gone, to go someplace else, to sit behind other two-way mirrors, in the same crisp white clothing, watching the next wave of local workers strip and bend.

Yakabuski could understand someone wanting to steal from bastards like that. Now, how were they doing it?

. . .

After seeing the staging area atop the mineshaft, Merkel took Yakabuski to the warehouse, where both a security official and a woman from the company's accounting department were waiting for them. The security guard explained how the diamonds were transported from the mine to the warehouse.

The accountant explained how the gems were inventoried, an elaborate cataloguing system that made Yakabuski's head swim. The woman went on to say she personally oversaw the daily inspection of the diamonds in the warehouse, making sure each gem matched the original intake documents.

"I haven't lost one yet," she said, and everyone standing with Yakabuski broke into laughter. After the warehouse, Merkel took him back to the airport terminal and into the departure lounge, which had a room identical to the screening room atop the mineshaft.

"There are no flights leaving tonight, so I can't show you how it operates, but it's the same drill as the staging area," said Merkel. "All the workers need to pass through here when they leave. They're allowed one checked bag and no carry-on. All sorts of complaints about that, but if you want to work here, there's no carry-on. And no complaining about the checked bag."

"What would they be complaining about?"

"Well, we just destroy those bags. After a while people figure it out. No lining. No outside pockets. The best thing to have, really, is a duffel bag."

. . .

At 10:35 p.m. John Merkel and Frank Yakabuski sat in a deserted cafeteria in a large corrugated metal building next to the terminal, coffee cups in front of them. The plane was being refuelled. It was scheduled to take off at 11 p.m. They were the only two in the cafeteria, which had tables spread out like classroom rows that could probably seat two hundred men. The only light in the room came from a row of vending machines on the left wall and two panels of fluorescent lights directly above their table.

"So, Detective Yakabuski, do you still think that diamond of yours was stolen from us?" asked Merkel, tilting his hard hat back on his head but not taking it off.

"Given the history of the victim, I have trouble believing anything else," he answered. "He was a man who rarely bought things. He preferred to take them."

"He was a criminal?"

"The former head of a gang in Springfield called the Shiners. An Irish gang. Been around nearly two hundred years. Yes, he was a criminal."

"Well, I can understand your suppositions then. You're thinking this man stole the diamond from its rightful owner?"

"I'm thinking he stole it from you."

"I have just shown you that is an impossibility."

"Some people say the same thing about life on this planet. Did you know that, Mr. Merkel?"

The general manager looked at Yakabuski but didn't speak and so he continued.

"Some supercomputer at UCLA has run the math, and the odds of human life evolving on this planet, the things that had to line up, at just the right time, at just the right place, the odds are about the same as a sea bass jumping in the middle of the Pacific Ocean and getting its snout caught in a plastic ring that someone had just tossed there. We would call that a statistical impossibility. Yet here we are."

Merkel chuckled and tilted the hard hat back a little further. "That would seem to be a stronger argument for religion, Detective Yakabuski, than it is for stealing diamonds."

"For some people, maybe they're the same thing. Have you heard of a man named Gabriel Dumont?"

"He filed a land claim against us last year. Our lawyers are dealing with it."

"He lives in a house about ten miles from here."

"Halfway between Fort Francis and the reserve. I know where it is. He claims to be some sort of Métis leader. Our lawyers aren't taking his claim very seriously."

"He's not just Métis, he's a Traveller. A North Shore Traveller."

"You believe that?" said Merkel, a surprised look coming to his face. "Our security people looked into Dumont when he filed the claim, and they tell me those are folk tales. That's funny — you won't believe me when I tell you we haven't been robbed, but you believe there are ghost gypsies on the Northern Divide. Why is that?"

Yakabuski didn't answer right away. He was thinking about the miners in the staging area. Remembering the insolent slouch to their bodies when they pulled up their overalls, the eyes that never blinked, looking right at the security mirror, the lazy-dog shuffle out of the staging area. No talking, no sign of camaraderie between them. Although the men had gone through their paces with the fatigued precision of a light infantry company marching away from a battlefield. A group of men that could work together and keep a secret.

"Maybe ghost gypsies are easier to believe than perfect security protocols," he said. "Tell you the truth, Mr. Merkel, they're a whole lot easier."

# CHAPTER
## TWENTY-THREE

The night sky was awash with stars when the plane took off for the return trip to Springfield. There was almost as much light on the ground: De Kirk was running three shifts, not enough hours in the day to pull out all the diamonds the company had found. There was the white glare of halogen floodlights ringing the fence around the perimeter, the head-lights of trucks travelling down the service roads, and earth-moving machines lumbering around the silos. Lights were turned on in every bunkhouse. Floodlights were aimed at the warehouse. A shoal of false light, on a peninsula jutting far into the Francis River.

When they had flown far enough away, the light on the ground faded and new light appeared. An arc of rose, purple, and yellow light that shone over the plane like a nighttime rainbow. The shimmering hues of the Northern Lights. So close it seemed as though the light were flying beside the plane, so palpable it seemed as though you could find a spot on the ground and sit dead centre beneath it.

In thirty minutes the plane lost sight of the Northern Lights and was travelling over the southern tip of the Great Boreal Forest, a swath of black-loam darkness without roads or towns, people or commerce. Yakabuski stared at the ground a long time and after a while thought he could pick out differences in the darkness, in the shading and texture. Perhaps he was looking at a river. Or a range of glacier-stunted mountains. Nothing man-made. Could not be anything man-made in that great pan of unexplored blackness beneath the plane.

Land was a funny thing on the Northern Divide. You could travel across ten thousand hectares of land no one wanted to own or live upon, and then you stumble upon a place like Cape Diamond, where civilization did a parachute drop of everything civilization valued: money, commerce, settlement.

Except for these rare occasions of interest, ownership of land on the Northern Divide was an exercise of the imagination. Yakabuski had an uncle who died several years back, and in his will he left his one-hundred-acre family farm to his grandson. But when the grandson went to get the land surveyed, thinking he would divide it into lots, he learned his grandfather only held a deed for four acres. The family had been swindled by the first railway agent who sold them the land. They had lived there for 150 years and no one had caught the mistake.

The only time land on the Divide had been coveted was in the heyday of square-timber, when any man holding timber rights could make a fortune selling pine to the British Royal Navy. The richest men in the British Empire, for half-a-century, were lumbermen from the Springfield Valley and the Northern Divide. The Shiners had their start back then, Irish labourers who couldn't find their way home and couldn't find work during the economic recession of the 1830s. Under the leadership of Peter Aylin, an Irishman with timber rights in the Upper Springfield Valley, the labourers learned how to rob a bush camp and set a timber crib afire, how to weigh down a man's body so he'd never be found if you threw him downriver from the Kettle Falls. The Shiners were running Springfield when the police arrived in 1847, their competitors fled from the city, travelling with their families upriver, where they hid in an abandoned seigneur estate with good battlements and escape tunnels leading north to the unincorporated townships.

Those were dark days on the Northern Divide. At night, people who had to journey through the region never strayed far from their fires; during day, they travelled in haste through the pine forests, anxious to be rid of this wild country, with its rolling mist and raging rivers, its night birds that swooped above their heads when they tried to sleep, the caves where old men lived, with long beards that hid everything but their eyes, which looked down on the world with fear and covetousness over clay pipes that burned in the night like fireflies.

No one knows how many people were killed in those years. Before Aylin was hunted down and executed. Before the rest of the Shiner leadership was rounded up and sent to the Perth Penitentiary. There were no newspapers back then. No civic records other than the allotting of timber rights and the selling of Crown land. It was a wide-open town. Four years ago, a mass grave was found near an old O'Hearn bush camp, thirteen men in the grave, all still clothed, workboots on their feet. Each had an axe stroke in the middle of their skull.

Trees had done that to people. Lumber, timber, forestry products, call it whatever you wanted to call it — you were still talking about trees. That's all it ever was. But for a brief while that's what people coveted and that's what the land held, so people became rich, people were killed, and history was written.

A land that held diamonds? It seemed to Yakabuski that was just asking for trouble.

. . .

An hour outside of Springfield, the pilot motioned for Yakabuski to come up to the cockpit.

"I've got a call from Chief O'Toole," she said, passing Yakabuski a set of headphones. "I've already given him an ETA of 1:45. If he asks, we can't make it any faster than that."

"You expecting him to ask?"

"He sounds a little agitated."

She smiled and passed Yakabuski her headset, flashed a sarcastic thumbs up. Good luck, buddy. Yakabuski put on the headset and pushed the button the pilot was pointing at.

"Chief, it's Yak."

"Yak, how far out are you?"

"Little more than an hour. Pilot says we'll be on the ground at 1:45."

"Can she get here any faster than that?"

"I don't think so. Why, what's happening?"

"The Shiners have struck back. I must have twenty patrol

cars on the North Shore right now, and it's not going to be enough. A bunch of them headed up there after the wake for Augustus. Just started beating on people. Like the old days."

"Is Morrissey up there?"

"We think so. We've got a bunch of them trapped in the service road that runs between Buildings A and B. We think he's in that group. But there are still a lot of them roaming around up there, so I don't know. We're going to have to tear gas the whole bluff to see what we've got."

Yakabuski looked at the darkness below him. The world seemed calm from up here. He wondered why he had never thought of becoming a pilot.

"There's something else, Yak. You know that Traveller you've been interviewing? The one with the brasserie on Tache?"

"Tete Fontaine?"

"We found his body fifteen minutes ago. He was hanging from that fence at Filion's Field."

# CHAPTER
## TWENTY-FOUR

They sat at a picnic table in Shawnee National Forest, playing cards. A retired machinist from San Bernardino, his wife, and the driver of a campervan with Texas plates.

The couple had arrived late to their campsite, pulling in after dark and then having trouble setting up the awning on their fifth-wheel. So much trouble Cambino, parked on the campsite next to them, had felt obligated to offer assistance. To do nothing would seem strange.

"This is the third night I've tried to set this thing up," said the retired machinist, who was wearing a Boeing Aerospace ball cap and would have been in his seventies. "If it don't get any easier, I'm throwing the gang-dang thing in the river."

"It's probably easier with two people," said the man who had come to help.

"It's a whole lot easier. Do you mind?"

"Not at all."

It took them ten minutes. Afterwards, the old man insisted on pouring drinks, to toast their success. His wife had already brought out a cooler and put it under the awning, along with a bottle of gin, a bottle of tonic, a bag of ice, and a stack of red plastic beer cups. They sat together at the picnic table.

"I was planning on being here three hours ago," the man said. "But there was some silly flea market Louise had to go to."

"I didn't hear you complaining when you bought that Hank Snow album," said his wife, who smiled at Cambino over the brim of her red plastic cup. An old woman nursing her first gin and tonic of the day. Her smile was beatific.

"I forgot about that. I should put that record on. It's been years since I've heard Hank Snow. I'll get us some fresh drinks while I'm up."

Cambino tried to beg off, but the couple insisted and he decided it was safer to stay. Surely they would be passed out before long. When the retired machinist brought the drinks, he also brought a deck of cards and a cribbage board. "Do you play?" he asked, and Cambino said yes, he knew how to play. The man dealt the cards as his wife got the board ready. From the fifth-wheel came the sound of Hank Snow singing "Miller's Cave." They sat by a campfire Cambino had started, the machinist saying he had never seen a man do it any better.

"So what sort of work do you do in Chicago?" he asked, peering over his glasses to take a look at his cards.

"I'm a facilitator. I help with labour disputes, corporate reorganizations. That sort of work."

"Where you from originally?"

"Many places. My family moved around."

"Just like mine. My dad was in the army. Were you an army brat?"

"Yes. I suppose I was."

After the first game, the old man suggested they start playing a nickel a point. He was on his third gin and tonic and insistent. Cambino said all right. They played for ninety minutes, which was a ridiculous amount of time to give the old man, who seemed smart and observant and for some reason, nowhere close to being drunk.

It happened finally when the old man was down two dollars and seventy cents. Not that this equated to the value of his life. Just something Cambino later remembered. The old man was down two dollars and seventy cents when it happened.

"Chicago," he said. "My brother used to live there. Right near the zoo. Do you ever go to that zoo?"

"Not that much."

"It's a beautiful zoo. Last time we went, though, they wanted an arm and a leg to get in. We didn't bother. It's a shame."

"It is a beautiful zoo. And it's a shame they charge so much."

The woman started to laugh.

"You two are so full of shit," she said. "You're thinking of the Los Angeles zoo, dear. When your brother lived in Los Angeles. Not Chicago. I don't think the Chicago zoo even charges admission."

The old man cocked his head for a moment, then snapped his fingers and said, "Dang, you're right, mother. It *was* Los Angeles."

He turned to look at Cambino. Not in a suspicious way. Not in a mistrusting way. Merely a curious way.

"*Is* there an admission fee at the Chicago zoo?"

Cambino looked into the old man's eyes and knew it was over. No matter what he said, the man's curiosity would soon turn to suspicion. After that, mistrust. Later that night, when they were alone in their fifth-wheel, the couple would start to think it was strange, a single man travelling alone in a camper-van. Before long Cambino would seem more Mexican to them than American. They would talk and talk, in the way of old people, and when the sun rose, they would be convinced there was something wrong with him. He would be reported to a park ranger as they drove away. The ranger would most likely ignore the old fools, but you never knew. And it didn't matter. Cambino was finished gambling for the night.

"You know what, that awning on your camper is a lot like mine," he said. "Would you like to see how it works?"

He rose from the table and started walking away. After he had taken a few steps, he turned to stare back at the old man. Who was still seated at the picnic table, not sure what to do.

But Cambino had been quick, the way he needed to be, and he waited patiently for the old man, who eventually stood up, unable to think of any good reason to stay seated.

"Well, I need to figure something out," he said. "If I have this much trouble every night, I'll just throw the dang thing away."

"I don't think you'll have to do that." Cambino placed an arm atop the old man's shoulder, steering him toward the camper. He turned back only once to see the man's wife, who held up her playing cards and gave a small wave. She took a sip of her drink. Cambino did not worry about her again. He unlocked the side door of the van, knowing she would be sitting there when he was done.

# CHAPTER
## TWENTY-FIVE

Thirty minutes after the plane landed, Yakabuski was back at Filion's Field, standing in the harsh glare of headlights turned to the south-side fence. The same panel of fencing where three days earlier the body of Augustus Morrissey had been found.

Unlike Morrissey, Fontaine was naked. His arms and legs were attached to the fence with what looked like chicken wire, with only slight bleeding around the ankles and wrists, which meant he hadn't struggled, was already dead when he was trussed up. His chest was covered in blood. Twenty-seven stab wounds Newton would say the next morning, some strong enough, wilful enough, to have fractured bones. A savage attack. Not a single cut looked tentative. Not a single cut looked doubtful.

The blood had trickled down his torso but left his arms and outer legs untouched, the harsh glare of the headlights giving sharp relief to the muscles, sinewy and perfectly proportioned, lithe and powerful.

He would have been wary, thought Yakabuski. On his guard. A twelve-inch Bowie knife beneath his lunch counter. Whatever firearms a Traveller would have considered wise to have around on the night of Augustus Morrissey's wake. He also had the high ground and the North Shore was as familiar to him as a path leading from his back door.

Who could have got the jump on a man like Tete Fontaine, he wondered. Yakabuski stared at the scene before him as though an attentive and appreciative patron at some Renaissance art gallery, the white marble statue with the finely cleaved muscles and tendons lit up like the gallery's prized possession. Disfigured though it might be.

. . .

O'Toole briefed him at the detachment at four in the morning. The official wake for Augustus Morrissey had been held at Adams Funeral Home, where visitors came to pay their respects to Sean and sign the condolence book. It was a closed-casket wake, which made the length of visit shorter than it may otherwise have been. When the visitors left the funeral home, they were escorted by black-arm-banded ushers to the unofficial wake, which was at the Silver Dollar, only a block away. The nightclub had closed to the public for the day. It had an open bar and a buffet that included Kobe beef, Russian caviar, and lobster flown in that afternoon, after having been caught in tidal pools off the coast of Maine that morning. The tavern tables were covered in white linen and the utensils were English silver. Entertainment was the choir from St. Bridget's Church and a well-known tenor from Toronto that Sean Morrissey hired the day before, paying three times the artist's normal rate because of the short notice.

As the sun went down the wake was in full swing, with people swelling and spilling out of the Silver Dollar, drinking and singing "Danny Boy," making drunken pilgrimages back to Adams to stand in front of the closed casket and curse the North Shore scum that had taken down Augustus Morrissey, a man who — six hours into an open bar — had become the greatest Shiner of all time.

The funeral home closed at nine, and O'Toole told the next part of the story in a start-and-stop cadence, halting and reflective, and Yakabuski knew he had spent a fair part of the night wondering if he could have handled it better. Maybe he had even been asked a direct question or two by the mayor.

"We were ready to shut down Cork's Town if things got out of hand," said O'Toole. "What we weren't ready for was Cork's Town getting up and heading to the North Shore."

O'Toole explained he had cordoned off most of the side streets around the Silver Dollar and most of the roads leading into Cork's Town. He had plenty of cops on scene, including a full tactical team. He even had a mobile command centre. But he didn't have Belfast Street cordoned off, as this was the main thoroughfare into Cork's Town, and the mayor said it was premature to cut off all road links to the neighbourhood.

At precisely 9:30 p.m., about fifty cars left the Silver Dollar and headed to the North Shore as fast as possible.

"It all happened so quickly," said O'Toole. "They just up and split, and we couldn't stop them in time. When the platoon commanders got orders to reposition, the Shiners were already over there."

And once they were there, as O'Toole had told Yakabuski in the plane, it was old school. Anyone on the street was assaulted. Cars were set on fire. The townhomes surrounding the high-rises were firebombed, and when the people inside tried to flee, gangs of laughing Shiners gave chase. O'Toole caught the last few minutes of the riot, before he ordered tear gas to be used and people started to disappear in the fog and haze.

"I've seen riots before," he said, looking directly at Yakabuski. "I was seconded for the G8 Summit in Québec City. There were anarchists there that you'd think were right out of a war film. Like they'd just had breakfast with Lenin and were looking for something to burn. Scary people with these vacant eyes that seemed more dead than alive. The North Shore was worse. That was pure hatred. That wasn't some political philosophy you'd learned in school and wanted to go to the wall for. That was a pack of animals wanting to kill something."

"Where was Morrissey when all this was happening?"

"That's a good question. I told you last night he was up there, but now we can't say. He wasn't picked up. He's not on any surveillance tape I've seen so far."

"How many did you arrest?"

"Twenty-seven."

"All Shiners?"

"All Shiners. We have twenty-two more in hospital. Six of them are Shiners, the rest live on the North Shore. A few of the people from North Shore are in critical condition with first-degree burns, but I'm told they'll pull through. So we only have the one death. Which seems like a miracle to me."

"Did anyone see Fontaine last night?"

"No one we've interviewed. He closed his brasserie early. Like he was expecting trouble."

O'Toole became silent. Several minutes passed before Yakabuski said, "That's not what you're thinking about though, is it? Where was Fontaine? Where was Morrissey?"

"You don't think so?"

"No."

"So what am I thinking about?"

"The cars."

O'Toole stared at him a long second before saying, "So you see it too?"

"Sure. How did that happen? All those cars leaving the Silver Dollar at the same time. Everything about last night seems like a drunken, spontaneous riot. Except for those cars."

# CHAPTER
## TWENTY-SIX

Donna Griffin had set her alarm for 5 a.m. and was sitting at her kitchen table ten minutes later, drinking instant coffee and staring at her laptop. She had asked the staff sergeant in Major Crimes if she could use the encrypted passcodes she had been given to work at home, and the staff sergeant had said he didn't know. Griffin was the first one to ever ask that question. Later in the day, he came and told her it would be all right.

"First one ever." Griffin had heard the phrase so many times she no longer felt insulted by it, as she once did, or proud, as she once stupidly did. Her teachers used the phrase often. So did her parents, who always added the word Griffin to it, as in: "You'd be the first Griffin in four generations not to go to university, Donna." Or: "You'd be the first Griffin to ever think that was a smart idea." One night, in a heated argument she and her parents soon came to regret, it was: "That would be a first, Donna. A Griffin walking a beat. Have you lost your mind?"

Her parents were what people called "old money," which meant they didn't work for it and their parents didn't work for it. The family money went back to her great-grandfather, who had started a shipping company in New Brunswick. That didn't seem all that old to Griffin, but that's all it took to be old money in Rosedale, and old money was what every auto dealer, pediatric surgeon, and business grad in the neighbourhood wanted to be. Donna Griffin, middle child tucked between two boys, never understood the cachet of old money. It embarrassed her slightly that her parents didn't work. That when other children's parents were rushing to work in the pre-dawn of a new day, hers were still in bed. And if it were a typical day, when they awoke the most pressing decision they needed to make would be tennis or mimosas?

Griffin had a utilitarian streak her parents couldn't understand, and they were just as embarrassed by their only daughter. Embarrassed when they arrived to pick her up at her riding lessons to find her mucking out stalls that had nothing to do with her, as though she might actually work there. Embarrassed by her desire for a part-time job at a clothing store, and most embarrassed by her fascination with police work, which started when Griffin went on a ride-along with a community police officer when she was fourteen. She started volunteering with Crime Stoppers the same month.

Griffin couldn't fully explain it, either. It wasn't an act of rebellion. She loved her parents, and she didn't have any shop-worn theories or philosophies on why their wealth should be despised. They subsidized the rent on her apartment, after all.

No, the fascination had something to do with how much work a police officer could pack into an eight-hour shift, how useful and needed they could sometimes be. There were many ways to describe what old money did to a person, but if you wanted to be fair and accurate, somewhere on your list of adjectives would be the world indolent. And indolent was something Donna Griffin could never be, even if most of her parents' neighbours had set that as their life ambition.

She stared at her computer screen and began scrolling again through the names in a Springfield city directory for 1974. She went through the Ms for a second time and then pulled up the directory for 1975. She was hoping to start on the provincial marriage registry before she left. With any luck, she would have something to report to the senior detective in Major Crimes by the time she got to work.

"Katherine Morrissey," she muttered, tightening the robes of her dressing gown and leaning closer to the computer screen. "It looks like you don't want to be found. Now why is that?"

. . .

Griffin was at Yakabuski's office at 6:45 a.m., his door open and a desk lamp turned on, although when she got there she found him lying on a couch with a parka over his head. She stood there a minute, wondering what to do, before walking quietly into the room and shaking his shoulder. On the second shake Yakabuski raised his right hand and slid the parka off his face.

"Two hours," he said, after he had sat up, arced his back, and looked at his watch.

"I'm sorry."

"Two hours' sleep. If I'm going to keep this up, I'll need a better couch."

"I'm sorry. Should I have let you sleep?"

"No."

"What all *did* happen on the North Shore last night?" she asked, and Yakabuski told her about the riot and the killing of Tete Fontaine. Griffin had heard on the radio that someone was killed, but didn't know it had been Gabriel Dumont's cousin.

"Hanging him on that fence seems like a pretty obvious message," she said.

"Too early to say what it means. So, Katherine Morrissey, what have you found out?"

Griffin sat on the chair in front of Yakabuski's desk. "It's a bit odd," she said. "That's why I wanted to see you right away. I tracked down four Katherine Morrisseys in Springfield and have ruled out all of them because of their age. Three of them are younger than Sean Morrissey, the other one would have been eight the year he was born. I can't find any record of Augustus ever having a wife and Sean seems to be his only child. That's a bit odd for an Irish crime boss, wouldn't you say?"

Griffin waited for the laugh that never came. Clearing her throat, she continued, "Sean Morrissey was born May 24, 1974, so, forty-four years old. Every document I've seen has Augustus listed as his only parent. There's never been another name."

"You've checked his birth certificate? Gone through the provincial registry office?"

"It's not there. Clerk says there was never one filed."

"What about school records?"

"Going all the way back to Mother Teresa's. So, grade school records. Only parent ever listed is Augustus."

Yakabuski stood up and re-tucked his shirt. Ran the problem through his head. "What about the rest of the family? Does he have any aunts or uncles we can interview?"

"No aunts. He would have had two uncles. One was killed and the other one went missing thirty years ago."

"I remember that. Augustus was charged for the killing, wasn't he?"

"He was. Brother's name was Ambrose, three years younger than Augustus. A good-looking man." Griffin took a black-and-white photo from the file folder on her knee and handed it to Yakabuski. He looked at the mug shot, dated 1985, which explained the white dinner jacket and pastel T-shirt. He was indeed a handsome man, looked a bit like John Dillinger, right down to the slicked-back hair and the dimples. "His body was found in the woods off Mission. Augustus was charged with first-degree murder, along with Paddy McSheffrey and Ricky Green. All three were acquitted in 1987. Weak link in the case was motive. State didn't have one. Just a lot of circumstantial evidence."

"Like the brother's blood in the trunk of Augustus's Caddy, if I remember the case right."

"Yes, that sort of circumstantial evidence."

"What happened to the other brother?"

"Baby brother Austin. No one knows. He went missing during the court case. Hasn't been seen since."

"That's it for the family?"

"For the direct family. Augustus had cousins — that's the Tommy Bangles connection — but there's no Katherine

Morrissey among any of them. I've also checked news sites, run searches on Augustus Morrissey and all known associates. I've run searches on the year 1974 and Springfield, to see if anything pops, but I can't find her."

"Well, Sean Morrissey has to have had a mother."

"You would suspect."

This time Griffin's comment was rewarded with a small laugh from Yakabuski. Encouraged, she went on, more animated this time, although she tried to calm her voice after a few seconds, thinking her enthusiasm might be too much for a man who had just awoken on the couch in his office.

"I can find this woman, Detective Yakabuski, I know I can. But I'm beginning to think computers won't be enough. We need to go back to primary sources. Hospital records. Church records. We need to find that birth certificate and I probably need to knock on a few doors to do that. How far do you want me to go with this?"

Yakabuski rubbed his eyes and considered her question. A thin red line had appeared on the eastern horizon, and he knew the sun was about to show. It was already hot in his office. He thought of Tete Fontaine's mutilated body lit up at Filion's Field like it was the statue of Champlain in the French Quarter, and the body of Augustus Morrissey tethered to the same fence three days earlier, his eyes cut out. The North Shore Travellers and the Shiners were apparently about to go to war, and he had no idea why.

"I don't think you can go too far," he said finally. "Do whatever it takes. You need to find that woman."

. . .

The sun was throwing a glare across Highway 7 when Yakabuski left the detachment, the highway busy now with morning commuters on their way to downtown Springfield, or to one of the sawmills upriver. He merged with traffic and headed east. On the radio, a DJ said the December heat wave was now in its twelfth day of record-setting temperatures, this after an autumn that never had a storm, never had bad winds of any kind, and never had a night that fell below freezing. It was like the seasons had stalled, the way an old car will stall and suddenly you're stranded by the side of the road, wondering if you should kick something. It was beginning to feel like that in Springfield.

The city had started as a mill town, cutting square-timber pine and floating the logs to Québec City. After that came the sawmills and the pulp-and-paper mills, the shake factories and the matchstick factories, so much sulfur in the air once in Springfield the bass leaves were always covered in yellow goo and any open flame would crackle and fizz and set off small, shooting sparks. You couldn't smell sulphur anymore, and the city had grown to 750,000 people, but Springfield still seemed a mill town to Yakabuski. It was loud and bawdy and the police were kept busy every Friday and Saturday night. It was also home to the Shiners and the Popeyes and many career criminals who loved the city, the Northern Divide being one of the few places left in North America where cutting a phone line and racing down a back road might actually work for you.

In many parts of Springfield, there was almost a laissez-faire attitude toward crime. Probably half the men working in the mills and truck yards had a criminal record. That didn't get you shunned the way it might some other places. Yakabuski remembered first arriving in the city, working patrol for nine months, then one night pulling over a car weaving its way out of Cork's Town. The driver was someone he knew, a mill worker who played on his beer-league hockey team.

He stumbled out of his car before Yakabuski got there, broke into a big grin at the sight of his teammate, and said, "Well, this is going to be fun, ain't it, Yak?"

Then the man took a swing at him. He missed, but followed up with a kick to Yakabuski's shin that connected well, and then the two men were rolling on the ground, punching each other, the driver laughing and saying, "That the best you got, boy?"

When Yakabuski had the man in the back of the squad car, he started to apologize.

"Sorry 'bout the tussle, boy. Didn't think you'd be any good. Bit of fun though, eh?" Three days later, the man phoned Yakabuski and asked for a drive to that night's hockey game.

"You still got my car impounded," he explained. "I ain't telling you what you gotta do, Yak. I wouldn't do that to any man. But the way I see it, you're sort of obligated."

That was Springfield. Yakabuski had yet to decide if he liked the city. Thought some days he might, other days that he needed to get back to the bush as quick as possible. But if you were a cop who liked to stay busy, you couldn't do much better than this hopped up mill town on the southern skirt of the Great Boreal Forest.

· · ·

When he was twenty kilometres east of Springfield, Yakabuski stopped at a trailer park, closed for the season. He unlocked the gate and drove to his ice fishing hut, up on blocks by the river's edge. He had begun to wonder if he was going to use it this year. When he was a boy, he helped his dad put out his fishing hut every year right after Halloween. Always the first week of November, and they probably could have put it out earlier, but the first week of November was tradition. That was High River, granted, but Springfield wouldn't have been much different.

When he unlocked the door to the hut, he found Jimmy O'Driscoll sleeping on a chair. When the boy was asleep, not awake and jumping around with his addictions, his debts and his fears, his forearms bleeding, that's just what he looked like: a boy.

Yakabuski shook his shoulder. O'Driscoll awoke with a start. Tried to jump out of the chair, but Yakabuski pushed him back down.

"Easy, Jimmy. You're all right. You're in my ice fishing hut. You remember coming here?"

The boy's eyes twitched a few times. Then he gave his head a couple quick shakes and looked around the hut. "We're fishing?"

"No Jimmy, the hut is still on the shore. You've been asleep."

"How long."

"Day-and-a-half."

"I don't remember."

"You needed some rest. Any idea when you slept last?"

O'Driscoll rubbed his eyes, looked around the hut again, at the bait buckets and manual auger, the gasoline cans and fishing equipment that Yakabuski stored in the hut when it wasn't being used. He yawned and said, "I'm not sure. It's been a while."

"I talked to your grandfather."

"How did it go? Do we have a deal?"

"We do. You need to come with me."

"Where are we going?"

"Ridgewood."

"Hold on, that's not the deal. You need to protect me. You need to get me someplace deep underground, where the Popeyes can't find me. Fuck, they'll know I'm at Ridgewood the day I check in."

"They probably will. And they'll leave you alone."

"Ahhh man, this was a mistake. I've got to get out of here."

O'Driscoll rose from his chair and Yakabuski pushed him back down a second time.

"Jimmy, you need to get yourself right-thinking again. Ridgewood will do that for you."

"I'll have my throat slit in the middle of the night. The Popeyes probably know half the people staying there."

"Which is why you'll be safe. Ridgewood is part of a court diversion program the Popeyes use all the time. They won't fuck with it."

O'Driscoll didn't say anything right away. Kept rubbing his eyes and yawning, looking around the hut as though it hadn't come to him yet. How he got there. "What's the program?"

"Hundred days."

"No fucking way. I can't do that."

"Your granddad thinks it's a good idea."

"Then get him to do the hundred days."

"Do you think he's got a hundred days?"

That seemed to wake him up. And because it did, Yakabuski had the momentary belief that he wasn't wasting his time with Jimmy O'Driscoll. That buried deep in his addictions, his fears and his mania, there was a part of the boy that had woken up and paused for a second. Saddened by the knowledge his grandfather would die soon.

"He wants to make it to spring," O'Driscoll said quietly. "He told me that the other day. Spring. He's counting what he has left in seasons."

"He's probably tough enough to make it. How tough are you?"

A salesman's close. Yakabuski felt a twinge of guilt for using it, for being that obvious, but he was at the start of what was going to be a long day, and what he needed right then was to be driving Jimmy O'Driscoll to Ridgewood.

"I'm plenty tough," said the boy, a note of hostility in his voice that did not worry Yakabuski, buoyed him, rather, because the boy needed to be a fighter now. Not a pleading, down-on-his-knees junkie.

"Then let's get going, Jimmy. We both have a busy day ahead of us."

O'Driscoll sat in the chair a minute longer, no longer yawning, no longer rubbing his eyes, thinking it through, one hundred days of sobriety, in a locked-down old house on the banks of the Springfield, miles from any bar, roadhouse, or street corner, the sweats and stomach cramps coming for him probably later that day, when the meth and Oxy began seeping out of his blood, the chemical mix about to go way wrong for him. His body shuddered at the thought of it.

Then he gave his head a surprised shake, looked up at Yakabuski, and said, "Why, what do you have to do today?"

# CHAPTER
## TWENTY-SEVEN

The funeral for Augustus Morrissey was held at St. Bridget's Basilica. Belfast Street was shut down for the service and there were patrol cars positioned on the side streets for a six-block radius. There were more patrol cars up on the North Shore. About fifty men who would have been attending the funeral were still in hospital, or still being questioned by police, but they weren't missed. Television stations later estimated the crowd inside the basilica at eight hundred, with another thousand on the street outside.

Sean Morrissey wasn't picked up on the sweep of the North Shore, and Yakabuski planned on questioning him as soon as the funeral was finished. It seemed an unnecessary provocation to pick him up beforehand. He stood in the back of the crowd that had assembled on Belfast Street, not surprised by the number of people who had come, as Augustus Morrissey was about as well-known as a man could be in

Springfield, and the Shiners were legendary. People gathered to catch a glimpse of his son, or some of the Shiners they had been reading about for years. Men like Harry LaChance, who once stole a shipment of gold on its way to the Bank of Canada, right off the tarmac at the Springfield Airport. Or Peter O'Reilly, tried in court three times for three different murders and acquitted each time. Came to see the out-of-town guests who had flown in for the funeral. Billy Adams, head of the Irish mob in Boston. The Derry brothers from Buffalo, a couple of psychopaths who ran a human smuggling operation so brutal it made Latin American cartels seem like finishing schools.

It wasn't just Irish. Italians from New York came. Latinos from Miami. They all came to say goodbye to Augustus Morrissey, King of the Shiners, a man many of the funeral guests had once envied, a gangster who ruled not a street, not a neighbourhood or a city, but an entire region. Held dominion over lands the size of New England. Augustus Morrissey had ruled a frontier and taken advantage of all the opportunities that offered — secret meth labs, secret transportation corridors, secret flight paths. Every man inside St. Bridget's had made money with Augustus Morrissey. Every man had envied his swagger, his success, his lumber-baron mien, which was part hedonist, part carnivore, a rapacious throwback to the days of gangsters like Bugsy Siegel and John D. Rockefeller.

The service was broadcast on speakers set up outside the church. A choir sang as the invited guests filled the church, then there was the reading of passages from the Old Testament and a benediction from Bishop Charles Guiges, a small grey-haired man who had travelled from Montreal to preside over the funeral service. After the benediction, the parish priest for St. Bridget's, Father Adam McCleary, spoke about Augustus, choosing to reveal only a fraction of what he knew to be true. He spoke of the generous donations to St. Bridget's. The faithful attendance on Sunday mass and his firm belief in the Father, the Son, and the Holy Ghost, in the Power and the Glory.

After Father McCleary, the choir sang another hymn, a beautiful song that came clean and clear through the speakers, which were expensive and positioned perfectly on pedestals so the sound didn't fade away but bounced back from the buildings across the street, so the people on the street were surrounded by the fine high rise of the verses, the swell of the chorus, a mid-December day with a hot white sun and not a cloud in the sky. It was almost possible to forget the choir was singing in praise of the most ruthless killer and bandit to ever live in Springfield.

· · ·

After the song was finished, there was silence from the speakers that lasted for several minutes, which seemed to confuse and startle the crowd on the street. People shuffled their feet in impatience. Stared at the reporters by the front steps, wondering if they might know what was happening. Stared at the floral tributes in a roped-off area by the front door, dozens of them, some as large as a grown man, looking for some sign of movement.

Eventually, they heard the voice of Sean Morrissey. He spoke for about five minutes, repeating some of what Father McCleary had said and emphasizing how pleased his father would have been, to see how much he was respected. He was sure his father was looking down upon them right then, and he knew his father was happy. To see his old friends. To know how much he was loved. To know that his death would soon be avenged.

There was a long pause after that, although this time the people on the street felt certain they knew what was happening inside the church. The son of Augustus Morrissey would have been casting his gaze across the pews, across the assembled tough men, the out-of-town gangsters, the cutthroats and bandits who had assembled beneath the gilded domes of St. Bridget's, letting each know that this problem — the killing of the King of the Shiners — would be handled the way Augustus Morrissey would have handled it. With speed. With clarity. With resolve.

"Enough said," Yakabuski muttered, and he continued to crane his neck and scan the crowd on the street, looking to see if anyone seemed like more than a curiosity seeker, a reality-TV watcher, more than an office worker taking a late lunch so they would have something interesting to say at the dinner table. More than a cop, scanning the crowd and asking the same questions he was.

Bishop Guiges gave the final homily, speaking in a reedy voice that seemed as thin and weak as strands of milkweed. The bishop praised Augustus Morrissey for his "great achievements in the community," and his "many successes," then he gave a final benediction and the choir started singing "Danny Boy." The song continued, through repeated verses, as Morrissey's casket was brought outside, left on the front steps of the basilica for a minute so photographers could take photos, then taken down the steps and placed in an idling hearse. The procession that followed the hearse must have been nearly a hundred cars, ushered into place by workers from Adams, who wore yellow vests and waved the cars down Belfast Street as though they were landing planes on an aircraft carrier. The choir sang through all of it, only stopping when the last car had left and altar boys started removing the floral tributes.

. . .

Yakabuski's sister came to see him before joining the procession to the cemetery. Tyler Lawson kept his distance, waiting in front of the church for a valet from the funeral home to bring around his BMW 430i.

Trish had met Lawson when she was in university and working as a hostess at the Baton Rouge, one of the more expensive red-meat-and-Scotch restaurants in downtown Springfield. Lawson was employed by a Chicago law firm that did work for the Shiners, and he arrived at the Baton Rouge one night stumbling drunk. Trish's boss told her he couldn't be thrown out, so she spent most of the night slapping away Lawson's hands and making sure he didn't fall on anything sharp.

He came back to the restaurant the following week, sober and apologizing for the "bloody fool I was the last time I saw you." He went on to explain the Clemson Tigers had been awarded a bowl game that very day, and Clemson was his alma mater, and then he shrugged his shoulders, ran his fingers through his already tousled hair, and flashed Trish a smile she had not noticed the week before. When he insisted

169

on giving her a one-hundred-dollar tip "to make up for being such an ass," she didn't protest long.

They dated off and on for the next two years, until Augustus Morrissey suggested Lawson quit the Chicago firm and move to Springfield. He promised the young lawyer enough work to bankroll the opening of his own law firm. Lawson married Yakabuski's sister within a year of moving to the city.

Trish had blinders on when it came to Tyler Lawson. Not that she was deceived about her husband being a mob lawyer. Just that she didn't let that play a major part in their relationship. They had two children — Jason and Sarah — that they both doted on. When Lawson wasn't working in his office, he spent most of his time at hockey arenas and dance studios, or tending the gardens around their home, a large Tudor on Mission Road.

If you let yourself forget it was Shiner money that bought the house and paid for the dance lessons, you could almost go skipping over the moon with Tyler Lawson.

"Frankie, how are you doing?" his sister asked when she was standing in front of Yakabuski.

"Just peachy, Trish. How do you think I'm doing?"

"I know. It's horrible what happened on the North Shore last night. A man was killed?"

"A man was killed. You want to know more, go ask your husband."

"Frankie, let's not do this right now. Work is work, and family is family. We've agreed. Even dad has agreed."

"Dad would go over Niagara Falls in his wheelchair if you asked him, Trish."

She laughed a perfect little laugh, the sort of laugh that

might be allowed on the front steps of a church after a funeral. Then she squeezed her brother's arms and said, "We should get together soon, Frankie. I worry about you. Dad worries about you. It's just a job, you know?"

Then she turned and walked to her car. The valet was holding open the passenger door. Lawson was standing beside the driver's door. Before he drove away, Lawson gave a small wave to his brother-in-law, then jumped into the car so quickly he wouldn't have had the chance to see if Yakabuski waved back.

# CHAPTER
## TWENTY-EIGHT

Cambino enjoyed the rhythm of a journey. It did not matter how he was travelling or where he was going. Every journey came with the soft hum and vibration of mechanical movement, with a world passing before his eyes like a tape that never looped back. He drove through the centre of North America, marvelling at a sky that never seemed crowded, even when filled with cumulus clouds. He passed within fifty miles of a reservoir that on his GPS looked larger than an inland sea and thought briefly of detouring so he could see it, then thought of his schedule and continued his journey north.

It was not only the schedule that kept Cambino on task. The journey had had complications. This needed to be acknowledged. The perfect journey would not have had an Arkansas state trooper with too much time on his hands. Would not have had an elderly couple that knew the admission price for the Chicago zoo. The perfect plan would have had a dead escort girl in a sugar beet field outside Corpus Christi and nothing else.

It was even possible, although unlikely, that a smart cop had linked the three crimes. The possibility did not overly worry Cambino — he had little respect for police agencies in the United States — but there had been complications, and he needed to acknowledge this fact and focus on his work. He turned his attention back to the two men from the North. To weigh and measure a man's future was a serious matter, and Cambino had been taught to take his time about it. He thought again of what he knew about the two men, for he did not know them well, business partners from afar who had come to him with tales of riches and schemes of betrayal.

They were both leaders of a criminal organization. Their gangs had existed for centuries. They were smart and daring and had the loyalty of their men. Cambino had done the research and knew this to be true. They were tough and brutal and in the old ways, with blood on their hands, no enemies they allowed to live, driving cars with trunks the size of storage sheds.

Those were the similarities. As for the differences: one of the men could spend many weeks in the bush. One would not attempt such a thing. One was a nomad, who appeared and disappeared. One was fixed to his village like a tree. He thought about his dilemma while the sun set to the left of him, a long, drawn-out strand of golden thread, fluttering and falling to earth.

After a while, Cambino tried tackling the problem from the other direction. Forget the two men from the North. What did Cambino abhor? He bore down on the question, slowing his breathing, repeating a mantra he had chosen earlier in the day. What sort of man could the planet do without? Covetous men. Weak men. False men.

He stopped and repeated what he had just said, this time moving his lips and saying it aloud, a soft whisper in the darkening cab of his vehicle.

"False men."

· · ·

Cambino pulled into the next rest area and went to use a pay phone. He turned his back to the steady stream of motorists entering and leaving the washrooms and placed his call. He would have appeared to the passing crowd as a slight man, wearing an old man's light-tan windbreaker and unfashionable running shoes, a Texas A&M cap pulled low on his face. The change was in his pocket, and his call was answered on the first ring.

"I was not expecting to hear from you today."

"I need a situation report," said Cambino, and he leaned his body forward, cupping the receiver so close to his chin it was nearly in his jacket. He listened for more than a minute, not moving, keeping track of the sounds on the phone, the sounds behind him.

When the man on the phone stopped talking, Cambino said, "It is not enough. You will need to do more."

The other man did not speak right away. When he did, he said, "I am not sure why. Everything is going as we planned. The police, they are working on nothing else."

"You have three more days. There's a chance that won't last. Even if it does, you should not risk it. There is a way to guarantee everything happens the way it must. Here is what you need to do."

Cambino's voice was so low it was not even a whisper that might be dimly heard amidst the shouts and chatter of the visitors' centre, the words more rhythm than pitched sound, the end of his instructions coming when he said, almost rhetorically, "You can do this?"

"Yes, of course. I'm just not sure it needs to be done."

"It is good insurance. None is better. It will also be a test for him."

"A test? What difference will a test make? He's dead either way."

"It will make a difference to me," Cambino said.

"You are sure of this?"

"I am. And he must know. He must agree to it."

"All right. Consider it done."

Cambino didn't say anything more. He hung up the phone and went back to his campervan.

# CHAPTER
## TWENTY-NINE

The Silver Dollar had a sign on the front door saying it was closed for the day and would reopen tomorrow. Eddie O'Malley stood in front of the door with his arms crossed, in case there was any misunderstanding about the sign.

"We're closed today," he said, when Yakabuski was standing in front of him.

"I'm not planning on staying long, Eddie. Is he in his office?"

"He probably is. But he's not taking visitors, Mr. Yakabuski. Did you not know it was his father's funeral today?"

"I know that, Eddie. I still need to see him."

The bouncer didn't speak for several seconds. Tilted his head, as though visualizing it, playing it out in his mind, how the fight would go once it started. He looked at the sign behind him, the police detective in front of him, and finally he said, "You sure about this? The place is full."

"I'm sure."

"All right. I'll walk you back."

Yakabuski followed Eddie's back as it weaved between the tables. The room was filled with men, and there was not an empty table. The women must have been taken someplace else after the funeral. The music was loud, some sort of Cuban music, the DJ in the booth a man Yakabuski had never seen before. They were almost to the hallway that led to Morrissey's office when Peter O'Reilly put out his leg and blocked their way.

He was sitting down, two other men seated with him at the round tavern table. If O'Reilly had been standing, he would have stood six-foot-four, although he always seemed a couple inches shorter than that because of an insolent junkyard slouch he had been walking around with since he was a teenager. He had a tuft of carrot-coloured hair, meaty lips that seemed out of place with the rest of his body's litheness, and Celtic crosses tattooed on the wrists of both hands.

When O'Malley stopped walking, O'Reilly looked up at the bouncer and said, "And what might you be doin', Eddie?"

"I'm taking Detective Yakabuski to see Sean."

"Are you now? And why, on such a sad and mournful day as this, might this bohunk dick need to see Sean?"

There were snickers from the two men seated with O'Reilly. And from some of the men sitting at nearby tables. O'Malley turned around and looked at Yakabuski. The expression on his face said: "That question was for you."

Yakabuski stepped around the bouncer to stand directly in front of O'Reilly. "This bohunk dick needs to see Sean about the riot on the North Shore last night. You wouldn't know anything about that, would you, Mr. O'Reilly?"

"The North Shore? I went there once to have a dump. Never went back," said O'Reilly, and after he said it he took a toothpick from the pocket of his sport coat and began working on his teeth. After a few seconds he took a napkin off the table, wiped the toothpick and put it back in his pocket. "On the day Sean buries his father, you come in here to roust him. You really are a prick, aren't you?"

"Don't know if that matters much. Are you going to let us pass?"

"No."

"You're going to stop me?"

"Not just me. Every man in here."

Some of the men at the nearby tables had started to stand. The two men sitting with O'Reilly leaned forward but remained sitting. Yakabuski wondered if they would stay that way. George McAllister and an out-of-towner with a French manicure. Yakabuski looked at them and figured they were going to stay that way.

"Just how quickly do you think they can get here, Mr. O'Reilly? Fast enough to stop me from breaking that leg you've got sticking out?"

"Talking tough, are we? I've got two good lads sitting here with me right now. No one has to come. It's already three to one. So why don't you piss off, and I'll tell Sean you came a-visiting."

"I don't see it."

O'Reilly put his hands in his pockets and stretched his body. Took the toothpick back out and said, "What don't you see?"

"The three to one."

"Are you a fuckin' idiot?"

Yakabuski figured that was as good a cue as any. His right hand flew across the table and smashed into the face of George McAllister. The man with the French manicure jumped up when the blow landed, but Yakabuski had anticipated that, already adjusted for the change in height and distance, and his left fist landed square on the man's jaw. He pulled both hands back at the same time, like an elastic band snapping back, and the two men wobbled for a second before falling forward, their heads hitting the tavern table with loud thumps, only a second apart. Like some sort of back beat.

No one moved. O'Reilly didn't move. O'Malley didn't move. The two men collapsed on the table didn't move. With everyone in the tavern looking at him, Yakabuski grabbed the bouncer and slid him into a half nelson. He planned to use O'Malley as a shield while making his way either to Morrissey's office or back to the front door of the Silver Dollar. He hadn't decided his direction. His eyes darted around the room, sizing up the men, calculating where the fighting would be toughest, and just then the silence in the room was broken by Sean Morrissey's yelling. "All right, Yak, you've made your point. You can come back to the office."

Morrissey was standing beside the bar, still dressed in his funeral suit of English twill cashmere, and after glancing around the tavern to make sure he had been heard, that no one was moving and about to damage his club, he added, "Eddie, you and Peter clean up that mess."

Yakabuski released his grip on O'Malley and let him go. As he passed the bouncer he whispered, "Sorry, Eddie. It was O'Reilly that screwed up the math."

. . .

Morrissey took off his coat and hung it on the back of his desk chair. Sat down, took the cufflinks from his shirt, and rolled up both sleeves. Yakabuski was surprised to see his arms were covered in tattoos, full sleeves, bright etchings of Celtic crosses and buxom angels and twisting serpents. He was starting to look less and less like the Jim Morrison jewel thief of his youth.

"So what can I help you with, Yak?"

"Why don't we start with the riot on the North Shore last night?"

"I hear it was quite the event. I wasn't there, of course. But you already know that. Otherwise I'd be sitting in a holding cell right now."

"Maybe you know something about it. Because it's the strangest thing, the people that started the riot all came from your nightclub."

"Did they now?"

"Yes. And it gets stranger. The men we arrested, every last one of them lives in Cork's Town. They all have criminal records, and most of them have you listed as a known associate."

"That *is* strange. You must think I had something to do with it."

"I must."

Morrissey leaned back in his chair, raised both arms, and knitted his fingers behind his head, his biceps stretching the linen fabric of his shirt. "And you have proof of this?"

"Not at the moment. A great many of your friends are still being interviewed."

"Well, as soon as one of them mentions my name, you come back here and tell me all about it."

He was smiling at Yakabuski, rocking in his chair with his bulging arms and his fou-hundred-dollar linen shirt, thoroughly enjoying himself.

Eventually he unknitted his hands, leaned over his desk, and said, "Here's something for you to consider, Yak. My father was much beloved in this town. I saw you at the funeral; you heard the service. Maybe those men you're detaining were doing nothing more than blowing off a little steam on the North Shore last night. It was my father's wake yesterday, as you know. Maybe things got a little out of hand and this has nothing to do with me."

"Nice speech, Sean. Problem is the cars."

"The cars?"

"The cars all left your nightclub at the same time. It was well coordinated. I don't think a military supply convoy could have done it any better."

"And you are telling me this because?"

"Because it was planned. Those men were following your orders."

"You can prove this?"

Yakabuski didn't bother answering.

"Ahh, I see. The same old problem."

"Do you know a man named Tete Fontaine?"

"Sounds like someone who would live on the North Shore."

"He did."

"Then no."

"That's strange too, because Tete Fontaine is a Traveller, and not three days ago I was sitting in this office, and you asked me if your dad had been killed by the North Shore Travellers."

"I don't recall saying that."

"You asked about your dad's eyes. Asked if I knew what that meant. Tete Fontaine was a cousin of Gabriel Dumont, and last night he was found murdered and hanging from the same fence where your dad was found murdered and hanging. Those are some mighty big coincidences, wouldn't you say?"

"I would. Some mighty big coincidences." He turned up his hands and shrugged his shoulders, didn't bother asking this time if Yakabuski had any proof, having gone beyond that, being dismissive now, giving the cop nothing more than an "and-your-point-is?" gesture.

Yakabuski chuckled and looked around the office, thinking again it was strange, and a little off-putting, to be sitting in an office in Springfield that had not a scrap of wood in it, only metal and chrome and Japanese prints of flowers you'd have to travel five thousand miles to see.

He thought for a moment of asking right then. Where's your mother, Sean? Or even, *who* is your mother? But if she were indeed the key to this investigation, it would be like showing Morrissey his hole card. Griffin would find her.

"So what are you two fighting about?" he said, once his gaze had come back to Morrissey. "A million-dollar diamond just thrown away to make some sort of point. Whatever this is about, the money that has to be in play, it must be your fantasy scheme."

"What do you mean by that?"

"I mean you're a schemer, Sean. You can't stop scheming. It's an adrenalin rush for you, no different than meth or coke, and it comes with the same problems, because if you scheme long enough you don't get better at it; you just start acting more and more like a junkie. Eventually you'll come up with a scheme so complicated and so outlandish it blows up on you."

"Is that so?"

"True gen. It's what some people call hubris. Something tells me it's coming for you."

# CHAPTER THIRTY

Yakabuski drove his Jeep out of the alley and made his way down Belfast Street. He stopped again at the corner of Belfast and Derry to stare at the cliffs on the North Shore, which were already in shadows, the sun starting to disappear down the backside of the escarpment. The scene was framed like a picture, like some painting you might buy from a street vendor at the Springfield Harbour. Although the artist would have needed to sketch quickly, for the scene didn't last long. Was already falling apart: the sun about to crush everything atop the bluff and cast the world into darkness.

Yakabuski felt like that harried artist. Trying to capture a true picture before it disappeared on him. He had begun to think nothing about this case was what it seemed. Investigating it was like watching a strip of silent-film celluloid, an old one that you might find in a museum, a twenty-second, black-and-white snippet with no beginning or end, just a mysterious middle with exploding chemical emulsions where there should have been credits and a final scene.

He started the Jeep and continued driving, left Cork's Town and drove along the shoreline, passing shanty cottages and warehouses that had sat empty for decades, with soot-stained brick and boarded-up windows. Some of the cottages had started to be converted into single homes, and a couple of the less decrepit warehouses had become office buildings, but most of the shoreline between Cork's Town and downtown Springfield remained what it had been when Yakabuski first saw it as a boy. A thing forgotten. Something left by the shore after everyone with money had moved inland. A strange demilitarized zone that separated the two sections of the city.

As he drove, he made phone calls. He called his dad and updated him on the case. Yakabuski knew this was something his dad enjoyed, the old cop being allowed to come out and play. And he had been a huge help in the Ragged Lake case. Had given his son the final clue that had found the final body. They talked briefly about the riot on the North Shore.

"The media hasn't released the name of the guy that was killed."

"It was Tete Fontaine."

"Holy shit. That would not have been an easy kill."

"I wouldn't think so. I'm just coming from the Silver Dollar."

"You spoke to Sean?"

"I did. He knows nothing about nothing. Come back when I have something. Did you know all the cars headed up there at exactly the same time?"

"So they were following his orders. Not quite the spontaneous, grief-stricken riot I've been reading about."

"Not exactly. Sean Morrissey's fingerprints are all over this. I just can't figure out what the game is."

He hung up and continued driving. He was in Centretown now, passing the Grainger Opera House, which as far as Yakabuski knew had never staged an opera, a music hall with pretentions since the day it opened in 1897. He drove past the courthouse and the turnoff to Kettle Falls.

He called his sister, who answered sounding drunk. "Frankie, we have some people over. Why don't you drop by?"

He pretended he had another call coming in and clicked off. Kept driving, in the French Quarter now, with the giant statue of Samuel de Champlain sitting on a two-storey marble dais, backlit with blue light. Past the dépanneur on Brulet Street and the Sisters of Charity convent. He stared across the river to the North Shore. Phoned O'Toole.

"Where are you, Yak?"

"Driving around. It seems pretty quiet in the city tonight."

"I'm betting that worries you."

"It does. We're waiting for something."

"For what?"

"I don't know, but I doubt if setting a few fires and killing Tete Fontaine can even the score with the Shiners for butchering Augustus Morrissey and putting him on public display on the North Shore. It's always Burke's Falls for those guys."

O'Toole understood the reference. In 1841, a miller at Burke's Falls, thirty miles upriver from Springfield, insisted upon charging his regular toll rate to a gang of Shiners bringing a load of timber downriver. The Shiners didn't want to pay the toll but needed to use the miller's log chute.

With several other river crews waiting to go downriver, the Shiners paid and continued on their way to Springfield. Three days later, with Peter Aylin leading the way, more than fifty Shiners returned to Burke's Falls, travelling at night down a corduroy colony road so they would arrive in darkness. Before the sun rose the next morning, the miller, his wife, and six children had been murdered. Their mill set ablaze. Their cattle butchered and left as feed for carrion birds that circled the falls for days.

Before heading back to Springfield, the Shiners also built a gate at the top of the log chute and left four men stationed as sentries, to start charging the tolls the miller and his family once charged. The Shiners doubled the old rate, but no one ever complained.

"It wouldn't be enough for them," said O'Toole.

"Not near enough."

Yakabuski clicked off the phone and kept driving. He was in the suburbs now. Passing single-family homes and modern schools. Big box stores and hockey arenas. Not many people were on the street. Not many cars. Last night's riot on the North Shore was frightening people even here.

Or maybe it wasn't fear. Maybe everyone was waiting for the Shiners' next move, same way he was. Waiting even if they didn't know they were waiting.

. . .

At 11:15 the waiting stopped. Yakabuski's cellphone rang and when he looked at the number he saw it was coming from the detachment.

"Senior Detective Frank Yakabuski."

"Yak, it's Bernie Dowds, down in Dispatch. I'm glad I reached you."

"Yes Bernie, what's up?"

"A woman called us this evening to report her daughter missing. She lives on the North Shore. Girl is twelve years old and never came home from school. Or at least that's what the mother thinks. She got home from work at 5:30 and her daughter wasn't there, the way she should have been."

"Shouldn't you be calling the detectives in missing persons, Bernie?"

"I'm pretty sure I'm calling the right person. No one picked up on it right away."

"On what?"

"The girl's name, Yak. It's Grace Marielle Dumont."

Yakabuski stopped driving. Pulled over and began making a three-point turn.

"Dumont? As in . . ."

"Yep. Gabriel Dumont's granddaughter. You should probably head over there, Yak. Patrol officers on the scene say there's a big crowd starting to gather around the girl's apartment building."

# CHAPTER
## THIRTY-ONE

The land had flattened and was no longer wild. Cambino drove by cultivated rows of corn with thick corrugated leaves and golden tassels, by soybeans and ginseng fields, mani-cured lawns that went on for hectares, with finely muscled horses cantering out on the horizon. Because it was flat land, there were many fences. Clapboard and chain-link, cedar rail and white picket — the fences ran beside Interstate 57 for mile after mile.

The towns he drove through now were large and leeched out from the exit ramps, a spill of shoddily built homes and neon-lit convenience stores. Traffic on the highway was a constant three-lane stream in either direction. This was prosperous country. The land here was being used. Not like the hills and mountains to the south.

He was making good time and was fifty-seven miles south of Chicago when his GPS binged. It was a special bing, one

Cambino had programmed into the GPS himself, picking the opening notes of "La Bamba" because it amused him to pick that song, a cantina favourite, a happy song, much the opposite of what the GPS had detected. Subterfuge when it was unnecessary, for Cambino never saw deceit and misdirection as things that should be avoided. He kept his speed steady and looked at the GPS screen. Saw the red line that lay across the Interstate. According to the GPS, it was seven miles ahead. As he looked at the red line, the opening notes of "La Bamba" rang out one more time.

. . .

The roadblock was set up fifty miles south of Chicago. The police had a good description of the campervan, and traffic was impeded as little as possible, the cops waving transport trucks through a lane that remained open, most of the cars waved through without any inspection.

But it was still a roadblock. It was still Interstate 57. And within thirty minutes of being set up, traffic was backed up for nearly a mile behind the barricades. Ninety minutes after it was set up, a cop manning a southern perimeter line saw the campervan, inching its way through the traffic jam. Within a minute of being spotted, every platoon commander and field commander in the mobile command centre was watching the campervan. What they were looking at surprised them.

"Do we have confirmation this is the vehicle?" someone asked over the police radio.

"Licence plate confirmed. Make and model confirmed," someone else answered.

"Visual on the licence plate?"

"We're close enough to read it. Plate number confirmed."

"Do we have a visual on the driver?"

"Negative. Tinted windows. We have a silhouette. That's all."

"Can you tell anything from the silhouette?"

"Looks to be male. Not that tall, judging by the sightlines. Looks calm. He's not looking around or anything."

The cop in the mobile command centre stopped asking questions and looked back at his vidscreen. With most road-blocks, the person being sought never reaches the barricades. Almost no one has the jam for that. At the first sight of a roadblock, most suspects take off in the other direction. Or they try to be clever and slip out of the car when they're stuck in the lineup. Occasionally, they will try to ram their way through.

But no one drives right up and rolls down the window. Certainly no one accused of the crimes the driver of this campervan was accused of committing. No one does that.

"If we move on him now, he may just blow the van," said the cop by the barricades, who had been answering the questions from the mobile command centre.

"Thermal shows no firearms in the van, no explosive material of any kind."

"Are we willing to go to the wall on that?"

There was static on the phone for a few seconds, but no one answered. The cop by the barricade said, "He'll see us coming a mile away. I mean that. We have cars backed up more'n a mile."

"Are you suggesting we just let him drive up to the bar-ricades? If he does want to go out in a blaze of glory, that's where he would do the most damage."

"I don't know if we have a choice."

It went back and forth like that, until indecision and fear did what it usually does. The moment arrived and the answer was what happened next.

. . .

"He's at the roadblock."

"Fuck, we can see that. What's he doing?"

"Nothing. He's stopped ten feet back. Like he's supposed to. Do I approach?"

"No. Stay where you are."

"That's going to seem odd in a second or two," said the cop by the barricade. In spite of himself, he looked over his shoulder, to where he knew the mobile command truck was located. *Get it together folks*, he thought. *People on the line here.*

Then he heard the voice from the mobile command centre say, "Wave him through."

"Without approaching the vehicle? We haven't done that with anybody yet. He may wonder why we're doing that."

"It's the safest option. Raise the arm on the barricade and wave him through. Direct him to the median. Everyone else on this channel, back up."

The cop by the roadblock looked behind him and motioned for the arm on the mobile gate to be raised. There seemed to be not a sound as it was raised. Every cop on the Interstate knew this was the vehicle they had been seeking. Knew the driver was a killer. Four people that they knew about, in the past four days, and how many more before that? For there would have to be more, from a man that killed this easily.

The campervan inched its way through the roadblock, the only sound its wheels turning on the pavement and the high caw of a black bird flying lazy circles above the jangle of cars below. A slow right turn as the van followed the trooper that was backing up and motioning with his hands to where the driver needed to go. The slop of tire over concrete and hardened mud when the van reached the median. Never a change in acceleration. Never a sideways glance from the driver.

An armoured personnel carrier followed the van down the median and when they had gone a hundred yards, the trooper held out his hand and the vehicles stopped. A half-dozen patrol cars popped the curb and repositioned on the median, in front of the camper.

"He's boxed," said the trooper.

"He just drove right in," said the voice from the command centre.

"That he did. This is one odd bird."

"Maybe he wants it to be over. Yell at him to get out of the van, hands on top of his head."

The trooper yelled. The driver didn't move.

"He's not responding."

"Give me a minute."

A few seconds later, the hatch opened on the APC and a black-clad tactical officer exited. He walked to where the trooper stood, unslung his snub-nosed rifle from around his neck, and pointed it at the windshield of the campervan.

"Tell him again," he said.

The trooper yelled the instructions one more time, but the driver paid no more attention than he had the first time. No one moved or spoke for several seconds, and in that time it came to resemble a scene, something static and rendered to memory: the Falcon Campervan with the roadside decals and the tinted windows; the police cars with their red and blue spinning lights; the black-clad tactical officer with the assault rifle; everyone standing on the median of Interstate 57, fifty miles south of Chicago. Even the circling crow seemed to hang suspended for a moment.

Finally the tactical officer reached for his shoulder microphone and said, "Can you confirm the vehicle has been cleared for explosives and firearms?"

"Confirmed. Nothing has shown on thermal imaging. There were dogs trotting right beside the van when it went down the median. Everything has been negative so far."

"All right. Let's go get this son of a bitch."

The tactical officer started walking toward the van, keeping his assault rifle aimed at the silhouette of the driver's head. He walked slowly but steadily, not in a straight line but in a wide arc so he approached the driver's door from the left. Not straight on. Making sure there would be a twist of the driver's body if he had a gun he wanted to fire. A twist that would be the last thing he ever did.

*Go ahead*, thought the tactical officer. *Make a move. Save everyone a lot of time.*

But there was no move. In the distance, the tactical officer heard the whirr of helicopter blades and knew a television station had finally arrived. He was surprised it had taken them this long.

The helicopter scared away the crow and seemed to give people freedom to talk, so there was a loud murmur in the air when the tactical officer reached in to touch the door latch of the van, a few shouts and "hurry up!" when his fingers touched the latch.

The cop pulled up on the latch, and the van exploded.

# CHAPTER
## THIRTY-TWO

The apartment was on the eighth floor of Building H, on the south side so the windows were looking onto Filion's Field. The white pine by the municipal garage was just tall enough to block any view of the river. At night, the lights from the sports field must have shone through the windows.

It was a two bedroom, with a living room, bathroom, open concept kitchen, and a balcony that resembled a concrete flower box. The walls were light brown, so neutral as to be unnoticed, a colour you would never recall. The furniture in the living room was a set you would buy at a big box store, a leatherette couch, loveseat, and chair.

She was waiting for Yakabuski in the kitchen. Rachel Dumont. Thirty-one years old. Government job with the federal Department of Public Works. She had long black hair and was dressed in what Yakabuski guessed would have been the clothes she wore to work that day. A dark-blue, mid-calf skirt. White blouse. Hair tied back with a cloth braid that looked homemade.

Yakabuski stood in the kitchen doorway and looked around. There were rosemary and sage plants in clay pots on the windowsill above the sink. Matching yellow towels strung over the handle of the oven. Dishes with a bright blue and yellow pattern stacked neatly in a tray by the sink. It was a tidy kitchen.

"Ms. Dumont, I'm Senior Detective Frank Yakabuski," he said, as he walked into the kitchen. "I need to ask you a few questions."

She took her eyes off the kitchen floor and looked up at him. "Shouldn't you be looking for my daughter?"

"We are, ma'am. But I still need to hear what happened today, and I need to hear it from you. Not from someone else. I know you've already told this to a few people, and I apologize for making you go over it one more time, but it's important."

She stared at him. His hair was long for a cop, she thought, curling over the collar of his denim shirt, streaks of grey by the temples, clear blue eyes that had yet to move off her face.

"Tell me please, Senior Detective, what you are doing to find my daughter."

"We've issued an amber alert, Ms. Dumont. That's country-wide. Not a regional alert. Every police officer in Springfield now has a photo of your daughter. Every first responder as well. It's the photo you gave us earlier. It's a good quality photo, and that will help a lot. Grace is eleven years old, do I have that right?"

"Twelve next month."

"She attends Northwood School, is in grade six, and is normally here when you return home from work, around 5:30 p.m. Do I have that right as well?"

She didn't answer. Stared at Yakabuski for a few seconds and then got up from her chair and walked to the sink, where she began filling a kettle with water. "Would you like tea?"

"That's very considerate. Yes, I'd like some tea. Would it be all right if I sat down?"

"Please. I have orange pekoe and Earl Grey. Some herbal teas as well."

"Whatever you're having will be fine."

"You're very polite, Mr. Yakabuski" — she placed the kettle on the stove — "and very good with your questions. People tell you things before they even know they're doing it. Does the trick always work for you?"

"Ms. Dumont, I'm not trying to trick you."

"Really? Then why aren't you asking me the questions that matter?"

"I'm not sure I know what you mean."

She placed a porcelain cup in front of him. The blue and yellow motif, he could see now, depicted sunflowers in the foreground of a blue summer sky.

"I mean, Mr. Yakabuski, that I'm a government clerk making thirty-two thousand a year. A single mother, living on the North Shore. My daughter has been missing seven hours. She's old enough to run away. Grace would never do that, but it happens often enough up here. Twelve, thirteen, girls start drifting away.

"Yet here you are, the fifth police officer to come to my home tonight and ask me questions about Grace not being in the apartment like she normally is when I got home from work. All of you investigating a missing girl from the North Shore, the daughter of a single-mother government clerk."

"Ms. Dumont, any missing child report is treated . . ."

"Be honest with me, Mr. Yakabuski. That's all I ask."

Her voice gave no hint of anger, or resentment, was as neutral as the paint colour upon her walls. Yakabuski took a sip of his tea, surprised to see it was white cedar, the winter drink of the Cree. Yakabuski took a long sip, the aroma reminding him of winter camping trips when he was a boy, far north on the Upper Divide, with his father and his cousins, not packing much so they slept beneath cedar boughs placed over burrowed snow, gathered berries before the sun went down, drank the ancestral drink of the Cree before going to bed.

"You and I both know why you're here, Mr. Yakabuski," she continued. "Maybe you should start asking me questions about it."

Yakabuski put down the teacup with the picture of the sunny day.

"Fair enough. When was the last time you saw your father, Ms. Dumont?"

A patrol officer stood in the doorway to the kitchen, to give them privacy, the small living room filled with other police officers, the dining table taken over with laptop computers and recording equipment. Waiting for a call from whoever took Grace Dumont. To demand whatever it is you demand when you steal an eleven-year-old girl.

"I haven't seen my father in eighteen years."

"Long time. You had a falling out of some sort?"

"That would be an interesting way of describing it. How much do you know about my father?"

"Not as much as I'd like. I know he's the head of a criminal organization called the Travellers. Some connection to the Traveller gangs in Europe, but not much. They're spread out along the old fur-trading routes. French and Métis, for the most part. Some people think they're gypsies. Your father is supposed to be their leader. He has the same name as Louis Riel's military commander in the North-West Rebellion. Don't know if he changed it or if that happened naturally."

She raised an eyebrow. "It was his name since birth. He has always been proud of it. You know more than most, Mr. Yakabuski."

"My father investigated the Travellers fifteen years ago. After he found one of their clubhouses in High River. It was sick, what he found in there."

Dumont sipped her tea. Stared at the back of the patrol officer. After a while, she said, "A lot of people believe the Travellers are the guardians of the old ways, great nomads from the past that were never brought under yoke. My father believes that. All I ever saw was a sick, twisted fantasy."

"Why do you say that?"

"Some people believe Gabriel Dumont used to wear the scalps of his enemies on a leather belt around his waist. Some buffalo hunters used to do that. The scalps of Sioux and the Dakota mostly. I don't know if it's true about Dumont. I suspect not, but my father believed the story. He tried it once. He had three scalps before he had to give it up. The smell was too much even for him. My dad may have known how to scalp a man, but he had not a clue what to do afterwards. I think you need to cure the hair."

Yakabuski looked at her over the rim of the porcelain cup and thought it was so common he didn't know why he continued to be surprised. By the things kept hidden in this world. By the damaged lives that are lived by people you pass on the street every day. Look at Rachel Dumont and you saw a composed young woman, the picture of self-decorum and rational, measured action. Raised by a man who kept scalps on a leather belt.

"How old were you when he wore that belt?"

"Twelve."

"You didn't have to think about that. I suppose that's not the sort of thing you forget."

"That's not the reason. I left home the following spring. I was about to turn thirteen."

"Where were you living at the time?"

"Cape Diamond. My father has a house there. I hitched a ride to Buckham's Bay and started waitressing at Ferguson's. I didn't look thirteen. So that's where I went."

"Did you dad try to find you?"

"I wouldn't have been hard to find. He never came."

"When did you move to the North Shore?"

"After Grace was born. I lived here when I was a little girl. I had Grace, and I didn't want to be a waitress for the rest of my life, so I came back and started taking night classes to earn my diploma."

"That took a bit of courage. A lot of people in your situation don't get clear of a family like that. What sort of work do you do for the government?"

"I'm a P6 clerk. The pay is so low I still qualify for a subsidized apartment."

Yakabuski took another sip of his tea. There was a stigma to being from the North Shore, most people from Springfield thinking a North Shore address meant you were indolent and dishonest and in some way a train wreck just waiting to happen. He wondered what those people would say if they met someone like Rachel Dumont, who right then was staring at Yakabuski with an intensity so strong and palpable it was like something pushing against his chest.

"Grace going missing, it has something to do with that diamond you found, doesn't it?" she said.

"It may," answered Yakabuski. "Do you know if your father has some way of smuggling diamonds out of that mine up there?"

"I wouldn't know. There wasn't a mine there when I was living at Cape Diamond. It wasn't even called that."

"A diamond mine opening up right on your dad's doorstep, that would get his attention, I suspect."

"It would. It looks like it has caught the attention of the Shiners too."

"Looks that way."

"And now my daughter is caught up in the middle of whatever this is. Tell me, Mr. Yakabuski, and please be honest — I think Grace must be more valuable to them alive. If this were straight revenge, you would have already found her body. That's right, isn't it?"

Yakabuski had started to wonder about that. If this were Burke's Falls, the Shiners would have hung Grace Dumont's body from a street lamp and been done with it. Put her on display, the way they had displayed Tete Fontaine. Why the hesitation? Why the shyness? It made no sense, the young girl's body not being found by now.

Which was the glimmer of hope Rachel Dumont was seeking, as weak as it was.

"That's right," said Yakabuski, staring directly into her eyes and nodding. "That's right," he said one more time, trying not to feel guilty at the meaninglessness of the words.

# CHAPTER
## THIRTY-THREE

The crowd on Tache Boulevard had swollen to more than a hundred people when Yakabuski exited Rachel Dumont's apartment building. Oil drums had been set alight at the cross streets and in the distance, under the lights of Filion's Field. Yakabuski could see several tents had gone up on the soccer pitch. People were arriving from other places.

*A child changes everything*, he thought sadly. In the Balkans, Yakabuski had seen a six-day standoff come to an end when a Serb sniper put a bullet through the head of a Muslim girl at the village well. Two hours later, the Serbs were in the village, picking off the Muslim fighters one by one as they charged in anger.

In Springfield, Papa Paquette once kidnapped a four-year-old boy because his father had owed the Popeyes money, and although the debt was quickly repaid, Papa held onto the boy, travelled with him, as though he were a pet, and in the next eighteen months the father was forced to rob three banks, make two mule runs to Montesano, and finally take a five-year manslaughter plea for killing a man he had never met. Papa released the boy to a shattered mother who left Springfield, vowing never to return. She must have kept her vow. The boy and mother were never seen again.

Yakabuski surveyed the crowd in front of him. A missing child was always a problem, and not in the ways you would think. For people with a guilty conscience, saving a child represented their best chance for absolution. "I may have done all these other things, Lord, but I rescued that fuckin' kid." It was the ultimate get-out-of-hell card. Also the reason why people not known for civic-mindedness were often the ones most upset about a child's disappearance, the ones shouting loudest at the public meetings, the ones calling for action and hatching feverish schemes of vengeance late into the night.

The media never got a missing child story quite right. It was always shown as the thousand volunteers walking a grid formation in some farmer's field, the candlelight vigil on a downtown street, the shattered innocence of the child's friends and schoolmates. When all the while, just below the surface, people were suspicious and fearful and getting ready to turn bat-shit nasty. Because there was a child missing. And you could do that.

The crowd in front of Building H was so thick Yakabuski had to push his way through, past unshaven men with long hair and flannel shirts, eyes you couldn't see unless the glare of the streetlight was directly upon them. A few of the men were wearing red sashes tied around their waists, the beaded tails of the sash dangling down their denim legs, the glass stones twinkling in the night. The old sash of the voyageurs. Not seen on the North Shore in more than a hundred years.

The men didn't speak as Yakabuski pushed past them. Didn't threaten or push back. Simply leaned back when Yakabuski approached, leaned back in when he had passed. Expending no more energy than necessary, to let the cop know he was that inconsequential to them.

Yakabuski expended the same amount of energy. To let the crowd know tonight was not the night.

. . .

Grace Dumont had never been to Cork's Town. Her mother forbade it. Just last year, her mother told her the story of how the North Shore Bridge was built, how people from Cork's Town arrived one morning and threw everyone from their homes. Her great-grandmother and great-grandfather had been two of the people left homeless that day. Her mother never spoke about them and had no photos, but they had been family. The girl had no one but her mother, and the story had haunted her.

That was the reason the spires of St. Bridget's, when she saw them, terrified her more than the kidnapping. That had been quick. Over in the time it took for a truck to stop in front of her as she walked the alley between Buildings G and H, and a passenger in the truck to jump out, lift her up, and throw her in the narrow back seat.

She had screamed, but she was inside the truck so quickly it made no difference. The passenger, a man with long blond hair and tattoos on his face, turned around and hit her, then shouted, "Shut the fuck up."

"Where are you taking me? Who are you?" she had demanded.

"Shut the fuck up. Lie down on the floor and don't move. Don't do a fuckin' thing."

She did as she was told. They drove for what seemed a long time, but when the truck stopped and she was taken out, there they were in front of her: the spires of St. Bridget's Basilica. From the window of her kitchen, on a clear day in the winter, with no leaves on the trees, she could see the spires. As she was led up the outside stairs in back of an old wooden house, she felt sad. Not terrified. Not confused. None of the emotions you might expect. Sadness. Knowing her mother was so close, but she had no way of reaching her.

It was the man with the long blond hair who walked her up the stairs. Unlocked the door. Shoved her inside and down the narrow hallway running through the centre of the apartment, all the way to the far end. The apartment was smaller than hers. One small bedroom. A living room that looked onto the street in front, just big enough for a couch and a television, a kitchen by the rear stairs, with patterned vinyl on the floor that was ripped and stained, a sink that was once white but was now more tobacco-coloured. The driver of the car had gone.

"Sit on the couch and shut the fuck up."

The girl did as she was told, staring around the living room when she was seated. Down the hallway, where it dead-ended at a wallpapered wall. The only entrance was off the kitchen.

The man gave her a nasty look and said, "I have to make some phone calls. You stay right where you are. If you move even an inch, I'll fuckin' know it."

205

In a few moments she heard his voice coming from the kitchen. He was angry. She heard him say: "I think it's fucking stupid." Later: "We don't need it. You should have told him to fuck off." And just before the call ended: "Well if it's a test, has he passed or failed?"

After that he was back in the living room. He had taken off his coat and was wearing a white T-shirt. He had tattoo sleeves on both arms. The girl had never seen a person with so many tattoos. He pushed strands of hair away from his face and said, "Are you hungry?"

"No."

"I'm going to make some supper. Are you sure?"

"I'm sure."

He gave her a strange look. Then he went back to the kitchen and she heard the sounds of pots being taken out of a cupboard, a gas stove being turned on, a faucet running. Several minutes later, he came back to the living room, carrying two bowls of Kraft Dinner. He put one of the bowls in front of her.

"That's all I'm making tonight," he said.

He sat down on the couch and started to eat. From time to time he would look over at the girl. When he was nearly finished his bowl of food, he said, "You're not crying and carrying on. Why is that?"

"Would it help me any?"

"No."

"Then why would I do it?"

"How old are you?"

"Almost twelve."

"Who told you to think like that?"

"My mother."

The man went back to eating. When he was finished, he leaned back on the couch.

"Why have you taken me?" the girl asked.

"Your grandfather. Because of some shit he's done."

"It's not because of me?"

"No."

"Then there's nothing you would want." The girl hesitated for the first time, searched for the right words before saying, "nothing you would want from me?"

The man stared at the girl a long time before he said, "I don't do things like that."

"Is that a promise?"

"That's a promise. You keep your mouth shut and don't try anything stupid, you'll be home with your mother in a couple days. This is all about your grandfather."

"I've never met him."

"Not many people have. I suspect that's about to change."

"You think he'll come for me? Why would he do that?"

The man laughed. "Fuck, you're a funny kid. What's your name?"

"You don't know?"

"No."

"Grace."

The man nodded. Stood up with his bowl and headed to the kitchen. Before leaving the room, he turned and said, "Sorry about hitting you in the car. I didn't know what kind of kid you were."

# CHAPTER
## THIRTY-FOUR

The detachment was chaos when Yakabuski arrived at four in the morning. Every patrol officer had been called in and people were running in and out of the dispatch room with such frequency, someone had wedged a crumbled takeout coffee cup under the door to prop it open. A tip line was being manned in the Crime Stoppers office by the front desk, and already a volunteer had asked if it were possible to get more phones. The night duty sergeant didn't know. Said he would look into it.

Reporters from news outlets already in town for Augustus Morrissey's funeral crowded the foyer in front of the sergeant's desk. Took photos with their phones of the handout of Grace Dumont, her sixth grade class photo from Northwood, her black hair pulled back in a ponytail, a smile that was both tentative and endearing. Some of the American reporters could not hide their excitement when they saw the photo.

Late that night, the Associated Press reporter made the connection between the missing girl and the recent murders on the North Shore. At 6 a.m. a story moved across the wires with photos of Augustus Morrissey, Tete Fontaine, and Grace Dumont, linking the child's disappearance to "recent gangland slayings in Springfield." After that the phone calls started coming from police agencies and newspapers across North America.

. . .

Yakabuski slept again on the couch in his office and was awoken shortly before 7 a.m. by his cellphone ringing. It was O'Toole, asking him to come to his office. When he got there, he found another man already in the office, a big Black man with a barrel chest and tight-shorn hair. The visitor eyed Yakabuski closely as he walked into the room.

"Yak, this is Lieutenant John Evans with the RCMP's anti-racketeering squad in Toronto," said O'Toole, and the man stood to shake Yakabuski's hand.

"I was part of the Ragged Lake investigation, Detective Yakabuski. I listened in on a phone call you made to an encrypted number we found on Tommy Bangles's cellphone. Not sure if you remember that call."

"I remember."

"Yes, I suppose you would. I have a few things I want you to look at." Evans took a highway map of North America from a briefcase open on O'Toole's conference table. He unfolded the map and spread it out. O'Toole came from behind his desk to stand beside Yakabuski while they looked at the map.

"The FBI has asked for our help in locating a serial killer that crossed into the United States from Mexico four days ago," said Evans. "His first victim was found just south of Corpus Christi, an escort girl from the village of Heroica. She went through the Brownsville border crossing at 11:13 a.m. Monday morning. Every guard at the border remembers her. She looked like Margot Robbie, apparently. Drove a Miata sports car. Working theory is she was a deliberate distraction for our serial killer, who crossed the border at the same time.

"Two days later —" Evans moved his finger from Corpus Christi up to Memphis "— an Arkansas state trooper went missing. His patrol car was found on Interstate 55, the dashboard camera ripped out, keys taken. There was no digital feed. A canvass of the truck stops in the area turned up a witness who said the trooper had pulled over a campervan with Texas plates, at the exact spot where his patrol car was found."

Evans moved his finger up the map.

"The following day, the bodies of an elderly couple were found in Shawnee National Forest. They had both been stabbed to death, their bodies found in their fifth-wheel. The campsite right next to them was rented the night before by a man that doesn't exist. Everything on the admission form was bogus. Other campers remember seeing a campervan with Texas plates on that campsite.

"Yesterday," said Evans, moving his finger further north, "a vehicle matching the description of the campervan was stopped at a roadblock fifty miles south of Chicago."

The room seemed to contract when he said that. Both O'Toole and Yakabuski felt it, although maybe it happened in the back of their throats and they mistook it for something happening to the room. What happened at that roadblock had been on the news most of the night.

"There must have been two dozen state patrol cars at the roadblock," continued Evans, "an FBI field unit from Chicago, another from Cooke County, ATF officers, and some local police. The media had helicopters in the air. When the driver didn't respond to several requests to exit the vehicle, a tactical team was sent in." Evans took a stack of photos from his briefcase and spread them out on the table next to the map.

"The bomb was detonated at 4:34 p.m., as soon as a tactical officer touched the handle of the car. He and four officers standing nearby were killed instantly. A news helicopter was blown out of the sky. Nine killed right there, and two more died overnight in the hospital. There are nineteen people still in the hospital. According to an FBI officer I spoke with an hour ago, not all of them are going to make it."

"But the driver must be dead as well," said O'Toole. "Isn't your investigation finished?"

"The person in the driver's seat is indeed dead," Evans said sourly. "It was the missing Arkansas state trooper. We got DNA confirmation two hours ago. No one else was in the van."

"How is that possible?"

"The van was being driven by some sort of remote control. They're still putting the device together."

When he said that, Evans looked at Yakabuski. A strange look. As though Yakabuski were guilty of something. He rummaged around his briefcase and pulled out a ruler.

"Detective Yakabuski," Evans said, and he tossed the ruler on the map. "Can you line up the crime scenes I have just mentioned, starting with Corpus Christi, please?"

Yakabuski gave Evans a look, then shrugged his shoulders and positioned the ruler on the map.

"It's pretty much a straight line," he said. "Heading northeast."

"That's right. Extend the line, please, keeping the same angle and direction. Tell me where you end up."

Yakabuski started to reposition the ruler. Before he was finished O'Toole was already talking.

"Don't know if this proves all that much, Lieutenant Evans. Your guy could have been going to Chicago. That's where the I-57 would have taken him. How can we possibly know where his final destination would have been?"

"Humour me, Chief. It's been a long couple of days. Where would you end up, Detective Yakabuski?"

"Somewhere on the Northern Divide," he said quietly. "Near Springfield."

"Yes, you sure as fuck would. Now here's the best part, the absolute best part about this whole motherfucking rat fuck." Evans turned back to his briefcase, pulled out a plastic baggie with what looked like a chunk of coal inside. He threw the baggie on the table. Yakabuski and O'Toole could see now that it was melted plastic. With some embedded glass. Some embedded metal.

"That was recovered from the van. It's the cellphone Detective Yakabuski called two summers ago."

O'Toole's head shot up. "It's the same guy?"

"That's a good question, Chief. What do you think, Detective Yakabuski? Is it the same guy?"

"What I'm thinking is you better start telling me why you're here."

"A little defensive? Well, I can't blame you. The guy you

212

threatened to hunt down one day seems to be heading your way. Killing people along the way. So I don't want any games from you, Detective, and I don't want any bullshit old-school vendettas. I need you to tell me everything you know about this motherfucker, and I need you to tell me right now."

# CHAPTER
## THIRTY-FIVE

Yakabuski rubbed his temples and looked again at the map spread out on O'Toole's table. Whoever was driving that campervan was heading north. A straight road trip. He could have been going to Chicago. He could have gone east or west once he reached the cloverleaf in Cooke County. Or he could have stayed on the line he was travelling and come where everyone thought he was coming.

Evans had left the map on the table but taken the rest of his files and left. O'Toole had given him a desk to work at in the general pool area of Criminal Investigations. No one was going to make him feel welcome, a Mountie from Toronto working a case that had nothing to do with a missing girl from the North Shore. Evans didn't seem like the kind of cop that would care all that much.

"He thinks there's been some sort of back channel communications between you two," said O'Toole, sitting behind his desk now, his feet propped on his windowsill, staring out his window. "There hasn't been anything like that, has there, Yak?"

"No."

"This guy hasn't been in touch with you, made threats, anything like that?"

"Nothing. I have no idea who he is."

"Well, he's a murdering motherfucking bastard is who he is. He killed two of my officers. Or he had a hand in it. Just like Sean Morrissey had a hand in it. I wouldn't blame you for going after the guy, Yak, if you had some way of doing that."

"I don't."

"All right. So what the fuck is he doing? He threatened to kill you, if I recall that phone conversation properly. Could this be payback time?"

"For Ragged Lake? That was nearly two years ago. Why come now?"

"That's what I was thinking. Does it have something to do with this war that's breaking out between the Shiners and the Travellers?"

"It must. The guy was a business partner with Sean Morrissey. We know that. One of the few things we do know about this guy."

"Extra muscle? Things are getting a bit dicey, so the Shiners put in a call and brought him up. Is that what he is?"

"It can't be. The timing is wrong."

"What do you mean?"

"If the FBI is right, he crossed the border at Brownsville at the same time we were finding Augustus's body hanging from that fence in Filion's Field."

O'Toole had yet to turn away from his window. He tilted his head, as though pondering what Yakabuski had just said. Beneath his window Highway 7 could be seen, just starting to fill with morning commuters. At this time of year, the highway should have been a line of cold exhaust smoke roiling through the heart of the city, winter mist and fog filling in whatever wasn't covered by exhaust fumes, so you couldn't see the cars and the city appeared as peaks and spires sticking out of a cloud. Should have been. Instead, there was an unobstructed view of the traffic. Another cloudless sky. Temperature twenty degrees above normal. The joy most people in Springfield felt a month ago when winter chose not to appear was long gone. People were restless now. Ready for the seasons to change. Unable to do anything to make that happen and so there was a surly frustration settling in.

"You're right. He was already on his way," said O'Toole as he looked away from his window. "So what the fuck is going on, Yak?"

# CHAPTER
## THIRTY-SIX

The explosion had lit up the late afternoon sky like an emergency flare. An eruption of fire that ensnared the helicopter flying over the campervan and sent it twirling to the ground, little more than a seared metal frame by the time it crashed. Cambino watched it happen through the binoculars he had taken from his packsack.

He watched for several seconds as hot metal fell to the earth, as the flames grew higher, black smoke starting to rise and then the secondary charges he had hidden in the commercial-sized freezer went off, sending what was left of his campervan soaring into the air one more time. When there was nothing more to look at, he put the binoculars away and started walking past the line of cars backed up behind the barricades. As he walked, he disassembled the driverless car control, throwing the parts away under idling cars. Not a person on the Interstate was looking in his direction.

It had been smart to keep the body of the state trooper. An old trick his father had taught him. Bodies did not need to be hidden right away. Not always. Sometimes they were good things to keep around; to send a message to your enemies at a later date, to confuse the police. A body had many uses. Strapping one into the seat of a driverless car was just one more example of how useful a dead man could be.

Cambino walked down the Interstate until he reached a small town, where he went to a 7-Eleven and purchased bread and sliced meat, some anti-freeze, a bottle of water. Then he started to walk north on a county road that he soon left, to walk through farmers' fields and down hydro-line corridors, keeping the Interstate to the left of him, fires burning as darkness fell.

He passed many abandoned farms and outbuildings, but it would be a mistake right then to put himself behind walls, and so he slept that night under leaves, on an old deer bed he found deep in the woods. He was up before dawn, his clothes wet from the dew, and he continued walking. With the sun just starting to appear he made his way to a county road and stole a newspaper from a mailbox. By the banks of a dried-up creek bed he made himself a sandwich and read the paper.

The *Chicago Sun-Times* had six pages on what had happened out on the Interstate. Police suspected the driver was wearing some sort of suicide vest he detonated when they tried to open the door of the van. There were a lot of photos. A sidebar with the names and short profiles of the dead. An editorial asking if the police were right to try to enter the van. The driver was trapped. Why not wait him out? Why endanger so many people?

It seemed a silly editorial to Cambino. Cops confront

criminals. They didn't set up lawn chairs and wait for them to surrender. He threw the newspaper away and continued walking. Shortly before noon, he heard the dogs.

. . .

The barking was faint and hard to hear at first. The dogs must have been miles away. But it meant the cops were no longer deceived. Cambino stopped walking and opened his packsack, took out the second loaf of bread he had bought at the 7-Eleven, along with the plastic jug of anti-freeze. He poured the liquid over the bread, took out a topographical map from the pack, and stared at it a moment. When he stood up he changed his direction and headed back into the woods. He walked for more than an hour, breaking off chunks of bread every fifty yards and throwing them as far as he could. When he reached the banks of the river he had seen on the topo map, he turned and walked back the way he had come.

He listened carefully to the barking, and when he figured the dogs were no more than a half-mile away, he found a tall pine and climbed it. Twenty minutes later he saw the first dog come running down the trail he had been walking, a police officer running behind, holding tightly onto the twenty-foot lead line. Within a minute, there were a dozen other dogs and police handlers running down the trail.

The dogs, as Cambino had suspected, were hounds and German shepherds, dogs that tracked by scent. A couple of them already looked sick and he knew they had found the bread. The cops should have brought field retrievers. A field retriever would have worked a grid and would have found him. But cops only used field retrievers when they were looking for bodies. Not when they were searching for armed killers.

So Cambino watched in safety as the dogs and cops passed him. He knew when they reached the river the cops would assume he had gone in the water, to try to hide his scent. In a few hours, that river would look like a beach in Normandy in 1944.

He waited until he no longer heard the dogs. Then he climbed down the tree and made his way back to the Interstate. Inside the restaurant at a Chevron station, he talked a truck driver heading to Detroit into giving him a ride, explaining his car was badly damaged in the explosions on I-57 the day before.

"You were there?" the truck driver said.

"Close enough to have my car totalled."

"Shit, that was something. A suicide vest. What is happening to the world?"

Cambino didn't answer. A half-hour north of the Chevron station, they passed a group of cops standing by the side of the Interstate. Two German shepherds were standing near them, throwing up on the gravel shoulder.

# CHAPTER
## THIRTY-SEVEN

Donna Griffin found Yakabuski in his office shortly after 9 a.m. She told him about the surly Toronto cop that had shown up that morning, sitting at the general pool desk right beside her, looking at every other cop in the squad room as though he wanted to hit them. Yakabuski filled her in on John Evans and the purpose of his visit.

"So there's a Ragged Lake connection to all of this?"

"Might be. We don't know at the moment."

Yakabuski thought back to that phone call. The man who answered the untraceable phone number sounded middle-aged at the start of their conversation, although by the end he wasn't as sure. He told Yakabuski not to pursue the murders of two Springfield police officers, forget what happened far up on the Northern Divide — "Consider Ragged Lake your lucky day." That's what he had said. When Yakabuski said a better idea might be to track him down and piss in his mouth, the man had laughed. Then he had threatened, in a voice as sweet and gentle as a telephone prompt, to kill Yakabuski's father and sister if he ever tried to find him.

You hear threats like that from time to time. Coming from the back of squad cars. The holding cells. The front steps of the courthouse. The phone conversation didn't rattle Yakabuski that much, although it was the first time he could recall thinking the person making the threat might not be a one-hundred-percent bullshit artist.

"So how's the search for Katherine Morrissey going?" he asked.

"You're not going to like it," said Griffin. "I can find no record of a Katherine Morrissey, in the age range we're looking at, ever living in Springfield or anywhere on the Northern Divide. I am at the absolute dead end of all known databases. There is nothing left for me to search."

"As for Sean Morrissey, who should have his mother listed on his birth certificate, he *has* no birth certificate. That's the long and the short of it. He has a passport, Social Insurance Number, all sorts of government-issued business and tax numbers, and they're all legitimate, but he has no birth certificate."

"How can you get a SIN without a birth certificate?"

"Baptismal certificate. That was allowed until 1988. Morrissey's certificate comes from St. Bridget's. Signed by Father Joe Maloney. Augustus is the only parent listed."

"The parish priest. That's amazing."

"It gets better. All the documents I've found for Morrissey have the same birth date. May 24, 1974. That date never changes. So I went to the Grace Hospital and asked to see the original birth certificates for May '74. April and June as well."

"That was smart."

"Thank you. But get this — the Grace had the original birth certificates for every day in those three months except one. And I'm talking perfect records. Nuns are good at that sort of thing, I guess. The missing day was May 24."

"Someone took his birth certificate."

"That's what I said. But the nun in the records room said, no, that couldn't be right; there had never been a mistake in the birth records at the Grace Hospital. She said it meant there were no births that day. So I asked if we could look at a few more months, just to confirm. Turned out she was right. There were days when the hospital had no births."

Griffin was smiling so broadly, Yakabuski wondered if her face was starting to hurt. He decided to do her a favour and play along. "But?"

"But the other days were still recorded. The official notation is 'no live births on shift.' The only day missing was May 24."

"So someone *did* take his birth certificate."

"Only thing that could have happened. Whoever Sean Morrissey's mother is, someone has gone through a lot of work keeping her a secret."

• • •

A successful murder investigation should move fast. It shouldn't meander or send you miles down a blind rush. The rhythm of a good investigation was the same as the rhythm to a Bo Diddley song, or an all-night road trip; it was the left-hand lane and the jingle jangle morning, intense and fast and about as right feeling as a thing can be in this world — the truth revealing itself.

Yakabuski sat at his desk after Griffin had left and was forced to admit this current investigation was none of those things. Five days after discovering the body of Augustus Morrissey, he was no closer to knowing who might have killed him than he was the morning he saw him hanging from a fence at Filion's Field. Same way he was no closer to knowing why a million-dollar diamond had been shoved into his mouth. Or who killed Tete Fontaine. Or where an eleven-year-old girl named Grace Dumont might be at that particular moment.

An investigation should always move forward, and this one had stalled. He had a company commander once who used to say, "When in doubt, sit it out." The man was a true-blue, live-to-fight-another-day guy, and he retired a two-star general, five years past his pension date and after a lifetime of too much sitting and absolutely no fighting.

Yakabuski never liked the argument. Moving things forward — acting when in doubt, rather than sitting down and stroking your chin — normally had good results for him. Those first few months after he went undercover, when Papa was having trouble accepting him, didn't he hang the Apache by his heels over the tenth-floor balcony of a condominium in Laval, annoyed that the meeting was entering its seventh hour and the questions were starting to repeat?

*Fuck it. Let's move this thing along.*

And in Bosnia, when a Croat general arrived at his checkpoint with an armoured company behind him, demanding entry into a Muslim village under UN protection, didn't Yakabuski refuse? Thirty minutes later, the general was still demanding to be let in, while posing at the same time for photographs that would appear later that month in a Zagreb military magazine. Tired of the charade, Yakabuski took his C-15 and fired a burst between the general's legs.

*All right, what are we doing here?*

Not everyone agreed with this approach. The world seemed to be run by close family members of that gutless commander, and there were certainly people in the upper offices of the Department of National Defence who said Yakabuski was wrong to fire his gun that morning, that it started a two-day battle with the Croats, five of whom were wounded, one badly, and DND had to call in every media favour it had just to bury the story.

Others will tell you that Croat general never got within ten kilometres of that Muslim village.

Sometimes you needed action, even if you weren't sure why, or what form it should take; just knew it was time to move things along. Time to rattle a few people, blow up a few schemes, and get a clear vista in front of you. Wasn't it Mike Tyson who once said: "Everyone has a plan. Till they get punched in the head."

Yakabuski laughed when he remembered the old quote. A few seconds later he laughed again, realizing who he needed to punch.

# CHAPTER
## THIRTY-EIGHT

Mission Road was in a gated community fifteen miles south of Springfield. The guard in the hut recognized Yakabuski and waved him through without even asking to see ID. He drove down the curving streets, still lined with hardwood trees in almost full foliage. Although the leaves on the elms looked like shrivelled appendages, and the ones on the maples were yellow and translucent looking. He couldn't decide if the trees looked sick or just hungover.

The lawns were a deep green, though, and he wondered if the homeowners were still fertilizing. Mid-December, but nothing would surprise him anymore about this lost season. He drove until he reached a large Tudor midway down a crescent street, pulled into the driveway, and parked his Jeep.

He knocked on the door and waited. Before long, Tyler Lawson opened, sheaves of paper in his hands as he was working at home today, something Yakabuski already knew. Lawson opened the door wide for his brother-in-law and was smiling broadly when Yakabuski punched him.

. . .

Lawson went back peddling down his foyer, both hands clasped to his nose, but that wasn't enough to stop blood from oozing through his fingers. Yakabuski took two giant steps into the foyer and hit him again. Square on the knuckles. When the fingers moved away in pain he hit Lawson one more time on the nose.

When his brother-in-law had fallen to his knees, Yakabuski turned away and closed the front door. He stood in the foyer and stared around. There was an open staircase, curving up to bedrooms on the second floor, and on the wall behind the staircase were family photos and awards, a vanity wall for dinner guests to gaze upon as they were removing their coats. Photos of his niece and nephew when they were babies, his sister giving a speech at some chamber of commerce event, a framed newspaper with a front-page story about Lawson getting a couple of Shiners acquitted of murder charges because of what the newspaper called tampered evidence. Yakabuski gave his neck a slight roll and took a handkerchief from his pocket. He started cleaning blood from his knuckles.

"Tyler," he said calmly, "this city is one bad incident away from blowing up, and it's all because of that man you work for. So you're going to tell me what the hell is going on around here, or I'm going to beat you so badly you won't be having sex with my sister for a very long time."

"You're fuckin' crazy."

"Crazy. Fed up and annoyed. It won't make much of a difference to you, Tyler."

· · ·

The two men sat on bar stools in the basement of Lawson's house. He had poured them Scotch and they were sipping their drinks. Occasionally, Lawson would blow his nose, wading up the tissue and placing it in a pile of red-stained bar napkins he had assembled near the ice bucket.

"What do you think I know, Yak?" he said angrily. "Do you think he tells me everything? Is that what you think?"

"You know nothing? Is that what you're telling me, Tyler?"

His brother-in-law didn't answer. Touched the bridge of his nose and said, "I think you've broken it."

"I know I've broken it."

"Fuck, Yak. You couldn't have just called? Honestly, you're fucking crazy some days. I don't know how you hang onto a job."

"Don't know if now is the time to be giving me career advice, Tyler. So — nothing? Is that what you're telling me?"

Yakabuski began to stand, and Lawson waved him back down. "I don't know what's going on, Yak, I really don't. I know it's not what it seems. You're right about that. This whole thing seems like some big scheme on Sean's part, but I don't know what the scheme is."

"They've kidnapped a little girl."

"Yak, you don't think I know anything about that, do you? Because I swear to God, there is no fuckin' way I would ever . . ."

"She's the same age as Sarah."

Lawson stopped speaking. His eyes seemed to glaze over for a second, and he reached for another bar napkin. Blew his nose until the tissue turned crimson red.

"Why do you keep doing it, Tyler?" said Yakabuski quietly.

"Why don't I quit? Is this career advice from you now, Yak?"

"You should consider it."

"You should consider it's not that easy."

Lawson stared at his brother-in-law with a tough man look, but his gaze wavered after a few seconds.

"Fuck, I saw how old she is," he said quietly. "You don't think I read that?"

"Then you should help me. I'm looking for someone."

"Who?"

"Sean Morrissey's mother."

"His mother? What the fuck would she have to do with any of this?"

"No idea. But I'm told if I find her, I'll know who killed Augustus."

"You believe that?"

"I do."

"Well, don't hit me right away, but I don't know where you can find her. I've never even heard about Sean's mother. I don't have a clue who she is."

"Neither do I."

"Really? You don't know who she is?"

"No. We've tried a few different ways to track her down, but no luck. So here is how you can help, Tyler — I want to find out who Augustus had for neighbours back in 1974."

"Why would you want to know that?"

"Because someone in this city knows who that woman is,

and I think an old neighbour of Augustus's from the year Sean was born might be the person."

Lawson nodded. Wiped his nose. "An original source. That's good. Why not the hospital?"

"Already tried."

"Friends and family would be tricky, because they're all criminals," Lawson said, sitting up straighter.

"You would suspect."

"So track down a neighbour. That is indeed good."

"I figure Augustus would have chosen his neighbours carefully. Associates, for the most part. Maybe one of them had a family. Any woman living on that street would probably know something. Know anyone who fits that bill?"

Lawson smiled. "Like I said, Yak, you should have just called."

He reached for another napkin, this time for a pen as well. He wrote something on the napkin and passed it to his brother-in-law.

"Paddy McSheffrey. Wife and five children. Lived next door to Augustus for years."

"Where I can find him?"

"He's dead. But his widow is still in Springfield. Don't know where. Her name is Fiona. You should be able to take it from there, right, Yak?"

"Fiona McSheffrey. All right, I'll check it out." He looked at his brother-in-law and added, "You should probably go to the hospital for that nose, Tyler. It needs to be set."

"No kidding."

"And I wouldn't bother telling Sean about my visit."

"You must think I'm an idiot. I'm cleaning up the foyer and pretending this never happened. This nose is going to have a hell of a racquetball story to go with it by the end of the day."

At the front door they shook hands.

# CHAPTER
## THIRTY-NINE

Yakabuski phoned Griffin from his Jeep and gave her the name Fiona McSheffrey. Neighbour of Augustus in 1974. Once married to Paddy McSheffrey.

"You think she'll know the mother?"

"I think there's a good chance."

Paddy McSheffrey. The man who replaced Terry Maguire as Augustus's right-hand man and chief enforcer, who stood trial with Augustus for the killing of his brother, both men acquitted for lack of motive. Before Tyler Lawson's time. Before Yakabuski's time. He had read about McSheffrey in one of Augustus's criminal files. He turned onto the highway and merged with the early-evening traffic heading out of the city.

One more coincidence in a murder investigation that was starting to have far too many. Like a killer heading to Springfield just as a war was breaking out between the Shiners and the Travellers. Like a million-dollar uncut diamond showing up on the North Shore, just when Gabriel Dumont was filing a land claim for all of Cape Diamond. A strange coincidence, and the only problem was Yakabuski didn't believe in either. Strange, or coincidence. Spend any time in the bush, and you stopped believing in strange. It wasn't strange that geese could fly in a half-mile V-formation, even though scientists were baffled by it and suspected everything from undetected sonar capabilities to primeval memory. The birds just had lousy peripheral vision. So they flew in forma-tion. Same way it wasn't strange that a she-wolf will kill her newborn cub if she knows the animal has no chance of sur-vival. Strange only if a wolf can't be sure of a thing like that.

Coincidence was no different. True examples of it were rare. There was normally something that connected random acts, some explanation for happenstance. If you looked long enough, you found it. Yakabuski often wished he could believe in strange coincidence. His life would be easier. He could give his mind a rest and sleep better at night. But he had found no way of doing it. He would stay with any investigation until it was solved or a priest in High River was throwing dirt on his casket. Not because he was more virtuous than other cops. Not because he was better. But because he felt uncomfortable and anxious when he didn't understand the world around him.

So assuming there was no such thing as strange, and no such thing as coincidence, what did he have? How could he explain the bomb blast in Chicago, the murders of Augustus Morrisey and Tete Fontaine, the kidnapping of Grace Dumont? What was the link that connected them?

He drove until he was at the gates of Ridgewood.

• • •

Jimmy O'Driscoll was in his room. Yakabuski had a bag of clothes with him, and he put it on the bed.

"Picked these up from your apartment, Jimmy. Thought you could use them."

O'Driscoll looked at the plastic grocery bag. A carton of Player's cigarettes sat on top.

"Why'd you do that?"

"Is that your way of saying thank you, Jimmy? You're welcome."

"I already told you I haven't made up my mind about testifying against the Popeyes."

Yakabuski looked around the room. It had wood panelling on the walls and some cheap prints showing scenes from the Old Testament, a single bed and nightstand, a chair in the corner. There was a window looking out on the rear grounds, and in the daylight there would have been a view of the Springfield River, a good view, probably, as the river was at its widest point near here.

"You know, Jimmy, as much as I like living around here, some days I think everyone is a little off. Do you honestly think the only reason someone would help you is if they want something?"

"What other reason would there be?"

Yakabuski looked out the window. He stared for a long time, thinking if he stared long enough he would be able to pick out differences in the darkness, different hues of black that would let him know there was a tree there, or the shoreline was fifty metres in that direction. But it stayed a uniform black. He thought it must have been the window. He could usually start breaking it down.

"Have you never done something for someone, Jimmy, just for the sake of doing something for someone?"

"Why would I do that?"

"Because it's a way to feel good about the world and about yourself. And I don't feel too good right now. I've been working five days, pretty steady, and I don't think I've helped anyone. That makes me feel useless. Makes me feel like a fraud. That make any sense to you?"

"No."

"Maybe it will one day. How they treating you?"

"It's all right. The food's good. The doctor isn't a complete jerk."

"High praise coming from you."

O'Driscoll laughed. Not a sneering laugh. Not a nervous or false laugh. Something genuine. Almost joyful. Yakabuski smiled and turned away from the window.

"I've known people who turned their lives around after leaving this place, Jimmy. Happened to an uncle of mine. He came in a mess, walked out right-thinking and ready to take care of his family. Same thing could happen to you."

"I don't know, Mr. Yakabuski. I like getting high."

"I know that, Jimmy. Everyone does. You just need to pick a better drug. Do you play cribbage?"

"Uhhh? Yeah, I guess I do. I mean I haven't played in a long time."

"Want to play a game?"

"We don't have a board."

"They do in the games room. I'll go get us one."

"You have time for that? Didn't some girl just go missing?"

"Never confuse a man running around with a man doing work, Jimmy. I need to think. Card games usually help me with that."

"Well, all right, I guess."

Yakabuski went to the games room and came back with a cribbage board and a deck of cards. O'Driscoll wasn't bad. He pegged well. Knew what cards to throw away. Yakabuski won the first game by only a few points. The boy was ahead in the second when Yakabuski saw something outside the window. The blackness was no longer total. No longer uniform. In the distance, far down the river, there was a light. Not a navigation light from a boat. Not a streetlight from the shore. Something else. Yakabuski stared for several seconds before he was sure.

A fire. Burning somewhere on the south shore.

"We're going to have to finish this game another time, Jimmy."

"You're about to get beat. You can't quit now."

"I think you're more right than you know."

# CHAPTER FORTY

The North Shore Bridge had patrol cars at each end of the span that night with lights flashing. Police officers scanned every vehicle as it passed. It was not an official roadblock, but cargo vans were being pulled over for spot checks, as was any large vehicle with tinted windows, any minivan with a driver who didn't look like a soccer parent. It had been twenty-eight hours since Grace Dumont was reported missing.

Because of the police cars, the Travellers left the North Shore by way of a footpath down the eastern flank of the escarpment. The footpath was a half-mile upriver from the apartment buildings, and the Travellers descended in darkness, not a man among them needing a flashlight to show him the way. They were two score in number, and they went down the cliffs as silently as mist rolling in from the river.

The path brought the men to an old ferry crossing, the land still cleared, though no ferry had run in more than a century. A half-dozen locked-oar skiffs were waiting for them. As they approached the boats, a large man dressed in the hide and skin of animals patted each man on the back. Most of the men had never met Gabriel Dumont. Just heard the stories. How Dumont had increased the wealth of the Travellers tenfold, by expanding their smuggling routes far down the Divide, almost onto the Great Plains. How he scalped his enemies and hung the hair from maypoles set up in the backyard of his home. How he had been given the sacred texts and talismans, was a true child of Riel.

To some men Dumont gave not only a pat on the back, but a two-armed hug. For a select few, a kiss on both cheeks, the men exchanging brief words from an old language as their lips touched the other's skin. Dumont wore a trench coat made of caribou hide tanned to a dark brown sheen, leather britches, and knee-high moccasins. Around his waist he wore a red sash with tassels that ran down his leg, as did each man who boarded the boats with him.

On the river, the boats moved just outside the arc of light cast by the North Shore Bridge. A shadow that could have been anything, the men hunkered below the gunnels, the oars moving in unison, the strokes cutting the water clean, creating no more disturbance than a ripple sent on its way by a summer breeze.

When they reached the south shore, they pulled the boats ashore and hid them behind some sumac bushes. They were standing on a service road that went from the shoreline to an unmanned hydro switching station, but the men turned away from the service road and began walking down the shoreline. Marched up and down the rocky grade. Through pools of water. Dense stands of chokeberry bushes. Never a misstep. Never a sound.

Ninety minutes after starting down the footpath, the Travellers reached their destination. A stretch of shoreline with a small dune in front of them. Without a word being spoken, the men formed two parallel lines. An old infantry formation that assured there was always a man to take the place of a fallen comrade. When the lines were formed, Dumont walked past each man, as though doing a parade inspection. A few times he stopped and a man would hold out his hands to show him what they were holding. A glass bottle containing gasoline. A length of cut wire. Woollen socks, packed with shards of metal that were sharp enough to perforate the wool.

After the inspection was done, Dumont said, "All right, let's go pay those bastards a visit."

The men strode up and over the rocky dune. Ahead of them were the bright lights and carnival sounds of Belfast Street on a Friday night.

• • •

The Travellers moved down the street throwing Molotov cocktails through the plate-glass windows of stores, and in the bed of any pickup truck parked on the street. People started to run, and the Travellers gave chase, falling upon anyone who fell or made a wrong turn. Within five minutes, Belfast Street was ablaze, from the shoreline all the way to the Silver Dollar.

The nightclub went up like a tinderbox, the wooden structure engulfed in flames seconds after the first Molotov cocktail hit the exterior walls. Customers fled from the front and rear doors, but the Travellers were waiting for them. Eddie O'Malley battled three of them before he fell to the ground and then disappeared from view, at the bottom of a red-sashed scrum, fists flailing. It was wrong to call what happened that night a battle. It was too brutal. Too cruel.

When Sean Morrissey came outside the nightclub, his hands were clutching a snub-nosed rifle, and he was firing rounds into the night. Peter O'Reilly followed him, also firing an automatic rifle. They fired at shadows running the other side of the flames. At any red sash. At a man in a full-length, buckskin coat, throwing back his head and laughing at them.

Ten minutes after the Travellers started their march down Belfast Street, above the gunfire and the screams, the hiss and crackle of burning wood, the explosions and the pounding of running feet, a whistle was heard. A high-pitched note that sounded five times and then faded away.

The Travellers' retreat was as fast and soundless as their attack. Within minutes they were running down the shoreline, pushing their boats back out onto the river, hunkering low and making broad, sweeping oar strokes, as soundless as a piece of driftwood floating downstream. They took a wider arc across the river on their way home. Needing to avoid not just the lights of the North Shore Bridge this time, but also Cork's Town as it burned through the night.

# CHAPTER
## FORTY-ONE

Grace Dumont saw the flames from the living room window. As she watched, her captor came into the living room, a cellphone pushed against his ear. He looked out the window and said, "I can see it from here. It's just on Belfast Street."

He didn't say anything for a moment. Nodded a few times and then said, "What if he screws it up?"

As he was listening to what the person on the other end of the phone was saying, he looked over at the girl. A strange look came to his face. Grace Dumont sat on the couch, wondering if her captor was a man who kept his promises.

"What do you want me to do if the cops come here?" he asked, then laughed at whatever the person on the phone had answered.

When he put down the phone, the girl said, "What is happening out there?"

"Your grandfather is burning down Cork's Town."

"Why?"

"He's pissed that you've been taken, I guess."

"But he doesn't even know me. Why would he do that?"

"You're family. That matters a lot to the Travellers."

"To who?"

"The North Shore Travellers. Do you not know *any* of this?"

"No. Should I?"

"Fuck, your granddad is Gabriel Dumont."

"I don't know his name. My mother never told me."

Later that night, visitors came to the apartment. They stayed in the kitchen and the girl never saw them. Two men who did not stay long, who argued with her captor, one man yelling near the end of their visit: "She should have been dead yesterday. What the fuck are we doing Bobby?"

When they left, the man with the tattoos came back to the living room and said, "Use the bathroom if you need to. We're out of here in two minutes."

She went to the bathroom. Ran the faucet and looked in the medicine cabinet, in the cupboard below the sink, searching for something she could bring, something that might help her. Outside the bathroom door, she heard her captor talking again on the phone.

"We shouldn't be that surprised," she heard him say. "They don't know what the fuck is going on. If you don't know, it makes sense, what they're saying."

There was a knock on the front door. "Wait a minute," her captor said and then she heard his footsteps going down the hallway. The girl found herself wishing again that there were two entrances to this apartment. How easy an escape would have been.

Then she heard a gunshot. Grace Dumont jumped away from the medicine cabinet and put her hands over her mouth. She heard more gunshots. And screams. And large objects falling to the floor. The noise lasted only a few seconds and then the apartment was quiet. She heard footsteps coming back down the hallway. She looked around for something to grab, something she could use as a club when the door opened.

When it did, the man with the tattoos and the long blond hair looked no different than he had when she went into the bathroom. He was not bleeding. Not sweating. If anything, he seemed happier.

"Forget what I said, we're staying here," he told her. Before walking away he added, "You should probably stay out of the kitchen."

. . .

When Yakabuski arrived in Cork's Town, the Silver Dollar was in full blaze. An aerial firetruck had its arm extended, and two firemen were in the bucket, directing a torrent of water down upon the club. There were red and blue flashing lights up and down Belfast Street, and paramedics were treating people lying on the pavement, white gurneys and ambulances scattered everywhere.

The roads into Cork's Town had been sealed, and there were reporters and television vans being kept on the other side of the blockade. The photographers weren't arguing with the cops who were keeping them away. A photo taken a mile away would have been the most dramatic photo many of them had ever taken. Flames reaching toward a darkened sky, the spires of St. Bridget's in the background, blue and red spinning lights anywhere there wasn't fire.

Yakabuski had been in Southern Afghanistan the night an American B-52 bomber accidently dropped a guided missile on a Canadian infantry company doing a night training exercise. Belfast Street seemed no different than that training range. Same shouts of terror and confusion, same blood stains, same paramedics hunched over men ripped apart the way God never intended a man to be ripped apart. In Afghanistan, to show the aftermath of the attack, to help the forensic team collect all the body parts, glow sticks had been used. So many glow sticks it looked like candles burning in a cathedral when Yakabuski arrived. He looked around Belfast Street looking for signs of this being different, but he didn't see them right away.

He found Sean Morrissey sitting on a curb outside the Silver Dollar. His rifle had been confiscated by a detective who told Yakabuski none of the paramedics had treated a gunshot wound. Unless someone turned up with a bullet, Morrissey wasn't going to be arrested. Same for Peter O'Reilly, who had been found firing his Uzi at shadows on the river.

"Even if we could arrest him," said the detective, "I don't think the charges would stick. If this isn't protecting your property, I don't know what is. It looks like a fuckin' bomb hit this place, Yak."

Morrissey stood up when Yakabuski approached him. His white shirt was soot-stained and torn, his hair singed, and there was blood on his cheeks. He stood with his arms by his side, his hands balled into fists, and when Yakabuski was five feet away he shouted: "Have you caught any of the cock-suckers who did this?"

"We're searching for them right now, Sean."

"Searching? Like you've been searching for my dad's killer? Dumont was here tonight, wasn't he?"

"I wouldn't know."

"Well I do. I saw the bastard with my own eyes. It's the North Shore Travellers who did this. The same bastards who killed my father."

"The death of your father is an ongoing investigation. Gabriel Dumont is a person of interest. If you had been more forthcoming with us, perhaps we could have made an arrest by now."

"You're saying this is my fault?"

"I'm saying you are keeping secrets, Sean. And that you probably know more about what has been happening in Springfield this week than any other person standing on this street."

"Fuckin' priceless. I can't believe you're the motherfucker who took out Tommy. How did you get so lucky?"

"I don't think luck has much to do with anything right now. What do you think?"

"I think this ends today. That's what I think." Morrissey spat on the ground, inches from Yakabuski's feet, before turning and walking away.

# CHAPTER
## FORTY-TWO

When he reached Detroit, Cambino caught a Greyhound bus to Petoskey, on the Upper Michigan Peninsula. It was early evening when the bus arrived, and he started walking right away. He avoided all highways and roads, kept to fields and forest, did not use so much as a footpath or hydro-line to guide him.

He had no bread left and so he ate berries and mushrooms he found in the forest, drank cool water from a spring that burbled in the darkness and that he found by following the sound. Whenever he heard a distant car, or any sort of mechanical sound, he stopped walking and waited for the sound to pass. Around midnight he came to a great river and swam its breadth, followed the shoreline on the other side until he could follow it no more, seeing smoke from a village that must have been around the next bend, and so he was forced inland.

For a while he followed the scat of a large cat, hoping to see the animal, but then he lost the trail and knew the cat had spotted him. Cambino sat on his haunches and did not move until he figured out how. Then he got up and continued walking. The forest he walked through was maple and oak, poplar and pine, the hardwood trees still holding most of their leaves, and so he moved in shadows and pools of darkness, the pine needles beneath his feet making a dry, rustling sound as he passed. The moon was high in the sky and offered little light. There were few stars.

He never heard a siren that night, never the bark of a dog or the sound of a human footstep. The darkness was near total and his isolation seemed complete. The world had been reduced to what he could dimly make out in front of him and whatever thoughts he carried in his head. Halfway through the night a feeling of great sadness overcame him, and Cambino knew it was because his journey was coming to an end. He had made his decision about the men from the North, which gave him a final destination, and when that happened there was always sadness. Decisions were a form of self-negation. Fences and boundaries erected around a world of possibilities, no more distant horizons, no more flights of imagination. This is what you must do. This is where you must go.

The sadness did not last long. It never did. As always, Cambino took comfort from the task he had given himself, knowing he was right in all the ways that mattered. The false man must die. Who could argue? It was a fantasy of Cambino's to live one day in a world where falseness had been cleaved away, where the physical world was nothing more than the physical world: no stories, no myths, the brutality of the wolf was merely the brutality of the wolf; the flood that killed a village was merely water searching for the sea. It was not tragedy. It was not a loving God who had fallen asleep.

He travelled through the night forest, and just as the moon was starting to slip away he crested a hill and saw the lake before him. A lake the size of an inland sea. With three shorelines he could not see and ships travelling down a distant channel, flying brightly coloured flags.

He had done well. The ferry terminal was at the bottom of the hill, not more than a mile away.

# CHAPTER
## FORTY-THREE

The sun started to rise the next morning at 6:51 a.m., another winter sun that didn't have the season to accompany it. Seventeen degrees Celsius when it had fully risen, with a predicted high for the day of twenty-eight. Windows in the detachment were already open, trying to catch a breeze that hadn't been around in weeks.

Twenty-seven people were in the hospital. All from Cork's Town. To everyone's surprise, there had been no fatalities. Eddie O'Malley was the most badly wounded, with a broken leg, six busted ribs, and a left eye that was hanging by its optical nerve when he arrived at the Grace Hospital in the middle of the night. At 8 a.m., O'Toole phoned and asked Yakabuski to come to his office.

"The mayor is considering asking the army to come in," he said, as soon as Yakabuski had sat down.

"Martial law?"

"State of emergency. It would work out to be the same thing."

"Maybe that's not a bad idea. The army was called in a couple times during the Biker Wars. It settled things down a bit."

"How would it affect your investigation?"

"Hard to say. Wouldn't be good news for any prosecution."

"Martial law would be a defence lawyer's wet dream."

"You would have to think so."

"That's what I told him. He asked if we could keep the city from outright exploding, and I said we could."

Yakabuski didn't bother answering. The two men stared at each other.

"We've got to find that girl," said O'Toole. "If we can find Grace Dumont, this situation might stop escalating."

"What if it's a body we find?"

"Then we're royally fucked, aren't we?"

O'Toole stared at Yakabuski with what looked like anger in his eyes. Then a startled expression came to his face, and he said quietly, "Listen to me. We're talking about a little girl. I should be ashamed of myself."

"You're not wrong. If Grace Dumont is dead, this whole town will go up in flames. The Travellers burned down half of Cork's Town last night just because she went missing."

"What is happening here? What in hell is happening?" O'Toole looked at Yakabuski, but his senior detective didn't bother answering. Because he didn't have an answer. Didn't feel remotely close to having an answer. And knew anything he said would be an annoying confirmation of that.

"The mayor said he would hold off making a request for

military assistance until tomorrow. He wants to see what happens tonight. He also said he'd like to see an arrest — pick your case — pretty damn soon."

"He'd like that?"

"His exact words. He'll hold off making the request, but he would like to see an arrest."

"Amazing."

"Not really. Rather generous, I thought."

O'Toole gave him a stern look. The two men had known each other for more than ten years, but right then, Yakabuski could not decide if he was serious.

The town was unravelling. You could feel it even here.

. . .

Evans came to Yakabuski's office shortly after 9 a.m. He stood in the doorway holding a sheaf of papers and said, "The FBI has found our serial killer."

He walked into the room and placed an 8 x 10 black-and-white photo on Yakabuski's desk. The photo showed a middle-aged man wearing a Texas A&M baseball cap, with short hair and a moustache, dressed in a windbreaker and collared shirt. He didn't look all that big.

"That's him?"

"The FBI thinks so. When they knew he got away in Chicago, they started watching the border crossings. Bit of a job that one because they don't have a fuckin' clue what he looks like. But they made assumptions. He would need to be in good shape, probably not young, probably not old, middle-aged man travelling alone, nothing distinctive about him to attract attention, but if you looked closely you might think he can handle himself. Seem logical to you, Detective Yakabuski?"

"Seems logical to me."

"That photo is a screen-grab from security video taken last night at the North Channel ferry terminal in Sault Ste. Marie."

The North Channel ferry used to run between the Upper Peninsula of Michigan and Sault Ste. Marie. It was busy enough at one time, with miners from Canada and the United States going back and forth to work at U.S. Steel or Stelco, both companies needing workers and no one caring much back then what country they came from. The workers went to whatever mine was busiest. Then the price of steel collapsed, terrorists flew planes into the World Trade Centre, and the daily, cross-border migration came to an end. Most of the passenger ferries on the Great Lakes were long gone, but a company out of Buffalo restarted the North Channel route last year, getting steady business from any motorist who had done the map calculations and figured out the ferry was the quickest way to get from Northern Ontario to the American Midwest.

"What makes the FBI think this is the guy?"

"Because there is no record of him being on the ferry. He didn't get on, he didn't get off, but there he is, on the security tape," Evans said.

"They've accounted for everyone else on the ferry?"

"They have. Twenty-three passengers in sixteen vehicles. All went through customs at the Port of Algoma."

Yakabuski picked up the photo and took a closer look. The man seemed to have a smirk on his face. Was looking directly into the camera. *He must have known it was there,* thought Yakabuski. But he didn't care. As though he were disguised. Or was planning on doing that later.

"How did the FBI account for all the passengers?" he asked.

"What do you mean?"

"You said the FBI had accounted for all the passengers and vehicles. How did they do that?"

"I just told you. Everyone that boarded the ferry went through customs on the Canadian side. No one is missing."

"So it was a computer check, of the passports and entry documents?"

"Right."

"He's in one of those vehicles right now."

Evans looked at him. The look on his face was half angry and half curious. "Impossible. All the cars were inspected when they cleared customs."

"He would have waved someone down on the road outside the terminal. Probably spent the ferry ride picking out his target. Snuck off the boat when it docked. You need to get in touch with every motorist on that ferry. Get cellphone numbers. Start calling."

. . .

An hour later Evans was back.

"The FBI reached fifteen drivers. No answer on the cellphone for this fellow. Harry Sloan. His customs declaration says he's a softwood broker from Sault Ste. Marie."

Evans put down another photo grab from the security footage. It showed a portly, middle-aged man in a thin, summer suit. No overcoat. His shoulders were hunched against the cold.

"Have they tried him at home?"

"An FBI special agent spoke to his wife. She's trying to reach him as well. She expected him back last night. It's a forty-five-minute drive from the terminal to their home."

"What sort of car was he driving?"

Evans looked at him and bit his lower lip. Didn't answer right away.

"A campervan," he said eventually.

# CHAPTER
## FORTY-FOUR

Harry Sloan stared straight ahead into the darkness. Too scared to turn his head. Not wanting the see the man who had kidnapped him. The man who held a gun pointed to his abdomen. The man who would . . . kill him?

The thought made his body tremor. His wife had warned him so many times. *This isn't the '70s anymore, Harry. You shouldn't be picking up hitchhikers.* But the man had been standing just outside the gates of the ferry terminal. Middle-aged. Wearing only a thin windbreaker. Probably worked at the terminal and was having car trouble. He stopped. The man jumped in. Pulled a gun.

That was two hours ago. The only word the man had said so far was "drive."

• • •

Cambino had never seen land such as this. For the first hour, it was as though they were driving through a cloud, a thick cumulus cloud that had been run to ground. Not the morning mists of Heroica. Not the fog that sometimes swirled in the harbour. A cloud that had fallen from the heavens.

The land, when it was glimpsed through this cloud, appeared to be nothing more than dark rock and distant gorges. Tall pine with needles as long and sharp as boar's teeth. Land that seemed as unwelcoming as land could possibly be, and he wondered if the people who lived here were grateful for the thick morning mists, for keeping hidden the land they had chosen to call home.

"What do you do?" Cambino asked, not bothering to look at the driver.

"I'm a salesman for North-Central Forestry Products," said Sloan.

"You sell trees?"

"Yes. You could say that."

"You have a family?"

"A wife and three boys. The boys are young, and I . . ."

Sloan stopped talking. He did not want to beg right then. Maybe when he was on his knees, with a gun pushed against his head, but not now. And he suspected it would make no difference to this man anyway. He did not seem in any way panicked by what he was doing. Did not seem uncertain. Did not seem like the worries and concerns of a salesman from Sault Ste. Marie would ever be his worries and concerns.

"So you survive from the bounty of this land?" said Cambino.

"Yes, I suppose," said Sloan.

"Did your company steal the land?"

"I'm . . . I'm not sure what you mean."

"Does more than one person claim the bounty of this land?"

"There are always land claims, I suppose. But I don't think there are any serious legal problems."

"Legal problems? Is that how you decide dominion of the land around here? By lawyers?"

"I'm . . . I'm sorry, but I don't understand what you're saying. What do you want to know?"

"Who owns the land?"

Sloan had been staring straight ahead, too scared to make eye contact with his passenger, but he risked a sideways glance when Cambino asked his question. Was surprised to see him with his eyes closed, his head resting against the passenger window, just starting to snore it seemed. Sloan looked at the handgun in Cambino's lap and thought, *This might be my only chance.* Thought of nothing else for thirty miles. Until he started to cry, knowing he was never going to chance it.

• • •

When Cambino awoke, he gave his body a long stretch, opened his eyes and saw that the mist had cleared. They were driving through a dark forest now, with thick stands of evergreen trees and rivers that twisted and turned and ran beside the campervan for many miles. They needed to be atop a hill, or midway on a span over a deep gorge, to see the sun.

"Where are we?" he asked.

"About fifty miles outside Cree Falls."

"Very good."

"What will happen when we get there?"

Cambino looked at the driver but didn't answer. Looked at the handgun sitting on his lap. He picked up the gun and examined it. "You are a smart man," he said. "For that, you get to decide."

"Decide what?" asked Sloan. "I've done as you asked. I've taken you where you wanted to go." He began to cry. Tried to choke it back, but couldn't. "Fuck, all I did was try to help you."

"Do you believe being helpful gives you the right to a long life? Why would you believe such a thing?"

"I have a family. I've already told you that."

"Fathers die every day, my friend."

"Please, take whatever you want. Take my camper. Take my wallet. I won't do a thing until tomorrow. I'll stay right where you leave me, and I won't move until tomorrow. I promise on the eyes of my children that I will do that."

"Promises mean little in this world. It is no different than being a father, or being a helpful man. Do you think God ever considers these things? Pull over here, please."

Sloan was crying and trembling and having a hard time focusing on the road, but he did as he was told. When the campervan was parked, he kept both hands on the steering wheel. Ten and two. He had always done that. Was teased about it from time to time. Doing things the right way, the proper way, was something he had always believed was important. Cambino looked at the hands on the steering wheel and said, "I am going to a land where they mine diamonds. Can you imagine? I think I have made the journey just so I can see it. A land that holds the light of the inner earth in stones you can pluck from the dirt and hold in your hands. Who do you think deserves the bounty from a land like that?"

"I wouldn't know."

"That is a good answer, my friend. I am not sure either."

"Please . . . what are you trying to tell me?"

"I am telling you it is random, it is happenstance, the relationship we have with the land we live upon. We wish it to be more, but it never is. The bounty of the Lord is decided only by the Lord." Cambino looked at the man sitting next to him, his grey suit wet from sweat, lines of moisture collected in the rolls of his neck. The salesman had not cried as much as he had expected. The drive had been rather pleasant.

"Would you like to decide now, or when we reach Cree Falls?"

"What are you talking about? Who the fuck, are you?"

"Perhaps now is best. You will roll the dice, and we will see what sort of God looks down upon you today. The decision will be yours and His. It is the best I can do, my friend. The next car we see — will it be coming from the north or the south?"

"What difference will that make?"

"Nothing. I have just told you that. You still need to choose."

# CHAPTER
## FORTY-FIVE

Yakabuski's sister was waiting for him at the Blue Bird diner dressed in an Armani suit and Jimmy Choo shoes. She belonged in the Blue Bird diner about as much as electric guitars belonged on a Hank Williams record. Yet she was having an animated conversation with a table of elderly ladies when Yakabuski arrived. The waiter, a dour man with the mien and personality of pencil-lead, must have refilled her coffee cup four times.

That was Trish. A force of nature that collected friends the way her brother collected bruises. She was in her early forties now, but looked ten years younger, with coal-black hair and hazel eyes, a full figure she liked to slip into summer dresses when she wasn't wearing business suits, a laugh that sounded like ice cubes tinkling at a summer cocktail party, slightly amplified because everything about Trish was slightly amplified. Her hands rarely stopped moving. She leaned in to hear what people were saying, leaned back to speak. The effect of all that motion was her body seemed to be constantly swaying. Undulating. Shimmering. A hopped-up heat mirage blowing right by you.

"Frankie, over here!"

Yakabuski walked to her table. He bowed to the ladies she had been talking with and took a seat. His back was turned to the other table, and he heard one lady say, "Now that's a gentleman," and then another lady say, "Do you know who that is?" After that there was whispering.

Yakabuski smiled at his sister and said, "So what did you need to see me about, Trish?"

"What do you think? You come to my house and punch my husband. That seems like the sort of thing a brother and sister should talk about."

"I thought Tyler was better than that at keeping secrets."

"Christ, Frankie, you broke his nose. How's he supposed to keep that a secret?"

Yakabuski looked over at the table of elderly ladies. They all looked away. One raised her hand for the cheque.

"I thought he had a racquetball story all ready to go."

"I'm his wife. I don't think Tyler even knows where his racquet is."

"So what did you do, beat it out of him?"

"No, big brother. I figured it out. Like a de-tec-tive."

She gave him one of her smiles. Yakabuski envied people who could make their faces do whatever they wanted. Who had smiles ready to go, whatever the occasion might be. He wasn't sure whether it was something innate or something you needed to practise.

"Your husband has a busted nose, and I'm the only one you can think of who might have done it?"

"Very funny. I guessed, and he admitted. With everything that is happening in Springfield right now, you in the middle of it all, and now that little girl is missing . . . I guess I know you, Frankie."

"You figured I'd be ready to punch somebody?"

"Something like that. You look like shit, by the way."

"Thanks. You look great."

"I really mean it. When was the last time you slept?"

"Got a couple hours earlier today. People have to stop burning things around here."

"On the radio they said the army might come in. Is that true?"

"It's possible. Sending a company in to the North Shore isn't the worst idea I've heard today."

"My God, what is happening to this city? The North Shore Travellers? I didn't think they even existed. Dad never found any of them."

"He never found Gabriel Dumont. He found plenty of Travellers. As you can tell by what happened last night, they're still around."

"I never knew. I don't think Tyler has once mentioned them."

"They like to keep a low profile. Or they used to. Burning down Cork's Town — I guess that's changed. So why am I here, Trish?"

His sister bit her bottom lip and lowered her eyes. Another practised mannerism. Or maybe it was natural, something she did when she was nervous. Again, Yakabuski wasn't sure how such things worked. All he knew for certain was that when Trish bit her lower lip, lowered her eyes, then looked up and asked for something, she generally got it.

She looked up at her brother and said, "Tyler told me you're looking for Sean Morrissey's mother."

"I am. Know where she is?"

"No. But I know you're going to have trouble finding Paddy McSheffrey's widow."

Yakabuski stared at his sister. "How much did Tyler tell you?"

"He told me you're trying to find neighbours of Augustus's from 1974, the year Sean was born. The McSheffreys fit the bill."

"Do you know them?"

"I know the widow," she said, and here his sister looked around the diner, seemed unsure what to say next. "I also know my husband is a good man, Frankie. I know you don't believe that, but he is. He loves me. He loves our children. His situation is — it's awkward, Frankie. He really would like to do something different, quit being a lawyer. We talk about it all the time. It's just . . . it's complicated."

"Why are you telling me this, Trish?"

"So maybe you'll understand the pressure he's under, what he's dealing with. And so maybe you won't hit him again when I tell you he wasn't completely honest with you yesterday."

"What did he lie about?"

"Not knowing where the widow is. She gets a monthly pension from Augustus. Or she got one, I suppose. Don't know how that will work now."

"How do you know this?"

"Because she phoned the house once looking for Tyler. She was quite drunk. She said her cheque was late. I spoke to her for a while. It didn't make a lot of sense, what she was saying. She insisted I take down her address, so Tyler could mail the cheque. Tyler already had her address, but she was drunk and she insisted on giving it to me."

"You *kept* it?"

Trish opened her purse, took out a yellow sticky-note and handed it to her brother.

Yakabuski looked at it. "She lives on the French Line?"

"Curious, isn't it? She doesn't go by McSheffrey anymore, either. There was a second husband who didn't stick. Fiona McGee. That's who you're looking for. If you're smart, Frankie, you'll show up with a bottle."

# CHAPTER
## FORTY-SIX

The French Line was an old colony road on the north shore. Surveyed and cut in the late-nineteenth century, by a provincial government that wanted more settlers on the Divide, one hundred acres was granted to any settler who built a cabin and lived on the road for five years. The land was gneiss and granite, covered by a topsoil of bad dirt, and very few settlers made the five years. The government struggled for many years to make the colony road a success — it doubled the size of the land grants and built a macadamized road to replace the original corduroy road — but nothing worked.

It was land you couldn't farm, not two running feet of it was level, and none of it was what you would call enticing, or made you think of easy days ahead. The land-grant program was quietly cancelled and the colony plans forgotten. What was left behind was a 103-mile gravel road, and log-cabin farms that were either abandoned or lived in by recluses and families too large and too poor to live anywhere else.

Although Yakabuski had an address, he drove by Fiona McGee's house. Tracked back and missed it again. There was no smoke rising from the bush, where the address should have been, which was usually the sign you were passing a house on the French Line: camp smoke rising from the spruce and pine. Except for the warmest days in summer, you needed an airtight stove burning to feel warm in those old cabins. He parked his Jeep and began searching, and after a few minutes found the mailbox hidden beneath a cedar that had fallen upon it. The driveway to the cabin was blocked by more fallen cedar. No way you could spot it unless you knew exactly where it should have been. Yakabuski pulled away a few of the cedars and walked back to his Jeep.

The driveway switchbacked for a quarter mile and then came out on a small ridge of cleared land. In the winter, the ridge would have a view of the Radisson River, a tributary of the Springfield that travelled from headwaters not that far away, an untamed river that could not be navigated and travelled through the unincorporated townships before falling over the north shore escarpment, twenty miles upriver from the high-rises by the North Shore Bridge. The Radisson Falls were a popular destination for sightseeing boats sailing out of the Springfield Harbour.

Despite the proximity of the river, there was nothing on the ridge to attract a sightseer. The cleared land was overrun with junk: empty oil drums, wooden crates, a rusted pedestal bathtub, two cars on cinder blocks, one of the cars more rusted than the bathtub. At the far edge of the ridge was the log cabin. The front door was off centre, and the mortar between the logs was a yellow wood-glue colour, so Yakabuski knew it was an original Colony Road cabin. Probably built in the 1880s. There was a vegetable garden to the right of the house, still not turned for winter, and garbage cans and green plastic bags lined up against the leeward side, to keep them sheltered from the wind that would come tumbling over the ridge, falling with the water to the edge of the escarpment, where it would shoot free over the open air above the Springfield River, turned to gust and gale and howl that would sweep its way down the valley. Only smart thing Yakabuski could see on that ridge. Keeping the garbage sheltered from the wind.

He parked in front of the cabin, next to a Ford Focus that looked like it could join the two other cars already on blocks. Yakabuski knew that for some people cars weren't things you traded in. You ran them into the ground because you couldn't afford the garage bill and you needed to get to work, so you kept moving and hoping for the best, until one day the car died and you had to start looking for another one. That's the narrative for more people than anyone wanted to admit. Planning was a joke. You just learned to keep on keeping on.

It took almost ten minutes to get Fiona McGee to answer the door. It was almost five o'clock and Yakabuski was pretty sure he knew what that meant. If Fiona McGee were a hard-core alcoholic, as his sister had warned, she would have spent the morning drinking. Passed out mid-afternoon. He walked around the cabin, banging on every window. Eventually he heard: "What the hell do you want? Who's out there?"

"Ms. McGee, it's Frank Yakabuski, with the Springfield Regional Police. I need to talk to you."

"What the hell for? I haven't done anything."

"It's for a case I'm investigating. I believe you can help me.

267

You were once a neighbour of Augustus Morrissey's, is that correct?"

"Fuck Augustus Morrissey. And fuck you. If you don't have a warrant, I'm going back to bed."

"Augustus is dead."

There was silence for a moment. When the woman spoke again her voice was quieter. "I didn't know that. When did it happen?"

"Six days ago. He was murdered."

More silence. Although not as long this time. And then Yakabuski heard laughter from the other side of the door.

"Fuck, that's the best news I've heard in years. I'm going to get up and have a drink. Toast the son of a bitch who finally had the stones to kill that fat pig."

"Ms. McGee, I need to talk to you. Can you open the door, please?"

"Fuck off."

Yakabuski straightened his back and let out a sigh. Trish had been right. He should have brought a bottle. He looked around the yard. There was a busted canoe leaning up against a cedar. Looked more like kindling than a boat. Yakabuski wondered when the last time Fiona McGee went canoeing might have been. No guess seemed right to him.

Yes, a bottle would have made things easier. But there were other ways to get a drunk's attention. He kept looking around. Eventually he walked over to Ford Focus. Circled it. Stooped to wipe some dirt from the back licence plate. Walked back to the cabin and knocked on the door.

"Ms. McGee, before I go I'm going to have to collect for your licence plate sticker."

Silence.

"It expired two years ago, so I'm going to have to collect for both years. Plus this one."

More silence.

"I can take cash or a credit card. I can't take a cheque, I'm afraid."

"What the fuck are you talking about?" the woman finally yelled.

"Your car, Ms. McGee. The licence plates are expired. I need to collect the money you owe."

"I don't have it right now. You'll have to come back."

"Not a problem, Ms. McGee. But the car can't stay."

Silence.

"I'll need to take the car if you don't have the payment. It'll go to the impound yard, and you can pick it up there when you have the money to pay for the plates."

More silence.

"Ms. McGee, are you still there? The law requires that I tell you how much the daily impound fees will be."

She started kicking the door. Yakabuski stepped back, thinking a house that old, with a drunk that mad, the door might come flying off. He watched the door shake and thud, bark from the crossbeam falling off, mouse droppings raining down from the termite-destroyed frame. Eventually the kicking stopped and Yakabuski could hear moaning. Then sobbing. He stepped toward the door and waited for it to open.

• • •

Fiona McGee stood about five-foot-six, with blond hair that looked as dry and brittle as corn leaves in October. No roots showing. She was wearing a dirt-stained housecoat and her forearms were milk white, with large blue veins so pronounced they looked like ink etchings. Her cheeks were sunken, and her pupils were dilated with washed-out blue irises that looked like faded denim when it was stretched too tight. Her mouth was thin and barely visible. Her nose, years ago, might have been what you called pert. Now it seemed angular and sharp, dangerous in some ill-defined way. She was yelling before the door was open.

"What the fuck do you mean take my car? I'm not driving it. It can sit in my driveway if I damn well fucking please."

"I'm afraid not, Ms. McGee. The law says I need to take the car." He gave her a hard stare. It didn't make any sense, what he was saying, but he knew it didn't matter. A bad drunk always assumed bad news was true.

"You can't do that. It's the only way I can get around."

"With expired plates?"

The woman's hands flew to her mouth. She shouldn't have said that. A bad situation just became worse. A trajectory she knew well.

"Ms. McGee, I don't want to leave you without a vehicle. If you say you can pay for the plates before long . . ."

"I can. That's not bullshit. I have money coming."

"How long?"

"Two weeks."

"Two weeks?"

"Maybe not that long. Maybe only a week."

"Well, maybe there's some way we can make that work. May I come in for a moment?"

She stood aside.

. . .

The inside of the cabin stank of sweat and pooled water, tobacco and spilled alcohol. There was an airtight stove in the corner of the living room, cold and black, not used any time recently, although it was now the middle of December. There were some flowered bedsheets hanging from the ceiling to separate the living room from the bedroom. The sheets were not fully closed and Yakabuski could see a box-spring and mattress on the floor, strewn with clothes and two sleeping bags it didn't look like she had bothered to zip together.

He sat on a couch in front of a circular coffee table that had once been a hydro-line spool. Fiona McGee's drink of choice seemed to be Ballantine's. There was an empty forty-ounce bottle, two twenty-six-ounce bottles and three mickeys of the Scotch strewn on and around the coffee table. The cabin seemed like the right sort of home to display empty brown bottles.

"So what can you do for me?" she said, sitting the other side of the hydro spool.

"If you can help me with my investigation, I think I can get the impound people to hold off on the car for a week."

"What do you need to know?"

"I need to confirm that you were a neighbour of Augustus Morrissey's in 1974."

"I was. Lived beside that fat pig for twenty years. My husband worked for him."

"Paddy McSheffrey."

"That's right."

"I'm interested in the Morrissey family. Augustus had only one child, is that correct?"

"Sean. Far as I know that's all he had. What is this all about? Didn't you say Augustus was dead?"

271

"Murdered six days ago."

"So why are you interested in stuff from forty years ago?"

"I'm trying to find Sean's mother."

"Why?"

"I'll know when I find her."

"Uhhh?"

"I just need to find her, Ms. McGee. There is no record of her anywhere."

For the first time, she smiled. Then she got up from the chair, went to her bedroom, and came back out with a mickey of Ballantine's. She poured herself a drink, not offering one to Yakabuski, took a long sip, and put down her glass. After that she laughed. "Why, that old bastard. I didn't know that. No record at all?"

"Nothing so far."

"Well, he didn't want people to know. I'm surprised he would go to that much effort, though. It wasn't that big a secret. Everyone on the street knew."

"Knew what?"

"That Sean's mother was the housekeeper."

. . .

The story was told between sips of Ballantine's, distilled from a memory that floated between the tenses of the English language, one moment back on Mission Road in 1974, then in a little cabin on the French Line, once looking at Yakabuski with suspicion and asking if he was with that cop who had threatened to take away her car the other day.

"We work together," said Yakabuski, and Fiona McGee flashed him a smile that decades ago might have been called flirtatious. She told him the other cop was a bastard but he seemed all right.

"The housekeeper, Ms. McGee. What can you tell me about her?"

"She was a looker, anyone on the street will tell you that."

She was a teenage girl from the Old Country, showed up one day as Augustus Morrissey's live-in housekeeper. She had the most beautiful black hair. Must have been one of the black Irish you find sometimes in the seaside towns around Belfast. If she'd ever gone to the Silver Dollar there would have been fights. But Augustus kept her close to home. Sean was born two years after she arrived. It was a spring birth, so the girl was well hid for most of the winter, but she was in the gardens right after the snow melted, and you could see it. The girl was pregnant. Sean showed up a few weeks later.

"No one talked about it," said McGee. "I don't know if people were scared to talk about it, but no one knew how Augustus would react if the topic were brought up, so no one ever did. Better safe than sorry. That was always the way you had to act around that bastard."

"So it wasn't a secret?"

"I don't know what you'd call it. People just forgot about the housekeeper. Sean was Augustus's son. Augustus was Sean's father. That was the family."

"What happened to her?"

"She went back to Belfast. Augustus's next housekeeper was an O'Rourke from Derry Street. Ugly girl that used to steal tomatoes from our garden. Can you imagine? As if Augustus didn't have the money to feed her."

She leaned forward to take a sip of her drink. Leaned back. Closed her eyes and began to snore.

. . .

As Yakabuski was leaning forward to give Fiona McGee a shake, his cellphone rang. He looked at the snoring woman, then at the phone number displayed on his phone. He leaned back and took the call. "Chief."

"Yak, where the fuck are you?" said Bernard O'Toole. "We have cars leaving Cork's Town."

"I'm on the French Line. What do you mean, you have cars leaving Cork's Town?"

"I mean every fuckin' Shiner in the city must be on his way to the North Shore. We've got dozens of cars already on the bridge. It's a fuckin' convoy that's passing me right now."

"Why don't you stop them?"

"Talk to your brother-in-law. He was in the mayor's office most of the day, threatening legal action over what happened last night. Says we let it happen."

"That's just Tyler rattling the old boy's cage."

"Well, it worked. Unless I see an illegal act being committed, I cannot touch a Shiner right now. What the fuck are you doing on the French Line?"

"Tracking down Sean Morrissey's mother."

"Getting anywhere?"

"I think so. I'll head to the North Shore as soon as I'm done."

"What's your ETA?"

"Hour. Hour-and-a-half."

"Come find me when you get here. I'll be in the mobile command centre," and O'Toole clicked off.

# CHAPTER
## FORTY-SEVEN

Yakabuski gave the old woman a shake. She reacted the way he knew she would. The way all bad drunks react when they are poked awake. Angry and scared, and Yakabuski was surprised by her strength, needing both his hands to keep her fingers away from his eyes.

"Ms. McGee, you're in your home. You're on your couch. Open your eyes and look around."

After a while Fiona McGee stopped struggling, opened her eyes, blinked several times, then reached for the bottle of Ballantine's and poured a drink. She put down two fingers of liquid in one swallow, straightened her back and said, "Who the fuck are you?"

Yakabuski didn't bother answering. Not having the time. Knowing it didn't matter much.

"What makes you so sure Sean's mother went back to Ireland?" he said.

The old woman scrunched her face. Her memory was liquid. Nothing solid or linear. For bad drunks it was always that way. He heard a psychologist once call it poetic aptness. When liquid became the most important thing in your world, everything eventually turns liquid. Yakabuski didn't know if the psychologist was right, but he knew you could waste a lot of time trying to reason with a drunk, or trying to hold a normal conversation. Might as well just throw them in the deep end and hope they can answer the one or two things you need to know.

"What makes you so sure?" he repeated.

"Because Paddy drove her and Augustus to the airport the day she left. Would have been late summer of '86."

Yakabuski couldn't keep the surprise from his face. "What makes you so sure of the year?"

"'Cause of what you guys did to Paddy right after that. You charged 'em with murder. You don't fuckin' remember that?"

"For killing Augustus's brother, right?"

"That's right. You guys arrested Augustus too. And Ricky Green."

"Do you remember Ambrose Morrissey?"

"Course I do. Best looking man I ever knew. Girls couldn't stay away from him. Paddy accused me once of having it off with him. Right bloody row that was."

"But your husband was acquitted."

"'Cause you guys had shit. Augustus looked guilty and so you arrested him and brought in Paddy, on account of he was such good friends with that fat prick. You had fuckin' shit."

Yakabuski stared at the old woman, laughing and snorting and weaving on her couch like a bowling pin that wouldn't fall. Walking would be impossible for Fiona McGee right then. Staying awake much longer would be impossible.

"You haven't told me the housekeeper's name," he said.

"Kate."

"Last name?"

"I never knew."

"What else can you tell me about her?"

"A right fuckin' looker. Not short, not tall. Hard-working girl. The Morrissey house was always neat as a pin. Paddy would razz me about it. Said I should be more like her. A fuckin' housekeeper. Can you believe it? Right bloody row about that one too."

"Anything else?"

The woman looked at Yakabuski. A confused look came to her face. Then surprise. "You're here about the car, ain't you? You can't take it away. I need it."

Yakabuski didn't bother answering.

"The housekeeper, Ms. McGee. What else can you tell me about her?"

"You'll leave the car?"

"Yes."

"She was a right looker."

"You've already told me that. What else?"

"A good dresser. The girl looked good in anything, so it shouldn't have mattered, but Augustus kept her in outfits. That was the only time you'd see 'em out in public. When Augustus was buying her stuff. She always had a lot of jewellery."

"Jewellery?"

"Yeah, she liked jewellery." The old woman opened her mouth wide, was yawning when she said, "Always had lots of necklaces and bracelets. And rings. She used to have this diamond ring, I'd never seen anything like it."

"What made it unusual?"

"The diamond wasn't cut. Or polished even. Looked like it came right out of the ground."

Yakabuski left Fiona McGee sleeping on her couch. He covered her with one of the sleeping bags from her bedroom, moved her cigarettes and lighter to the kitchen counter, and ran to his Jeep.

# CHAPTER
## FORTY-EIGHT

When he thought about it later, Yakabuski would remember his drive down the French Line that night as something that seemed to happen in a dream. A hallucinatory experience. No linear recollection of it. His thoughts seemed to fill the Jeep, physical objects pressing down on him, the Jack pine and the birch flying past his window and losing distinction, so it seemed as though he were flowing through white-green space. Untethered. Driving too fast. Way too fast.

Sean Morrissey's mother had owned that diamond. It came from Cape Diamond. She had it more than thirty years ago. Was John Merkel right? Did this have nothing to do with the De Kirk mine?

He couldn't be right. "Who tosses away a million-dollar diamond?" he muttered, then waited a few seconds and gave himself the answer: "Someone who knows he can get more." He phoned O'Toole to get on update on what was happening on the North Shore, was told there might have been as many as eight hundred people gathered around Rachel Dumont's apartment building. Shiners, Travellers, and cops. Lines had been formed. Cops in the middle. Shiners and Travellers to either side.

"If this blows, it is going to be the fat fuck to end all fat fucks," said O'Toole. "When are you getting here, Yak?"

"Twenty minutes," he answered and clicked off the phone.

Sean Morrissey's mother had gone back to Belfast around the same time as his uncle was murdered. One of the flaws in the criminal case against Augustus had been motive. Why would he suddenly kill his brother? The cops had no good answer to the question. The mother of Augustus's only child had left town at the same time. No one knew.

A girl from the streets of Belfast, hired as a maid but used for something else, Augustus deciding he had the right to choose the services she would offer. Maybe there was something more to it. They had been together a dozen years. Augustus spoiled her. Kept her hidden. A woman of memorable beauty. So much so, the image of Kate had stayed in the addled brain of a bad drunk who couldn't remember much else.

Yakabuski rubbed the brow of his forehead and concentrated on the road ahead of him. The French Line switchbacked and dipped and his right hand was constantly moving the gearshift on the Rubicon. Pumping back and forth, stepping on the gas, touching the brakes, getting air at the top of the tallest hills. Why wouldn't the pieces of the narrative snap into place? Why did every geometry figure he tried to build blow up halfway through construction?

How did Sean Morrissey's mother have that diamond?

There wasn't a mine at Cape Diamond in 1986. And where had it been for thirty years? He repeated the question, aloud this time: "Where has that diamond been for thirty years?" Had the mother returned from Belfast to kill Augustus? An act of long-plotted revenge that Yakabuski would find difficult to investigate in the wholehearted way a cop should investigate a murder as gruesome as Augustus's. Better if he never found her. Better if everyone went home. He could live with an ending like that.

Through the forest he saw a flash of red and blue spinning light and knew he was getting closer to the North Shore. To the battle lines in front of Rachel Dumont's apartment. To the dank cesspool of hate and fear the Shiners and Travellers had been swimming in all week. Closer to all of it.

Not closer to answers. A diamond. Two dead men. A kidnapped girl. Where was the connection between them? He drove. He thought. He placed one last call, getting O'Toole on the phone and telling him he would be there in five minutes, then asking, "Do we have eyes on Sean Morrissey?"

. . .

Tache Boulevard was lit up with false light when Yakabuski arrived. Halcyon strobes in front of Building H. Red and blue swirling lights atop the scores of parked patrol cars. Flourescent light, mounted on garage tripods, surrounding the tactical vehicles. The apartment building was lit up from the inside as well, each apartment window with a light showing.

All shadows had been burned away. Depth of field was flat and misleading and the cops nearest the building were shielding their eyes. Don't give those bastards an inch of darkness. That's what O'Toole had said he was going to do, and as Yakabuski had his Jeep waved to the front of the police line, he was impressed with the plan. Nothing had happened yet. If you could keep a spotlight shining in the face of every person on this bluff, maybe nothing would.

"Glad to see you, Yak. We've got a restless bunch out there," said O'Toole when he was inside the mobile command centre. "We haven't been able to find Morrissey."

"Is he here?"

"We're not sure. You would think so. This is rather his play, isn't it? I hate these bastards by the way. Did you see what they're all carrying?"

"I did."

"They're not weapons. That's what this asshole told me." He pointed at a video screen, at Peter O'Reilly, smoking a cigarette and twirling a baseball bat. "The bats are for a late night baseball game they're thinking of having at Filion's Field. And the tire irons? Some of their cars are having mechanical problems."

"Cute."

"Yeah, right fucking cute. Your brother-in-law put the fear of God into some people today. We can't do a fuckin' thing until someone actually makes a move."

"Looks like the entire force is up here tonight."

"Pretty much is. All hands on deck. Holidays cancelled. Leave cancelled. Court duty tomorrow cancelled."

Yakabuski nodded. A show of force made sense. He stared at another video screen inside the trailer, this one showing the Travellers, who were also getting ready for a midnight game of baseball. Who were also driving vehicles that might need urgent mechanical attention. He went back and forth between the video feed showing the Travellers line and the Shiners line.

"You need me to do anything right now?" he asked O'Toole.

"We're just waiting."

"I'll see you in a few minutes, then."

"Where are you going?"

"To see that little girl's mother."

. . .

The Travellers let Yakabuski pass the way they had let him pass two days earlier. Not by clearing a path, but by leaning back when he approached, then leaning back in when he had gone. So he was always surrounded. So he had to feel the flannel shirts and the denim jeans as he brushed past, had to stare into their eyes, had to smell the dried sweat and sense their anger. Although no man swore at him. No man spoke under his breath. He was inconsequential. If Yakabuski burst into flames right then they would turn the other way. If he fell, they would stand atop his prone body. It was loathing in its purest form. What you reserve for a bug you find vexatious, but you still didn't stand up and hunt it down. Because it was a bug.

The foyer of the building was empty and he rode the elevator alone to the eighth floor. When he knocked he heard Dumont say, "Come in." He turned the handle, surprised to find the door unlocked. After the chaos of noise and light that was outside the building, walking into the apartment was like walking into a sanctuary. There was the scent of lemon and cinnamon — from candles burning in the living room or baked goods in the kitchen, Yakabuski wasn't sure. The candles in the living room cast a weak yellow light that left most of the room in shadows. He moved noiselessly over the Mandala rugs, already knowing where he was going to find her.

Rachel Dumont sat at her kitchen table with the overhead light turned off. There was a fresh-baked cinnamon loaf cooling on a cutting board beside the stove. More candles burning on the windowsill above the sink. A teapot and cup were in front of her and another teacup was at a place setting across the table from where she sat.

"I made chamomile," she said. "I hope you don't mind. I suspect chamomile wouldn't be one of your favourites."

"Not normally. Maybe it's right for tonight."

Yakabuski sat and poured himself a cup. He leaned back in his chair and crossed his legs. "You knew I was coming?"

"I suspected. I thought you might have been here already. It's quite the crowd outside."

"I'm just getting here. I was doing an interview on the French Line. A woman who used to be a neighbour of Augustus Morrissey's."

"Did she know something about Grace?"

"In a roundabout way, I believe she did."

"What do you mean by that?"

Yakabuski took a sip of his tea. Smacked his lips slightly and gave her a smile. She was right. He didn't care for it much. "I can't explain this to you, Ms. Dumont. It's just a feeling I have. And I hope I'm doing the right thing by telling you this, because I have no proof of what I'm about to say. But I've never been wrong about these sorts of things.

I don't mean to sound boastful, but that's the truth. If something feels right and true to me, it is. If something feels the other way, then that's what it is. And right now, I don't think Grace is in any danger."

Dumont didn't react the way Yakabuski thought she would. Not much of a reaction at all. She raised the teacup to her lips, and when she put it back down she said, "Why do you think that?"

"Because I'm starting to think this war between the Travellers and the Shiners is fake. It's never going to happen, and we're all being played. I don't know how. I don't know why. But it doesn't seem real to me anymore. Which means your daughter's kidnapping could not have been an act of vengeance by the Shiners."

"What was it then?"

"I'm not sure. Part of whatever this is. But I don't think she's in danger."

The candles seemed to dim slightly. Or the night darkened. A change that was hard to pinpoint. Yakabuski continued talking. "Do you know if your father is outside this building?"

"I have no idea."

"No one has seen him. We know he was in Cork's Town last night. No one has seen Sean Morrissey either. Makes you wonder who's in charge out there."

"I suspect no one is. It's more of a mob, wouldn't you say?"

Yakabuski tried another sip of his tea, then pushed the cup aside. "Ms. Dumont, you're not reacting the way I thought you would. Why is that? The mother of a missing child should be relieved by what I just said. She should have questions."

"Maybe because I have the same feeling, Mr. Yakabuski. None of this makes sense to me anymore. Why would the North Shore Travellers go to war for my daughter, a child they did not even know at the start of the week? Why would my father care? He's never even met Grace."

"Good questions. Have you come up with any answers?"

"They both want the same thing, the Travellers and the Shiners, and my daughter can help them get it. She is part of someone's plan."

"Any idea what they might be after?"

"I suspect what people are always after around here. The spoils of the land. It used to be trees, used to be fur, now it's diamonds. That's what people fight and kill for; I don't think there has once been a face on the Northern Divide that launched a thousand ships."

Despite the foreboding of the evening, Yakabuski could not help but smile. "You may be right about that. Have you been back up to Cape Diamond since you left?"

"No. I have no interest."

"This has everything to do with that diamond mine. That feels right and true to me. I just can't put the puzzle together."

"Perhaps you are looking in the wrong place. Deception is probably my father's greatest skill. More so than violence. He told me the Travellers had survived as long as they had because their enemies could never find them. The trick was to make sure they were always looking in the wrong place. Learn that, he told me, and you can disappear. It's an old magician's trick. The rabbit never vanishes. It's just hiding where you're not looking."

"I'm not sure I'm following."

"It's a feeling *I* have, Mr. Yakabuski. I have never been

wrong about mine, either. When I feel like I've been cheated, or deceived in the sort of way my father used to deceive me, then that is the truth. That's how this feels to me right now. As though we've all been summoned here, but we're standing in the wrong place."

# CHAPTER
## FORTY-NINE

As Yakabuski was walking back to the mobile command centre, he was surprised to see John Evans huddled behind one of the tactical team's armoured personnel carriers. He was wearing a flak jacket, although he had taken off the combat helmet that had been given him and was sitting on it.

When Yakabuski reached him, Evans smiled and said, "So is this a typical week up here? You don't really need television, do you?"

"Why are you here?"

"I actually thought I might be able to help out. It's pretty quiet, though, isn't it?"

"It is."

"That's odd," he said, taking a quick glance at the line of Travellers in front of Dumont's apartment building, then the line of Shiners on the other side of the APC. "I also wanted to let you know we found Harry Sloan, the driver of that campervan, and get this — he's alive."

"He hadn't been harmed?"

"Might take a few doctors to get you the answer to that one. He hadn't been physically touched. But he's in shock."

"Can he give us a description of the man who kidnapped him?"

"I'm told he couldn't spell his name right now," Evans said sourly.

"Where was he found?"

"Cree Falls. Parking lot of an Irving station. People working the eight-to-four shift say he was sitting on the curb when they got to work. People on the midnight shift don't remember him. No sign of the camper. I Google-mapped Cree Falls."

"It's a seven-hour drive from here," said Yakabuski.

"Yes it is. Our boy may be joining the party tonight."

"He may already be here. How would we know?"

"That's right. How would we know?"

. . .

It seemed to Yakabuski that in a northern country you spent half your life waiting. For seasons to change, rain storms to end, road trips to finish; you wait for fishing season, hunting season, freeze up, the next portage sign, the plane ride home, the snow plow to come down your street, the leaves to fall. The North is country borne of anticipation, the people who live here always gazing down a long road or a coursing river, wondering what might be coming their way.

Yakabuski wondered if it was the same for other countries, other places. His experience was limited. He had travelled abroad, but only to war zones. Which skewed everything. Maybe anticipation, the white-knuckle days of waiting, was a common thing. Although he didn't think it was. You needed seasons. You needed forests and lakes and open space. In a city with no seasons, what would you be waiting for? The bus?

So when he returned to the mobile command centre, he joined the cops inside that were waiting and didn't think that much about it. Situation normal. He stared at the video screens and waited for someone's first move. Waited for the lines to move. Or six hours to pass, the sun to appear over the Springfield River, and Bernard O'Toole to say, "We're calling it a night, let's pack up and go home."

At 12:15 a.m. there was a rustling on the Travellers line, some men moving from the back of the crowd to the front, and the tactical squad cops tensed and took the safeties off their tear-gas rifles, but several men switched places for no apparent reason and nothing more happened.

Everyone went back to waiting.

At 12:45 a.m. a cop on the front line reported seeing a Molotov cocktail in the hand of Peter O'Reilly, and four members of the tactical team surrounded him and led him away, to the jeers and curses of the Shiners standing near him, who did nothing more than jeer and curse. O'Reilly was searched, but the cops found nothing, so they had to let him go. O'Reilly walked back to the Shiner line, slouching and pursing his meaty lips and giving the cops the finger.

The Shiners applauded. Everyone went back to waiting.

• • •

Yakabuski rubbed his eyes, trying to remember when exactly he had slept last. Yesterday morning. Three hours on his couch. And the day before? That answer didn't come to him as quickly.

*"It feels as though we've all been summoned here, but we're standing in the wrong place."*

Rachel Dumont's words kept rolling through his mind. She knew her father better than anyone, certainly better than most, and she thought he was playing everyone. His greatest skill was deception, she had said, misdirecting people's attention, being able to disappear by standing where no one was looking, the stock trick — maybe the only trick — in the magician's handbag.

Even if she were not the daughter of Gabriel Dumont, if it had been nothing more than a casual observation by someone on the periphery of this case, the words would have resonated with Yakabuski. Because it felt that way to him as well. And he knew, by looking at O'Toole's increasingly angry face, that it was beginning to feel that way to the chief of the Springfield Regional Police Force as well.

It was beginning to feel to Yakabuski as though everything that had happened in Springfield that week — the killings of Augustus Morrissey and Tete Fontaine, the kidnapping of Grace Dumont, the riot on the North Shore, the riot in Cork's Town — had led to this moment, to this scene he was looking at on the video screens inside the trailer. It did not seem like happenstance or bad breaks coming one after another. It seemed like something that had been built. Had been envisioned. A plan of some kind.

He tried again to figure it out, ran the known facts through his mind, careful not to include speculation or assumptions, things that seemed logical yet were unproven, just the known facts:

Augustus Morrissey had been murdered, and his body had been trussed to a fence on the North Shore. His eyes had been cut out, something the North Shore Travellers used to do. Two days later, the Shiners came to the North Shore, started a riot, and killed Tete Fontaine, a cousin of Gabriel Dumont, leader of the North Shore Travellers.

The Travellers did not retaliate right away. They only did that after Dumont's granddaughter had been kidnapped. Yakabuski included the kidnapping of the girl as a known fact, which wasn't technically true — she simply wasn't where she should have been — but he knew it to be true and included it on his list.

What else was known with certainty? A diamond worth more than a million dollars had been found in the mouth of Augustus Morrissey. The stone was from Cape Diamond, where Gabriel Dumont had lived for many years. Sean Morrissey's mother once owned a ring that was made from an uncut diamond. She disappeared when Morrissey was twelve years old. A killer was making his way north, a business partner of Sean Morrissey's, his last known whereabouts a seven-hour drive from Springfield.

The known facts. In the false light and anticipation of that night, Yakabuski kept running them through his mind. The link, when he found it, would be as tangible as a known fact. Would *be* a known fact, because that's the way it always went.

When nothing came to him, Yakabuski tried to expand his list of known facts. Gabriel Dumont was violent and probably delusional. Tete Fontaine had been hung on the same fence panel as Augustus Morrissey. Sean Morrissey was a thief. No one throws away a million-dollar diamond unless he can get more. Tyler Lawson couldn't keep a secret to save his soul. His sister needed a divorce.

Yakabuski stopped. He had lost the path and stumbled off into the woods. He didn't have the fact he needed to solve the puzzle. There was still something missing. Or something he had not picked up on, a known fact whose significance he had missed.

*"It feels as though we've all been summoned here, but we're standing in the wrong place."*

# CHAPTER FIFTY

Yakabuski left the trailer and went back to the police line. The moon and the stars could not be seen that night because of all the false light on the bluff. He looked around at the two lines of potential combatants assembled in front of Building H; the Coyote APCs and steel-plated patrol cars in-between; a half-dozen ambulances lined up in the alley beside Building G; the small knot of men in grey uniforms and old-fashioned cowboy hats, smoking beside one of the ambulances.

He found Evans, who was telling the tactical team sergeant a story about raiding a crack house at Jane and Finch once: he'd thought it wouldn't be a problem, but there was a steel door to the upper floor that would have made the Bank of Canada proud. A hundred feet of steel chain and a Coyote solved the problem.

Yakabuski stared at Peter O'Reilly, who gave him the finger. Then at a Traveller standing on the front line of potential combatants who was bigger than he was and hadn't moved all night, not so much as a finger, according to the cop who had been watching him on video since 10 p.m.

When he returned to the trailer he asked O'Toole, "Those guys outside with the cowboy hats, where are they from?"

"Special constables. They're normally stationed at the airport. The feds called them in around 9 p.m. Any cop within a hundred miles of Springfield is up on this bluff tonight."

Yakabuski slammed open the door of the trailer and started running toward his Jeep.

• • •

The Springfield Regional Airport was to the south of the city, a forty-five-minute drive from the North Shore, but Yakabuski made it there in under twenty. He brought the Jeep to a screeching halt in front of the security kiosk by the arrivals gate, where a startled security guard with a face covered in pimples told him nothing unusual was happening.

"All quiet," he said. Then thinking that more needed to be said, added, "Even more than normal."

Yakabuski was told the same thing at the security office inside the terminal. A quiet night. A plane from Toronto had landed four hours ago. Passengers were long gone. A plane from Buffalo was arriving at six in the morning. The terminal was about as quiet right then as it was possible for an airport terminal to be. None of the ticket windows were manned. The carousels were not moving. A janitor with a floor polisher was swinging it around at the far end of the terminal, so far away Yakabuski couldn't hear the swoosh of the brushes.

Yakabuski asked to be brought to the control tower and was told the same story one more time. A quiet night, said the duty controller. There were probably not more than a dozen people working in the terminal right then. Good luck getting a coffee.

"Nothing out of the ordinary has happened tonight?"

"Nothing," said the controller, who hesitated a second after he said it, and then added, "A commercial flight landed about an hour ago. Called in a change to its flight plan while en route."

"That's unusual?"

"Not really. Although it's not the sort of thing the bigger companies tend to do."

"Whose plane is it?"

"That De Kirk plane over by hangar five." When he said it the controller stood up, looked out his window, and added, "That's strange. The back cargo door is open but there's no one around."

# CHAPTER
## FIFTY-ONE

The light in the room was dim and shadows had settled, lying unmoving between the furniture. The two men in the room were seated and still, only occasionally raising crystal rock glasses to their mouths to take sips of Scotch. Cambino looked at the man seated on the other side of the metal desk. The man had been his business partner for many years, but this was the first time they had met.

"I was not expecting you until tomorrow," the man said, and he gave Cambino a curious look. "Did anything go wrong during your journey?"

"No."

"I still don't understand why you drove. You could have taken a plane."

"I like to travel."

The man took another sip of Scotch. It was fine Scotch and burned his throat only a little while going down. Once there it sat in his stomach like a late-night ember, the same comfort and worth as a hearth at the end of day. After a while he asked, "Why have you come here tonight?"

"You don't know? That surprises me."

"We have a deal. Did he make you a better offer?"

"He offered me nothing."

"Then why are you here?"

Cambino did not answer. The only light in the room came from a shaded lamp upon the desk, and shadows settled further into the room, curling under the furniture and hiding in the corners like animals bedding down for the night. The room was still. Neither man reached for a glass. No finger tapped. No lash moved across the iris of an eye.

"So I am betrayed."

"I would not call it that."

"They used to hunt us down like vermin, did you know that? As soon as we were of no use to the fur trading companies and the lumber companies, we were hunted down and executed. Burned on our timber cribs. Banished and shunned. You should consider that. If we stole every diamond, tree, and chunk of ore on the Northern Divide, we would still not have taken what is owed to us."

"That is a nice speech, my friend. And if it were true, you might get what you wish."

"It *is* the truth. How can you doubt it?"

"I have no doubts," said Cambino. "Let me ask you a question. When you kill a false man, what do you think you have killed?"

The other man gave him a strange look and then thought about the question. In time he said, "I think you have killed a sinner before God, like any other."

"And what about a false prophet?"

The other man felt something wet and ancient move in the bottom of his stomach. He took a long sip of his Scotch before saying, "This is about the girl, isn't it?"

"You do not wish to answer my question?"

"I was told it was necessary. That without the kidnapping of the girl, the police would not care as much. The murders of two gangsters would not be enough to scare them. The airport would be left protected."

"I know what you were told. The message came from me. But you are a man of free will, yes? The decision to put your family at risk, it was yours, correct?"

"You are making a mistake."

"Never. And a false prophet is more than a sinner before God, my friend. He is a shadow of a man. He is nothing. When you kill a false man, you kill nothing."

"I can pull a gun right now and shoot you."

"But you won't."

"What makes you so sure?"

"Because you know the old stories. Because you knew I would come one day. And because you know it would be useless. Your throat would be slit before you had the gun out of the drawer."

"You think so?"

"It is a certainty, my friend."

The voice was pleasant and reassuring and the cold chill that had passed earlier through the man's body changed suddenly to a warmth and calmness that startled him. He closed his eyes. Already in God's sweet embrace.

Neither man spoke for a long time. Eventually, Cambino asked, "Do you have a request?"

"No."

"Most people have a request. It makes no difference to you?"

"No. We are done here."

Cambino gave a deferential nod and rose from his chair.

# CHAPTER FIFTY-TWO

The feeling of coming to the end of a long, hard trail was so palpable when Yakabuski fell asleep that night it might as well have been a living, breathing person caressing his cheek. It was a deep sleep, but not long. By 7 a.m., he was already showered, dressed and driving back to the detachment. He was not looking forward to the day, knew that Springfield was awakening that morning not with a sense of relief at news the Shiners–Travellers war had been averted, but with a sense of disappointment, a vague feeling of emptiness that was hard to describe and that would turn to surliness by noon.

Most people who lived along the Northern Divide were familiar with tragedy and its many stages, and they had done the prep work for whatever the gangland war might bring. Had rationalized things in their mind, getting ready for the tough days ahead, and so they would feel cheated. Like doing a half-day portage, following the signs the whole way, and then ending up back at the trailhead. It pissed you off. Hard work was never considered a problem on the Divide. Death and violence weren't even considered problems a lot of days. But being cheated and tricked — one more time — that drove people crazy.

He took a detour and drove through Cork's Town before reaching the detachment. The neon sign for the Silver Dollar, once proudly displayed right on Belfast Street, fifty feet from the actual nightclub, was an ingot of melted chrome and busted neon. The façade of the nightclub was badly charred, though it was still standing. The maintenance shed out back did not fare as well. It had burned to tinder, and so there was a clear view that morning right down to the river. Further down the street, a gang of boys was searching through the rubble of what had once been a dollar store.

A middle-aged man in white T-shirt and factory pants was sitting in a folding chair in the rubble in front of O'Keefe's, drinking a quart of beer and giving Yakabuski's Jeep a nasty glare as it passed. *Never seen a man drinking in the morning, asshole?*

Yakabuski looked at the man in his rear-view mirror, lighting a cigarette and flashing him the finger. He didn't seem to mind being outside. Yakabuski wondered if O'Keefe's was actually open and serving, or if the man was just a creature of habit. Seven a.m. was O'Keefe's normal opening time, to catch shift workers before their day started.

When he got downtown, the city had a dank, dirty feel to it. Soot particles floated in the air, a light wind just strong enough to make them spin and converge but not strong enough to blow them away. The scent in the air that morning was of wet, charred wood, a charcoal sort of scent — a fat, smudge of a scent you could not avoid. Nothing about the day was appealing. And it was going to stay that way. O'Toole had scheduled a full criminal investigations departmental meeting for 8 a.m.

. . .

In the conference room were eleven nervous people, laptops opened in front of them, because the laptops held all the intel that had been collected since Augustus Morrissey was found dead and hanging from a fence in Filion's Field one week ago. The computers had the situation reports and wiretap transcripts; the surveillance photographs and minutes from previous meetings; the complete criminal records of at least twenty men, with corresponding mug shots and cross-referenced files of all known associates. It was meticulously categorized information. A complete compendium of the known facts and revealed secrets of the investigation into Augustus Morrissey's murder, what law enforcement people needed to collect so they could feel good not only about their work, but also about their place and purpose in the world.

All of it useless.

Not suddenly useless, either. Not the-investigation-just-went-bust, or the-state-won't-prosecute sort of useless.

Always useless.

It still hadn't sunk in for everyone. Those that had figured it out shuffled their feet beneath the conference table and tried to avoid eye contact. They were embarrassed. Already wondering if this had ruined their careers. But they hadn't been the only fools. You have to remember that. They had been up most of the night and that was what they had come to work with, what they were hoping might save them — *I wasn't the only idiot.* Yesterday, they had walked with confidence. Today, they avoided eye contact and waited for others to speak.

Yakabuski sat to the right of O'Toole and Donna Griffin sat to the left of him. As a patrol officer seconded to Major Crimes for the week she didn't need to attend the meeting, but Yakabuski thought she deserved to be there. She had put in the work. He didn't want to cheat her out of the ending.

O'Toole motioned for the lights to be turned off and started the security footage tape from hangar five. It was displayed on an old-fashioned white screen set up at the front of the room, a black-and-white video with night-vision turned on, so that most of the objects appeared pallid and ghostlike. The De Kirk plane taxied into view, according to the time stamp, at 12:43 a.m. Came into the frame moving right to left, so that the cargo doors at the rear were in the middle of the frame when the plane stopped. The view could not have been better if you had blocked it out for a movie.

The cargo doors opened, and a tall, thin man dressed in a grey pilot's uniform with piping on the legs and a crest on his shirt pocket was standing there. Next to him was a cargo container on wheels, measuring about six-feet-by-three, the sort of container you see roadies wheeling into concerts. The doors were open only a few seconds before a Ford Econoline van drove into view. No markings on the vehicle. Rear licence plate covered with some sort of cloth. The driver's door and the passenger's door opened at the same time and two men got out, wearing balaclavas and windbreakers over turtleneck sweaters, black jeans tucked into workboots. One man had blond hair sticking out the back of his balaclava, and it was this man that approached the plane, while the other man went to the back of the van, opened the doors, and pulled out a metal ramp.

Although it wasn't caught on the videotape, the pilot must have done something to begin lowering the ramp of the plane. The man with blond hair waited until it was down, grabbed the cargo container and began pushing it to the back of the van. The second man took over the job and the first man ran back to the plane, then up the ramp and disappeared inside the plane with the pilot. The man in the balaclava was in the plane for fifty-five seconds before he reappeared, pushing two more of the cargo containers. The pilot was not seen again.

It took one minute and ten seconds for the two masked men to load the new containers into the back of the van, and then the Econoline made a three-point turn and drove away. Total elapsed time was two minutes and fifty-six seconds. The final shot — the De Kirk plane with its cargo doors open and no one around — stayed on the screen for almost the same length of time, as though O'Toole wanted it to sink in a little bit more. Finally, he stopped the tape and motioned for the lights to be turned back on.

"The pilot was found dead inside the plane," said O'Toole. "He'd taken two .38-calibre slugs in the back of the head. His name was Rene Charlebois, and he lived just outside the Kesagami Reserve. He must have had something to do with the robbery because the co-pilot had been drugged. We found him sleeping on the plane. He's one lucky guy. We have no idea who the two men in the van might be. The plane was on its way to New York City."

"Where is Gabriel Dumont now?" asked one of the RCMP officers who had shown up earlier in the week.

"We can't locate him."

"And Sean Morrissey?"

"Can't find him either."

"So this was nothing but a hustle? The war between the Shiners and the Travellers, it was just a diversion for a jewellery heist?" said the Mountie in disbelief. "Shit, the army was almost called in. That's a hell of a lot of work to go through just for an armed robbery."

O'Toole looked at the RCMP officer for a long second. Then he picked up a piece of paper lying atop the file folder in front of him.

"De Kirk has sent us the bill of lading for the plane," he said, his voice sounding as distant as some radio signal skipping over the dark side of the planet. "The insured value for those three cargo containers is one-point-two billion dollars."

•  •  •

The people in the room were too tired to give it the import it deserved. Or too fearful. Each person just starting to comprehend how badly they had been played, just starting to feel the vertigo that overcomes people when they have once and for all, truly and for all time, fallen off the edge of the known world.

One-point-two billion dollars. Nobody was going to survive this.

Donna Griffin turned to Yakabuski and mouthed the words "holy fuck."

It was the only motion in the room until Yakabuski

leaned forward and said, "The guy driving the van is Sean Morrissey."

Each person turned quickly to look at him. The first quick movements of the morning.

"The other guy," Yakabuski continued, "if I didn't know for a fact he was dead, I'd say it was Tommy Bangles."

"How do you know this, Yak?" said O'Toole. "Ident has not found a single distinguishing feature on either of those two men, except for the blond hair, which they think is probably a wig. They have been going through the tape for five hours now."

"Ident should go down to Cork's Town and see how people walk. It's Morrissey. I don't know about the other guy, but he's a Shiner. We should start checking to see just how many cousins Sean Morrissey has."

"Does that make any sense, Yak? If the Shiners and the Travellers were in this heist together, wouldn't the second man be a Traveller?"

"The Travellers already had someone. They had the pilot."

Yakabuski gave them time. Looked around the table to see who would figure it out first. Was surprised to see it was Evans, nodding and muttering, "Well, I'll be a son of a bitch."

O'Toole and Griffin seemed to get it at the same time, although it was O'Toole who spoke. "Shit, Yak, are you saying there was a back end to all this?"

"I am. It wasn't just De Kirk that got ripped off last night."

# CHAPTER
## FIFTY-THREE

Evans came to see Yakabuski in his office shortly after the meeting ended. He didn't walk in but stood in the doorway, swatting his knee with a file folder he carried in his hands.

"One-point-two billion dollars," he said with a laugh. "I don't fuckin' believe it."

"Believe it."

"Any idea where my psycho fits into all of this?"

"The back end, I would think."

"Yeah, you would sort of have to think that."

He kept swatting his knee, looking down the hallway that led to Yakabuski's office. After a while he said, "I spoke to a Mexican ranger this morning who knows the guy. Says his name is Cambino Cortez. He's Mayan. His family runs one of the cartels in Heroica, and he's a wealthy and powerful man, according to the ranger, but he likes to disappear from time to time. His father did the same thing.

They just up and vanish. Ranger spoke about the guy like he was some sort of demon. He didn't think he would ever be caught."

"Sounds like that guy has got inside the ranger's head," said Yakabuski.

"Can you blame him? I'm beginning to wonder about the guy myself. Harry Sloan — he hasn't said a word yet. Catatonic shock and not a scratch on him. Doctors have no idea when he might snap out of it."

"I've seen Popeyes put the fear of God into people so bad, they didn't know which side was up. Didn't make them demons."

"Yeah, I suppose," said Evans, a faraway look in his eyes, and then he straightened his back and said, "Listen, I'm sorry for rattling your cage when I first got here. I didn't know what you were dealing with."

"No one did. That ranger, did he have a photo of Cortez?"

"What do you think?" And Evans walked away.

. . .

Yakabuski phoned Ridgewood and was told Jimmy O'Driscoll was sleeping. He was put on hold, and a woman from the accounting department came on to confirm Yakabuski's mailing address. He phoned his sister but couldn't get an answer. He phoned his father, who answered on the first ring.

"Thought it might be you," he said.

"Have you heard what happened last night?"

"One-point-two billion dollars. Am I hearing that right?"

"You are. A reporter told me an hour ago it might be the largest armed robbery in history. They're trying to confirm it."

"Well, that's going to put us on the map, isn't it? And they're both missing — Sean Morrissey and Gabriel Dumont?"

"No sign of either one. Although one of them is probably dead. It looks like the Shiners tried to get away with all the diamonds, cut the Travellers out on the back end."

"Can't trust a thief. I'm surprised to hear that."

"Where would you stash one-point-two billion dollars in stolen diamonds, Dad?"

"On that private island I just bought, the one with the good stone breakweater and the warehouse full of RPGs."

"Think that would be enough?"

"Fuck no. You coming over tonight?"

"I'm going to try." Yakabuski hung up the phone.

• • •

At 12:30 p.m., the day-duty sergeant from the RCMP detachment at Fort Francis phoned Yakabuski to tell him Gabriel Dumont was dead. His body had been found that morning, in the office of his home outside Cape Diamond.

"You guys have been phoning up here looking for him," said the sergeant, explaining the reason for his call. Yakabuski asked how Dumont had died. He heard the sound of rustling paper and then the sergeant said, "He was murdered sometime last night. Serrated knife was the murder weapon, not recovered at the scene, minimum six-inch blade to have hit some of the bones that were broken. Either that or the killer struck with such force he was burying the hilt. No way of knowing because of the mess. It was a vicious killing."

"Any suspects?"

"No one so far. Not even sure who we should interview. You knew he was a Traveller, right?"

"I did."

"Those guys have been keeping secrets for centuries. I've got granite up here that would be more talkative."

"Who found the body?"

"A girl that worked for Dumont as a housekeeper. She phoned it in a little past nine. There's a lot of security at that house, but no cameras. Go figure."

"Can you tell me anything about the crime scene?"

"Let's see," he said, and Yakabuski heard more paper being rustled. It lasted longer this time and when the sergeant spoke next, he said, "There are a few oddities. There were no signs of struggle inside the office. And all the blood found at the scene belonged to Dumont. For a killing this violent, I've never seen that before."

"Could Dumont have been drugged, or passed out?"

"Anything is possible, although Dumont was known to us, and he didn't have a reputation for being a drug user. Or as someone that could be easily tricked."

Yakabuski thanked the sergeant again for phoning and hung up. He sat at his desk with his eyes closed. When he opened them, he reached for his phone and started making calls.

His first two calls were brief, but the third lasted nearly fifteen minutes. Halfway through, he took a steno pad from his desk drawer and started taking notes. When he was done the call he stood up, took his coat from the couch where he had thrown it, and left the detachment. He phoned O'Toole from the parking lot, as he was backing up his Jeep.

"I'm out for a few hours."

"Where are you going, Yak?"

"Going to bring in Sean Morrissey. And we can stop looking for Gabriel Dumont."

# CHAPTER
## FIFTY-FOUR

Grace Dumont was released at 1 p.m. She'd had a dreamless sleep the night before, fallen asleep right after her captor gave her a hot chocolate, awoken with the sun nearly full in the sky, and been taken back to the Dakota pickup truck. The man who had held her captive the past three days drove over the North Shore Bridge and then down the service road behind Filion's Field.

The truck stopped. The young girl pushed open the passenger door. Before stepping out, the man placed something in her hand.

She watched the truck make a three-point turn and take the service road back the way it had come. When she could not see the truck anymore, she counted to one hundred, as the driver had told her. She looked around while she counted. On the western horizon she could see high cumulus clouds.

For the first time in many weeks, the sky was not a light blue. It was cobalt and getting darker.

When she reached one hundred she began the short walk to her home. She cut across the soccer pitch and entered the rear door of Building H. Rode the elevator with an elderly woman who stared at her strangely but never spoke. It was mid-afternoon, and she was surprised to find her mother at home, sitting in the kitchen, and when Rachel Dumont heard the door open she ran to her daughter with tears streaming down her face. The little girl also started to cry. She was picked up in her mother's arms, kissed on the cheek, the mouth, the nape of her neck, her mother saying nothing more than her name for several minutes. Then the girl was put back down, and her mother looked closely into her face.

"Are you all right?"

"Yes."

"Did anything happen to you? Did anyone harm you?"

"No. I did what you always tell me to do, Mommy."

"What's that?"

The girl looked up at her mother in surprise. She hadn't been gone that long. She put her hands on her hips, gave her little body a twist, and doing a poor impersonation of Rachel Dumont, said, "Get through the tough days, Grace. Tomorrow will be different."

The mother's tears came rolling down her cheek. What a child she had. What a remarkable, smart, tough, you're-going-to-be-all-right-up-here little girl.

Grace looked at her mother and remembered what she had brought home. "I have something for you."

"Something for me?"

"I think you'll like it."

The girl unclasped the hand she had been holding tightly clenched since stepping out of the pickup truck. Shoved in her pocket for the walk across Filion's Field. Balled up while she rode the elevator. She unfurled her tiny fingers, and there in her palm was a diamond.

"The man said we could have this."

. . .

Yakabuski took Highway 7 to the turnoff to Buckham's Bay and then headed west, travelling beside the Springfield River. The temperature had begun to drop, and he could see high cumulus clouds on the horizon. The radio said snow was in the forecast. A storm of about twenty centimetres, coming tomorrow morning, although Yakabuski knew, by looking at those clouds, that it was coming earlier than that.

He drove through Buckham's Bay, and then the tiny hamlet of La Toque, where there used to be a voyageur portage past a set of bad rapids. The rapids were no longer there, but an old cemetery was still by the shore, where they used to bury the drowned. Past the cemetery the river widened, and for a time Yakabuski could not see the far shore. The hardwood trees he drove past were black and the last leaves were finally falling. When the far shore came back into view it came as a black line sitting atop grey water.

When he reached St. Bernard he stopped at the post office and asked for directions, as the place he was seeking could not be found on his GPS. The postmaster wrote the directions on the back of an envelope, saying he used to drive

315

a rural route that took him past that place every day. Did Yakabuski have family there?

"No."

"Well, it's a lovely place," said the postmaster, and handed him the map.

The turnoff was five minutes outside St. Bernard, poorly marked as the postmaster had warned. A secondary road that turned quickly to gravel, the stones just starting to freeze into place so the driving wasn't bad. Yakabuski drove past hoarfrost fields and crystallized vegetables missed in the harvest, corn and wheat mostly, the stalks looking like icicles that had fallen and impaled the earth. Drove past abandoned homesteader cabins with timbers black and cracked, the off-centre door long gone, nothing but a black hole the wind rushed through. Drove until he reached an wrought-iron fence with a gate announcing he had just arrived at Ste. Anne Cemetery.

He parked and let the car idle. In the northwest corner of the cemetery stood Sean Morrissey.

# CHAPTER
## FIFTY-FIVE

The wind was getting strong, and leaves were twirling around the tombstones as Yakabuski began walking down the row that would take him to Morrissey. Dark brittle leaves that had finally been torn from their branches, with edges so sharp they could cut a person if they blew across their face. Morrissey turned once to see him approach, then turned away. There was a wheelbarrow near the tombstone he was standing in front of, and two men sat near it, smoking cigarettes.

When Yakabuski was standing beside him, Morrissey said, "How did you find me?"

"Your uncle is buried here. After your dad made sure he couldn't be buried anywhere in Springfield. Were you close to your uncle, Sean?"

"Not really."

"Close to your mother though."

"Is that a question?"

"I reckon not."

The tombstone on the freshly dug grave read: *Katherine Anne Morrissey, August 15, 1954–September 10, 1986; May She Forever Rest in Peace.* The two men stared at the tombstone. The men smoking cigarettes looked at them and then looked away.

"You figured it out just from that?"

"No. Last night I started thinking your mother was probably dead. I phoned some of the memorial companies this morning. Robertson's was my third call. They told me you'd ordered the tombstone last Monday. Needed it to be here today. Not a day before. Not a day after. Where did you find her body?"

"Miller's Crossing. Off a trail in the conservation area."

"On the way from Cork's Town to the airport."

"That's right."

"Is that how you got the date for the headstone?"

"No. He told me."

*He told me.* Yakabuski shuddered. He could just imagine. "They were legally married?"

"Private ceremony at home. Father Joe did it. I was there too. Just the four of us. I still don't know why he did it."

"Maybe he loved her."

"He never loved anything. He possessed a great many things. I think that's how he saw it."

"So you waited thirty years to kill him."

"Don't believe I've said that."

The leaves were now falling so fast and in such numbers they had begun to obscure the sightlines to the river. The wind seemed to be coming from many directions. Yakabuski knew that if you were out on the river fishing right then, it would be a bad wind. A lost season always ended with bad wind. It was why the best guides in High River refused to work during one.

He looked over at Morrissey's Cadillac, parked next to the workmen's pickup truck at the end of the row and said, "Got any diamonds in that car, Sean?"

"Would you like to search it?"

"I'm sure someone will. I'm thinking I have better things to do."

Morrissey didn't say anything. Bent down and wiped some leaves away from the tombstone.

"Your mother wasn't from Belfast, was she? She was from Cape Diamond. She was Cree. That's why she had that ring. Probably the reason your dad kept her a secret."

"I wouldn't know anything about that, Yak."

"Why not keep the diamond? I can't figure that part out."

"Speaking hypothetically, and with no knowledge of this crime, maybe it needed to be returned."

Yakabuski looked back at the tombstone. Tried to think of a follow-up question. Nothing came to him and so he said quietly, "I'm wondering where you go from here, Sean. I can follow everything up to now. I can see the scheme you and Gabriel hatched. Start a war as a distraction to a jewellery heist. You both need to have skin in the game, so you sacrifice a father; Gabriel sacrifices a cousin and kidnaps a granddaughter. Might be about even. But you're a Shiner and a thief, so that wouldn't be good enough. You needed to add a rip-off to the back end. And you brought that lunatic up here to get rid of Gabriel for you."

"Another interesting theory of yours, Yak. And the proof of this would be?"

"I'm not trying to prove anything today. I'm just trying to get ready for what's coming."

"What do you mean?"

"Remember what I said in your office about schemers? How they always go too far? That's what you've just done, Sean."

"You're speaking in riddles, Yak. Why don't you just tell me what you want to say?"

"Cambino Cortez. He'll be coming for you. You've brought him right to Springfield."

Morrissey didn't speak right away. Cocked his head a few times, as though lost in thought. Eventually, he said, "We need to stop talking, Yak. There will be plenty of time to talk when I get back to Springfield. Have you called it in?"

"Soon as I saw you."

"Then come see me in the holding cells. Bring a coffee. That would be friendly."

"You're going to need some friends, Sean. The Travellers aren't going to like the way they just got played. I doubt if the Popeyes are going to much like you becoming rich with a scheme you never told them about. And I don't think those are even your biggest problems."

"What makes you so sure he's coming?"

"Because you've got one-point-two billion dollars in stolen diamonds stashed somewhere. Because Cortez was seven hours from here last night. Do you really think he's taking his cut and going home?"

The wind was now strong enough to be pulling leaves from the trees and sending them out over the river in funnel formations. Spiralling lines of frayed colour that twirled for a moment and then were blown away. In the distance they heard police sirens and Morrissey looked up the road, waiting for the cars to appear. Yakabuski reached behind his back for the handcuffs.

"Turn around, Sean, left hand on your shoulder," he said, and when Morrissey turned to look at him, saw the handcuffs, he did as he was asked. Yakabuski put the cuffs on and started leading him down the row of tombstones. When the first police car arrived, two cops jumped out, their guns drawn, but when they saw Yakabuski they holstered their weapons and stood by the car waiting. Just as they reached the gate, a light snow started falling.

# EPILOGUE

The snows had come and gone, and it was now spring. Cambino Cortez had never seen snow and so he had stayed for the season. For the new sensations it offered. The brace of cold air on his skin. A sun that travelled flat across the sky. A new world.

He journeyed far that winter, never staying in the same place more than two nights. Walked through forests with pines so large and towering he could not see the upper branches when he stood beneath them. Walked the girth of one tree and counted twenty-three paces. Walked a frozen lake that creaked and groaned beneath him, as though a thing trapped.

He followed a grey jay that brought him to a ridge of high land, where he stood for most of the day, letting the wind pass over him. The high land ran east to west and he could see it easily, unfurling in either direction, a raised spine of rock that separated the water. He walked upon the Divide for many days, before following a river that led him to the bay of a giant ocean. Once there he saw men in boats made from the hides of animals, fishing far out in the bay. He watched them until the sun fell and the world became dark. The boats never came ashore.

He travelled through storms he had never imagined, never dreamed, snow falling so heavy it was like a curtain had been dropped, separating one world from another. It felt like a physical passage, walking not through air, not through wind or rain, but something as palpable as walls. The sky hidden. The ground swirling. It was a world that tried to push you around. One night, in one of those storms, he heard a wolf howling, and he wondered what sort of animal would venture outside during a storm like that. Not hunker. Not hide. Howl into the maw of the storm. Such disdain for the physical world. Such power and confidence the animal had.

He kept walking and the days lost distinction. Time slid off his back. He saw frozen bays the size of small seas and mountains with not a tree growing on any flank. An elemental world. Nothing superfluous. Just what was base and strong and forever. The migratory birds returned when the snow was still deep on the ground and Cambino guessed that meant it had been a long winter. He had no way of knowing. The birds flew in circles. Bright colours that spun in the sky. Many looked familiar. The birds that arrived in Heroica during the Festival of Lights, when sculptures of a baby and a virgin mother were carried on poles down crowded streets.

Soon after the birds arrived, the snow started to melt, and the world became pooled water and mud. Trees started to talk to him, late at night and early in the day, the juice beneath the bark burbling and oozing and making small child sounds. He saw black bears and white geese. A patch of blue appeared in a sheet of ice one day, and he sat and watched as a lake materialized. Creaking and snapping and moaning as the ice broke apart. The labour of nature. He had only seen it before with animals.

When it was time, he returned to the campervan.

. . .

Cambino hit the rewind button on the laptop computer and watched the video one more time. It had been several months, and he wanted to confirm his memories were correct.

The tape had been purchased from an old business associate of his father's, a Shiner who had managed to get a message to Cambino, saying the tape was for sale. A high price had been asked but Cambino did not haggle; information about your business partners, knowing what they wanted to keep secret, was usually worth the asking price.

He watched a boy's bedroom come into focus. The camera was shooting from above, hidden in a light or a ceiling fan probably. The old Shiner had been head of security, and he had bugged the bedroom without the knowledge of his boss, he told Cambino during their one phone conversation. Just doing his job, but when he told his boss about the tape, he knew he had made a mistake. He left Springfield the same day.

For several seconds the camera picked up nothing but a young boy lying on a bed. Twelve or thirteen years old, it seemed to Cambino. Then a door opened, and Augustus

Morrissey strode into the frame. He walked to the end of the bed, and in a frustrated voice said, "She's gone, Sean. I don't know what wind picked her up, and I don't know where she was cast to, but she's gone. The sooner you accept that, the better off you'll be, lad."

The boy looked at his father and said, "She just left us?"

"I'm afraid so."

"She didn't say anything to you, before she left?"

"No."

"Didn't leave anything behind?"

Cambino hit the pause button. Leaned in so he could take a close look at Augustus's face. There was no mistaking it. His memories had been correct. There was fear in the man's eyes. He hit play.

"No, she didn't leave anything behind, Sean." When Augustus said that the boy leaned back on the bed and slid his arm beneath one of the pillows. Left it there a second. When the hand reappeared, it was holding a wooden box.

"What do you have there, lad?"

"You know."

"And where did you *find* it?"

"In your safe."

"You've been in my safe, Sean?"

"Took me less than ten minutes."

Augustus gave his son a hard look. But the boy did not turn away. Rather, he opened the lid of the box and held it out so his father could see inside. The small arm as solid as a beam, not a quiver to it, the box held out like a communion offering.

"Why would she leave this behind?" he said.

"I don't know. You'd have to ask her, Sean."

"She always wore this ring."

The pause button was hit one more time. Cambino leaned in to look closely at the boy's face. After a few seconds he smiled and nodded. Then he looked at Augustus's frozen face. Not needing to lean in this time. Seeing it clearly. There was still the glow of fear in his eyes, but there was something new there as well: a look of hatred, the unbalanced twitch of combat. It was a look he had never seen a father give a son.

He hit play and watched as the boy took a diamond ring from the wooden box. Rolled it in the palm of his hands. Held it to the light.

"She left this for me," he said eventually.

"Hold on, Sean. That's an expensive ring you've got in your hand. Hell, that ring could be cut into a dozen expensive rings."

"I would never do that."

He said it with such conviction Augustus was taken aback. You could see it on the tape. A twitch of the big man's body. A straightening of his head.

"You got a thing for diamonds, do you, Sean?"

"I do. I think they're beautiful," and he closed his fingers over the ring, slid it into the pocket of his pyjamas. "Like my mother was — before she *left* us."

Augustus stared down at the boy with a rage so palpable, so immense, any viewer of the tape would have thought the next thing to happen would be a blow from the father to the son. Instead, the boy smiled sweetly and said, "Don't worry, Dad. It's just for safekeeping. I'll give it back to you one day."

• • •

*"I'll give it back to you one day."* He chuckled. He had not known Sean Morrissey had a sense of humour. Nor that he enjoyed the issuing of veiled warnings. This was useful information. He did not know what he would do with the first, but men who took joy from the issuing of warnings, from being prophetic, these were men easy to defeat. Often, you needed to do little more than convince them their deaths were heroic and destined.

It was a pity, in a way, that they must become enemies. He could not blame the son for avenging the death of the mother. It was the killing of the father that was unnatural. That could not be accepted.

He thought of what he must do. Wondered, briefly, if his course of action would be any different if he had never seen the video. Never paid the price requested by the dying Shiner — enough money to pay off a grandson's drug debt. Would he have taken his cut of the diamonds and gone home? Would he be sitting in Heroica today, having left half the bounty of Cape Diamond in the hands of a Shiner from Springfield?

Cambino thought, not for the first time, about the motives of men. How often they are kept secret, he marvelled, revealed only in early-morning dreams, or the darkness of empty streets, or at the commencement of great battles, with the sun not fully risen and mist swirling around the feet of men whose future could be measured in hours.

*The motives of men.* Perhaps it assumes too much. Perhaps it is one more false thing. When the truth is, we all do nothing more than play the cards we found waiting for us.

Cambino closed the laptop. Went back to the driver's seat of the campervan and started the engine. Around the first corner, he passed a roadway sign saying, *Springfield, 92 kilometres.*

**Ron Corbett** is an author, journalist, and broadcaster living in Ottawa. He is the author of seven non-fiction books. His first novel, *Ragged Lake*, the first book in the Frank Yakabuski Mystery series, received rave reviews and was a finalist for the Edgar Award by the Mystery Writers of America. A father of four, he is married to award-winning photojournalist Julie Oliver.